Fatal Lesson

A Karen Fowler Mystery

by

Kathy Johnston

To Barb,
Happy reading!
Kathy Johnston
2020

For information, email Cozy Cat Press, cozycatpress@aol.com or visit our website at: www.cozycatpress.com

COZY CAT
PRESS

ISBN: 978-1-952579-08-0
Printed in the United States of America

10 9 8 7 6 5 4 3 2 1

To Stan,

Who believes books must have solid plot lines with no holes

To Holly,

Who tirelessly edited and offered suggestions

!

Chapter One

Early Tuesday Morning

Karen rolled over and hit the alarm that was blaring music near her ear. Just five more minutes, just five more minutes, she pleaded with herself, and pushed the button on her phone alarm. Minutes later, she woke again with a start when Gabby, her 16-year-old daughter, shook her shoulder. "Huh, what?" she muttered.

Gabby continued to shake her arm insistently. "Don't you have to be at school early? I thought you said last night you had to meet with your school principal and those needy parents, those Watsons."

Karen sat up, alarmed. "Oh my God, oh my God! What time is it?" Grabbing her phone, she moaned, "7 a.m. I'll never make it. I must have hit the stop button. Darn this phone." She leaped out of bed and dashed for the bathroom.

Yanking her closet door open, she pulled out a shirt and skirt, grabbed some hose, and put on her comfortable shoes. So what if women didn't wear hose any longer? She loved the way her legs looked in hose. Dragging a comb through her tangled hair, she applied makeup with her other hand. Glancing in the mirror, she frowned at her trim figure and forty-year-old face. *I'm definitely aging*, she thought, as she examined the wrinkles around her eyes and noticed that her light brown hair was slightly speckled with strands of gray.

Her phone rang. Glancing down, Karen saw that it was her friend Rhonda. Grabbing it with one hand, she picked it up and said, "Rhonda, I've only got a minute, I'm late."

Inaudible sounds came from the phone. "I can't understand you. I've got to get going. I'm late."

"I'm so worried about my observation," said Rhonda in a whispery, shaky voice.

"Are you okay? You sound funny."

"Oh yes, just fine." Rhonda's voice started to break up. "Just fine."

"You don't sound fine. Listen, I'll see you at school. Calm down. Trandon is just trying to intimidate you with her evaluation of your teaching. Principals do that sometimes. You're going to do a great job." Rhonda had no confidence. She was a good teacher but always let the principal get to her. *I wish the woman would get a backbone,* Karen thought.

Unfortunately, Sherry Trandon was a bad-tempered woman hypercritical of all her teachers, so it was fairly easy to lose confidence. In the past two years that Karen Fowler had been an assistant principal at Kennedy Elementary in Chaldea, a small town in southern Iowa, she'd seen every teacher in the school cry due to Sherry Trandon's sharp comments. Rhonda, in particular, was sensitive and fragile. And she certainly got no support from that lousy lay-about husband. Karen had met him only once but had not been impressed. His demeanor was sour, and he spent most of his time making snide comments about Rhonda's inefficiencies.

Gulping down some coffee, Karen prepared to dash out the door. Gabby was eating cheesecake in the kitchen. Her dark curly hair, slim figure, and long legs reminded Karen of her late husband, Cliff. He had died in Iraq when Gabby was a tiny baby. *But those clear brown sparkly eyes she got from me.*

Kissing her on the top of her head, Karen said, "Have a good day, honey." Gabby, who had a mouthful of cheesecake, just nodded. "Even if I'm in a hurry, I can see you're eating cheesecake for breakfast, Gabby. That's a lousy breakfast."

"But it's got eggs and cheese in it, delish," Gabby hollered as her Mom ran out the door. The only answer was the slam of a car door and the vehicle accelerating down the driveway.

The tires screeched as Karen rounded the corner too fast and slid into the last available staff parking space behind the school. The back alley was almost empty because everybody always forgot it was there. *I can't believe I didn't remember I had to meet with the Watsons this morning,* she thought. *Life is difficult enough without forgetting a meeting with a parent who happens to be the business manager for the school district. And he's such a flaming know-it-all. I'm the educator, not him. He's so convinced his kid is a genius he can't comprehend the kid's having trouble.* She envisioned Mr. Watson pacing in the hallway, and Mrs. Watson irritably glaring at her fancy new Apple watch. Karen's stomach churned uneasily. "This will certainly not endear me to Sherry the intimidator," she muttered.

A vision of her principal, graying bangs falling over her left eye, pencil-thin lips fixed permanently in a scowl, and hands placed on her hips flickered through Karen's mind. The woman was tall and muscular, and that penetrating stare she gave everyone didn't win her any friends. *Why, oh why can't I be an assistant principal in a school where a young, pleasant principal is in charge?*

Karen sighed, hopped out of her cherry-red sports coupe, and pulled two dilapidated book bags from behind the front seat. The sports coupe had been a birthday present to herself on her fortieth birthday, and Karen loved the sporty car. Slinging both the book bags over one shoulder, she balanced three large pieces of cardboard between her arm and side. Then she grabbed her lunch, purse, and coffee with her free hand, and slammed the car door with her foot. As she staggered across the back parking lot, she attempted to open the back door. "Locked, I can't believe it," Karen groused, and continued around the corner toward the front door.

She stopped in shock. The teachers were milling around in a group near the far end of the parking lot in front of the school and all three local police cars were straddling the entrance to the school. The perky new first-grade teacher appeared to be retching in the bushes, a few teachers were leaning against some cars, and the rest were huddled in small groups. Usually, the Kennedy Elementary School staff was pretty loud and energetic, but today Karen could only hear a soft murmur of voices.

Something terrible must have happened. Karen hurried across the parking lot and was met by two friends who taught third grade, Noreen Peck and Rhonda Burgess. They gazed at her with stricken looks. Rhonda was leaning against a car, looking sick. Her unruly dark brown hair had come out of her bun, and she looked even paler than usual. She was clutching her shapeless gray sweater to her body as if her life depended on it. Noreen, always the kind helper, was attempting to hold her upright.

"What is happening?" Karen asked. "Is someone hurt? Rhonda's faced whitened and she abruptly slumped against Noreen. Ever practical, Noreen supported Rhonda with one arm and took hold of Karen's arm with her other hand.

"Karen, something terrible has happened. I mean it's awful, it's really truly horrific." Noreen couldn't seem to stop saying "It's terrible, it's so horrific."

Karen continued to stare at Rhonda and Noreen with a guarded look, prepared for a catastrophe. *My God, if Noreen can't gossip about it, the world must have ended.*

Bobbi Nelson, who had taught fourth grade for twenty-eight years, glared over at them. Tall and imposing, her grating voice could always be heard. "Oh, spit it out," she barked. Leaning against the oak tree, she looked as if she had just swallowed a mouthful of sourballs. "Sherry went and got herself murdered," she said in a piercing voice.

Karen froze. "She... she what?"

"Sherry's in the office sprawled across her desk, with a knife in her back, or so the teacher gossip mill says. Personally, I didn't see it."

Karen's book bags slid to the ground, and she too leaned against a car, breathing rapidly. "My God, oh my God," she moaned. "I can't believe it. This is awful." Karen closed her eyes and tried to comprehend the enormity of the situation. *Sherry Trandon, my bossy leader, whom everyone tacitly disliked, is dead on her desk.* She squelched a burbling desire to start laughing hysterically. Sherry had always seemed so indestructible, so larger-than-life. How could she be dead? Who would kill her? *Probably, lots of people. She was such a bitch, it could have been anyone.* Karen's mind raced with thoughts.

She glanced around at the teaching staff. Most of them looked like lost sheep, just milling around aimlessly, looking for guidance. Well, almost everyone. The tall, willowy fifth-grade teacher, Glenda, was glaring at her watch and tapping her foot. The woman was a ball of nervous energy. Turning to those around her, she said, "We've got state testing next week. We can't let this distract us."

"The principal has been killed. We really can't worry about state testing right now," her teaching partner said plaintively. Others jumped in to back her up.

"Let's forget testing for five minutes. Even the state of Iowa will stop the march of testing for this, surely," growled Bobbi. She was the oldest teacher at the school, and although she had stopped being an effective teacher years ago, she understood the politics and logistics of public education.

"Let it go, everybody," Michael, the other fifth-grade teacher, boomed. "The principal's dead, dead, dead." And turning dramatically to the crowd, he said, "And who did it? Mistress Teacher Tina, in her classroom, with her scissors, or Master Teacher John, in the library with the dictionary?"

"Stop it, Michael. Just stop it. Sherry's dead and it's terrible," Noreen said. "You're always joking around at the wrong time." A few teachers started to cry.

Karen turned to Noreen. "Are the police in the office?"

Noreen nodded toward the window of the principal's office. "They're all in there, with the body," she whispered. She continued, "And the superintendent might be there."

"Are you kidding?" snapped Bobbi. Derisively, she continued. "It's only 7:45. Why would a superintendent arrive for work anytime in the vicinity of school starting?" She snorted and turned away.

Everyone knew there was no love lost between the superintendent and Bobbi. Rumor was, the two of them had been involved years ago, but the superintendent's wife had put a stop to the affair; there was plenty of bitterness left over for everyone involved. Unfortunately, the superintendent's wife, Mary, also worked as an aide in the school, so it was all a bit too close for comfort.

Karen straightened her shoulders, shuddered involuntarily, and spoke to the group. "The busses will be rolling into the parking lot in approximately five minutes. And the carpool line is ready for the teachers to unload kids. What do you propose we do? Have the police said anything?"

Suggestions were tossed about for debate.

"Keep them on the bus. Don't let the carpool kids out of the cars yet. There'll be pandemonium."

"Send everyone home."

"Put the kids in the gym."

"Wait," Bobbi interrupted the group, "there could be a dangerous killer hiding somewhere in the school. The kids will have to stay on the bus and in cars until the police give the all-clear."

"The question is," Michael interjected. "What would Sherry do?"

"Oh, shut up, Michael," the teachers shouted in disgust.

Just then a grey sedan screeched into the parking lot and the superintendent for the Chaldea School District, Dr. Nash, bustled out of the car and stormed into the school. Usually impeccably dressed, the handsome superintendent looked downright disheveled. His silver-gray hair was mussed,. and the tail of his shirt was hanging out. He was missing both his tie and suit jacket.

Suddenly, the front doorway was crowded with police. The Chief of Police stepped forward. "Okay, listen up, everyone. The building is being searched and secured by the police. I suggest you wait on the busses with the children until a decision is made about what to do with students and staff. And round up those children on the playground," he growled. "Get them on a bus. I saw some little kid out back on the swings a few minutes ago. And I'm sending an officer over to tell the carpool parents to keep those kids in their cars."

Right on cue, three busses turned into the parking lot. In a daze, the teachers started to shuffle toward the busses. The students, who were used to their routine, began spilling off the busses and surged across the parking lot toward their respective entry doors. "No, no, get back on the busses," shouted several teachers, but no one was listening. Kindergarteners and first graders skipped to the front door and older students were walking around to the side doors. Some of the younger students stopped to admire the police cars. The police looked horrified as the kindergarteners and first graders descended on them at the front door.

Karen looked around at the complete chaos. As the students realized that something was wrong, they started to shout and run about. A few boys started chasing each other, and one student pulled out a soccer ball and started kicking it around with his friends.

"What's going on?" some students asked. "Why are the police cars here?"

"Why are all the teachers outside?" asked an observant student. "There must be a terrorist in the school." A teacher quickly shushed him.

"Did someone rob the school?" asked a towheaded young boy with freckles. "I bet the robbers were from Missouri. My dad says all the bad guys live in Missouri."

The police chief put his arms up and hollered loud enough to be heard on the town square, "Everyone is to stand still right where you are, close your mouth, or... or I'll arrest you." Turning toward the carpool line, he shouted, "Not one child or parent is to get out of their cars." The chaos from moments before turned into children frozen on the spot, mouths suddenly closed. It was as if the entire school was playing freeze tag. Turning to Karen, the Chief said, "They're all yours, Mrs. Fowler," and stepped back.

Karen looked out at the crowd and for an instant wished she could just leave them all there, frozen in space. Then she collected herself and said in a firm voice, "Teachers, collect your students." Karen watched as teachers lined up children and sent them to the buses. Karen placed her hand on Noreen's arm and guided her toward one of the buses. Rhonda trudged behind them.

"Rhonda discovered the body," Noreen whispered to Karen. "She said it was gruesome."

Karen stopped, put her arm around Rhonda and gazed at her friend sympathetically. "Oh, you poor thing, that must have been awful. It's so hard to believe Sherry's dead. It just seems so surreal."

"Well, I believe it. I saw it." Rhonda shuddered. "What I can't believe is that all I could think was—" She stopped and gulped. "Well, I guess I won't be observed for an evaluation today." Karen started to giggle at the absurdity of it all, but then quickly assumed a more serious face. Reaching over, she rubbed Rhonda's back. "People think all kinds of crazy things when they're shocked. It's okay, Rhonda."

Rhonda, Karen, and Noreen climbed on the bus and plopped down in the front seats. The children began bombarding them with questions.

"What's going on?" asked the two girls behind them.

Three boys in the back hollered, "Who got hurt? Where's the ambulance?"

"I have to go to the bathroom, now," whimpered Beth.

Suddenly there was a chorus of "I have to go to the bathroom."

"Oh, there's an ambulance pulling up but there are no lights or siren. That means there's a dead body to transport. I saw it on a TV show," said Ken, the know-it-all, as he stared out the window.

Karen stood and faced the students. Putting a hand up for silence, she announced, "Listen, kids, there's been an incident in the school. We can't use the bathrooms right now. I don't have any more information. When I do, I'll share it with you." Sinking back down on the seat, she sighed, "This is going to be a very, very difficult day."

The bus driver, a wizened, elderly man turned to her. "You can't expect me to sit here with this busload of kids. I've got to make a run to Lincoln School. You all just get off."

Karen looked calmly at the bus driver. "Police orders! We stay on the bus until the police decide what to do with the children. Radio the District Office, tell them there's an emergency at Kennedy Elementary and they need to let the other school know." Gazing out the window at the other buses, she added, "Better let the other drivers know too."

Sinking back in her seat, too overwhelmed to discuss the happenings with Noreen and Rhonda, Karen reflected on the morning's events. Ten years of teaching elementary school, she was now partway through her second year at Kennedy Elementary. She loved being an assistant principal, and she genuinely enjoyed the students and parents at the school, but in her gut, she knew most parents and students would react hysterically to the news of Sherry's murder. *And rightly so. Murders aren't supposed to happen in elementary schools. Everyone is going to think a killer is on the loose and parents will panic about their children. I don't blame them. Perhaps a killer is on the loose. It's going to make running a school pure hell.*

She wondered how the administration was going to manage this mess. That was an opportunity to watch their ineffectual superintendent in action. What would the district do about the state testing that was scheduled for next week? *I ought to be thinking about poor Sherry. After all, she's the one who is dead. But first, I've just got to get through this day. I'll think about Sherry later.*

Karen came to with a start. Noreen and Rhonda were gazing at her. "I'm sorry; this is such a shock that my mind is going a mile a minute. What happened? What do you know? Are you okay, Rhonda? You look really pale." Looking around, Karen whispered, "Let's stand outside the bus. Little ears, you know." The three of them climbed off the bus and huddled against the side. Fortunately, the windows were closed, so young eavesdroppers couldn't hear. "Are you all right, Rhonda?" Karen asked again.

"I think so. I'm not sure," replied Rhonda in a shaky voice. She trembled, sighed, and gulped some air. "I was here early, around 6:40 this morning, because, you know, I was being observed and I just get so nervous. I had so much to carry that I went straight to my room. There wasn't anyone around, not even Jorge was sweeping the floor."

She stopped, gulped in some more air and continued. "You know, now that I think about it, the office lights were off; it was dark in there. Anyway, I puttered around my room getting ready for the big day of observation. It was really quiet. I think Jo went by on her way to her classroom, but I'm not sure." Rhonda heaved an enormous sigh. "I was just so preoccupied."

"Then what?" Noreen nudged her. "How did you manage to see—you know—the body?"

"That would be Sherry," Karen responded dryly. "Not the body."

"Well, you know what I mean. It's less frightening to just say 'the body'. Makes it impersonal, you know. Otherwise, it's just too horrible to even think about." Noreen's voice ran down. Rhonda started to shake; Karen rubbed her back and offered the cup of coffee she still had in her hand.

She shook her head and continued her story. "So I... I walked down to the office to use the photocopier. I thought I should just check in with Sherry, you know, break the ice, and find out what time this morning she was coming. It was really weird though. Now that I think about it, I had to turn the office lights on. Still, in my mind, I was sure Sherry was here. Because you know, Sherry is always here. Anyway, I knocked on her door, although that was strange too because her door isn't usually closed." Rhonda suddenly leaned against the bus as her legs started to buckle.

Putting her arm around Rhonda, Karen spoke, "I'm sorry, Rhonda. We're being insensitive. It's just that we're all so darned shocked. You're upset about finding Sherry and I don't blame you. None of us would be prepared for what you saw." Rhonda turned her head and threw up next to the bus.

Karen looked up to see Kenny with his head pressed against the window. "Mrs. Burgess is barfing outside the bus," chirped Kenny as he opened the window. "I've never seen a teacher barf before." Several children ran over to peer out Kenny's window.

"Let's move away from the open window. Perhaps you should just lean against the bus door and we won't talk about it," Karen suggested. "It's been too much of a shock for you."

"Thanks, guys," Rhonda swallowed hard. "But let me finish. It might make me stop shaking and it will get it all out of my head." Leaning against the side of the bus, she continued, "The police will be so angry. I'm sure I destroyed evidence by turning the doorknob. I listened at the door to make sure I wasn't interrupting a conference and I called out hello and walked right into the middle of her office. Then I just stood there shaking."

Rhonda stopped and breathed hard. "She was sitting at her desk, bent over, with her head on the desk. There was a knife sticking out of her back and blood—oh my God—blood on her clothes, and the desk and the floor. So much blood! Who would have thought there would be so much blood? It just spilled out all over. There were puddles of it on the floor, and—and blood was dripping off the desk. Sherry would have hated the mess." Sobbing, she sank to the ground.

Karen and Noreen bent over Rhonda. "Oh, Rhonda, this is awful. Are you okay?" Noreen wailed.

Just then a police officer approached the threesome. "I'm looking for a Mrs. Rhonda Burgess."

"That's me," Rhonda whispered. "I don't feel good."

The officer bent over and helped hoist Rhonda to her feet. "Come inside with me, Mrs. Burgess. I'll get you some water and then the police chief would like a few words with you." Turning to Karen, he said, "Mrs. Fowler, when the buses depart, the superintendent would like to see you in the office." Taking the police officer's arm, Rhonda stumbled toward the school.

"Oh my goodness, this is just too much for me. I think the school should be closed." Noreen began wringing her hands. "Who knows who's in there? And what about poor Sherry? We haven't even grieved."

Karen's thoughts reverted back to Sherry. It was perfectly dreadful what had happened, but Sherry wasn't that well-liked. She was sarcastic with students, abrupt with parents, and downright mean to the staff. She was efficient and saw procuring needed equipment and supplies from the central administration office as her own special personal mission. Of course, lately, supplies had certainly seemed to dry up. Last week there wasn't even one new dry erase marker in the supply cabinet. When asked, Sherry said she was working on it and she'd gotten red in the face. She had even shaken a file and said the district office had some questions to answer. The whole interaction was weird, Sherry was known as a fighter who won, a real Atilla the Hun.

On a more positive note, Karen acknowledged to herself that Sherry was also insightful into children's behavior and was often painfully honest with parents and children, which could be helpful. She would be missed, but no one was going to grieve for her. With a choking feeling in her throat, Karen realized someone would have to notify her family. She shook her head in a perplexed manner. Who was Sherry's family? Good heavens, was Sherry's father still alive? Wasn't her father in poor health sometime last year? Belatedly, Karen realized that she didn't have a clue about most of Sherry's family. She only knew about the brother out in Last Chance who Sherry didn't speak to. Maybe someone else on the staff knew more about Sherry's personal life.

Just then, the school door opened, and a police officer walked toward Karen. "The students will be bussed to Lincoln School where they will sit in the gym until a parent or guardian can pick them up."

Karen climbed back on the bus.

"Why do we have to go to Lincoln School? I don't like Lincoln, it's old," complained a kid near the back of the bus.

"Super," announced another boy near the back. "No school, I can watch TV all day. Why can't accidents happen more often?"

"I want to go home now," sniveled a petite girl near the front, starting to cry. Her ponytail swung back and forth with each sob.

Karen looked down to see little Tina Ogby tugging on her dress. "What about Fluffer? We need to feed him, and I brought carrots." She shoved the carrots at Karen.

Several other students started to clamor. "Yeah, what about Susie Q, the hamster in Mrs. Gawler's room? And what about the fish in Mr. Temble's room?"

Again, Karen put her hand up for silence. "Students, there's a serious problem at our school and we must do what the police say. The animals and the fish will be okay for one day. If we're not allowed back in the school tomorrow, we'll arrange for someone in authority to feed the animals. Now sit down and be quiet."

"Eww..." Kenny announced to the bus. "Just as I thought, they're opening the door of the ambulance. I bet there really is a dead body in the school. We'll know if they bring out the stretcher with the dead body in a duffel bag." At this, the two girls at the front of the bus started crying in earnest. Tired, Karen climbed back off the bus and began walking toward the school door.

Kenny's head popped out the window. "Mrs. Fowler, Mrs. Fowler!" Kenny shouted. "You'd better stop the bus. I just saw Joey Demper in the bushes. I think he's playing hooky." Karen stared in horror at Joey as he dashed behind another bush.

Karen shouted at the bus driver to stop. "Joey Demper, you come here right now!"

Joey appeared from behind the bushes at the front of the school. "Sure, Mrs. Fowler, I'll be right there," he hollered back and came running over. "Hi," he said excitedly. "I've been looking for clues."

"Joey Demper, you are supposed to be on the bus."

"Oh, that explains why Marty never came to find me. We were playing hide and seek before school." Joey hit his forehead. "He must have gotten on the bus. You see, I was hiding behind the steps to the side door, in that kind of cubbyhole. That's when I heard this man tell this other man there'd been a murder. Was there a murder, Mrs. Fowler? Wow, like, that's scary, so I thought I'd better start detecting. I heard one man say a woman had done it, I think it was that student teacher woman. But why is everyone on the bus? Is there a field trip today?"

Karen just stood and looked at Joey in dismay. "Joey, you're one of a kind. All I know is, you almost got left behind. The school is being evacuated to Lincoln due to an incident at Kennedy. Now get on the bus. And not a word, not one word to any of the kids about a murder. I—I think you misheard that information and I want no rumors floating around. Do you hear me?"

"Why?" Joey asked forlornly. "I want to tell Marty what I heard."

Tapping Joey on the shoulder, Karen said, "You will do as I say, Joey. I don't want you upsetting the other kids."

Looking at Joey's sad face, she explained, "There's been a terrible incident at school today and we can't discuss it yet until all the facts are known. As a future detective, surely you understand that." Joey nodded.

Karen headed for the office. It seemed as if she'd been at school for hours, and it was only 8:10. Noreen peered out the window at her and mouthed, "Rhonda never came back. I hope she's okay."

Karen ran into Kat, the office manager, in the hallway. The barrette which usually held her long, black hair back from her face was falling out, and her normally placid demeanor was shaken. She had a computer tucked under one arm and her jacket over her other arm. "I'm on my way to Lincoln to help with dismissal. I was told they needed my authoritative voice." She shook her head in disgust. "Those teachers need to develop some gumption." No one messed with Kat and survived at Kennedy Elementary. She was tough with students, parents, and staff. "The district office has decided that we'll use the emergency forms to contact all parents that Kennedy Elementary is closed today and children must be picked up at Lincoln as soon as possible. They want all pick-ups signed out. Paper trail, paper trail, that's all the district office is interested in. I can only hope we get each kid to the right place."

"Good luck with that, you're going to need it. Before you go, have you seen Mrs. Hart's student teacher? The young woman has already missed the allotted number of days for student teaching and never showed up out front when the school was evacuated."

"Oh yeah, I've seen her. She's in big trouble with the police. When I announced that all staff members were to leave the building immediately, our least favorite student teacher, of course, stayed in the classroom. She was escorted out by the police, and I think they're still holding her."

Looking down the hall, Karen grumbled, "Well, they're not holding her now. There she is."

Jessamyn Babcock was sauntering down the hall as though she hadn't a care in the world. Her long blond hair was swinging from side to side, and once again she was dressed inappropriately in a tight blue sweater with a low neckline and an unbelievably short skirt. The outfit was completed with three-inch hot pink high heels.

Karen shrugged at Kat, who responded with, "How does a student teacher plan to teach in that?" Karen made a wry face and started down the hall toward her.

"Jessamyn, why didn't you exit the school with the rest of the staff? Didn't you hear the announcement?" Karen frowned at the student teacher.

Jessamyn spoke in an irritated voice. "The announcement said school staff. I'm not school staff; I'm just a student teacher. A police guy did look around the classroom, but I was behind the reading loft, looking for a book. I saw him, but he didn't see me. Then I started to wonder why there was a police officer in the school and where everyone was, so I went out in the hall and there was another policeman. Boy, they sure do get ticked off easily. Some police guy got pissed at me for being in the school. His face was red and everything."

Karen told herself to be patient and drew a deep breath. "Jessamyn, that announcement was for everyone. There's been a terrible incident at the school. And, for Pete's sakes, how many times have you been told—YOU ARE SCHOOL STAFF." She was almost shouting at that point. Then she suddenly lowered her voice, "Sherry Trandon is dead."

"Oh." Jessamyn looked horrified. "That's why the policeman hustled me out of the school and made me stand around on the playground. Oh, and that's why he said a detective would interview me later. This is just awful, poor

Ms. Trandon. She was quite ancient. Perhaps she died of old age. Crap, I'm not feeling good. I think I need to go home."

"No, that's not what happened to her." Karen looked at the student teacher in disgust. "And you are not going home. You're staying at school and you're going over to Lincoln to help Mrs. Hart with her students as a dedicated student teacher should." *I would love to wring her neck but we can't have two murders in one day.*

"Oh, so no class today. Hmm, probably no class tomorrow." Jessamyn could hardly keep the excitement out of her voice. "I guess I won't have to teach that language lesson today."

Karen turned abruptly and started back toward the office. Jessamyn trudged along beside her. Irritated, Karen thought, *why does this woman even want to be a teacher? She doesn't like children, she's not interested in teaching, and she's a pain in the neck.*

"I love your outfit, Mrs. Fowler. Those bangled earrings are all the rage and the print on your skirt looks great with your dark blue silk shirt, even for someone your age."

Karen gave Jessamyn a perplexed look. "Maybe you should think about going into clothes design. You seem to have a passion for it."

Jessamyn rolled her eyes. "Yeah, like my dad would approve of that. All he does is tell me that teaching is safe and has a pension."

Turning around before she entered the office, Karen said, "You must have gotten to school pretty early if you ignored the announcement to evacuate the building."

Jessamyn turned away and mumbled, "Yeah, I got here early to, you know, get ready for today's lesson and catch up on that grading Mrs. Hart wanted me to do. After all, you both said I might not pass student teaching if I didn't do a good job on this lesson."

Before she lost her patience, Karen instructed, "Hurry on over to Lincoln. I'm sure the teachers need help with the students."

Chapter Two

Tuesday morning

Opening the door, Karen walked into the office and was greeted by her tearful office assistant, Chloe. An angry Superintendent Nash was standing in the middle of the office, bellowing in rage. "Why wasn't I called sooner, Chloe, and where the hell is Kat? As office manager, she should be here."

"She's over at Lincoln, helping with the dismissal. It made sense for her to go because she knows all the parents and kids."

"I need her here at Kennedy. She's terribly efficient. I can't believe something like this could happen and I wasn't contacted immediately. District emergency policy must be followed."

As soon as Chloe saw Karen, she burst into tears. At eighteen she didn't have the experience to handle an angry and distraught superintendent. Her mascara had run down her face, her lipstick was smudged, and her pencil-thin body was shaking. Karen put her arm around her. "Go take a bathroom break and then we'll figure out what to do."

"She's too young and inexperienced for this job," said Dr. Nash, brushing back his gray hair and straightening his tie. Karen was tempted to retort with a suggestion that if the District paid more than minimum wage, they'd be able to get an experienced office assistant, but she didn't. One did not argue with the superintendent.

"Chloe's a hard worker and she's shocked that Sherry has been murdered. Give her a few minutes, she'll be okay."

"Oh, all right. This is a fine mess, Karen. I need you to contact Watson at the district office. I'll need a statement for the parents and make sure the district lawyer approves it." With his finger outstretched and pointed at her, he commanded, "And you need to notify the teachers there is a mandatory meeting for all staff after student dismissal. Where was everyone taken? To Lincoln?" Karen nodded. *Patience, patience! Soon the gray-haired scarecrow will be back at the district office and then I can start getting things done.*

A police officer stuck his head into the office. "The detective for the murder investigation is here."

Dr. Nash gave Karen an appraising look. "Now, look, you're to help this detective with his investigation. You'll need to stay close, answer questions, and don't leave him alone in the building. We need to manage the narrative for this investigation; there are bound to be PR issues."

"I'll do what I can to be helpful, sir. But I am sure the detective won't want me around all the time."

"Yeah, yeah. Don't be such a girl scout, Karen. Nose around, find out what he knows and what he's doing. This is a terrible thing that's happened, and the district needs to stay on top of it. We're all in this together, we're a team." *Good heavens, is the man going to thump me on the back like a good team player?*

Karen took a step backward. "Certainly, I'll do what I can." She tried hard not to slam the door on her way out. She was so angry at the superintendent she wanted to stomp to the front door but managed a more sedate walk. *The man is such a pig-headed idiot. Really, I'm supposed to trail around after this detective. Give me a break. With Sherry Trandon dead, I'm acting principal and I've got better things to do, like manage the school. Jeepers, creepers, the man makes my blood pressure skyrocket.*

Karen looked out the front door and saw a rusty sedan with a good-looking guy sitting in it. He had his driver's seat reclined and seemed to be studying the building. She stepped forward and waved. There was no acknowledgment. She moved over and tapped on the driver's window. The man sat up with a jerk. He had nice curly brown hair, brown eyes, and a friendly, kind face. Glancing down, Karen saw long legs. *Her friend Lucy would say he's a hot tamale. I wonder if he's single.*

Karen waited for the man to roll down his window and then said, "Hi, I'm Karen Fowler, Assistant Principal here at Kennedy Elementary School."

"Oh hi, I'm Brian Kerns, Acting Detective for the case. Sorry, I was lost in thought. I attended Kennedy Elementary many years ago, and driving here brought back a few memories. I just don't remember the school being so small, but," he smiled, "I guess, maybe, it's just that I've gotten bigger."

As Brian continued to examine the building, Karen looked at it through fresh eyes. The red brick of the original structure was still two stories high and rows of large glass windows twinkled in the sunlight. However, that single row of classrooms that had been attached to the back of the main structure made the whole building look like a lopsided T. Unfortunately, the school was surrounded by badly marred concrete, which had to be used for both parking lots and playgrounds. There was still an old metal play structure, although the PTA was working to raise funds for a new playground. No landscaping softened the harsh appearance. The original front door no longer functioned, and the side door was used as a front entrance. Karen loved the school even if it needed major work.

Brian climbed out of the car.

"Pleasant memories, I hope," said Karen.

"Hmm, that's difficult to say. As with most experiences, there were good and bad parts. I was one of those kids who couldn't sit still, so school was mostly agony for me. Do you still have a little black wooden chair that sits outside your first grade?"

"Nope, we got rid of that chair just last week. I decided it just didn't work to keep little boys quiet," said Karen, smiling.

"Enough with memories, on with the business at hand. I understand the Chaldea Police Chief has come and gone, the Major Crimes Team for the county has taken pictures and preserved the crime scene, and the body has been removed." Karen nodded.

Brian stopped suddenly. "I'm being so rude. I jumped right into business when I needed to tell you I am sorry for your loss. Sudden death is a shock and murder makes everyone sad and anxious at the same time. Were you and Ms. Trandon close?"

"We worked together and I admired Sherry Trandon for her efficiency, but no, we weren't close." *Close, are you kidding? Being friendly with Sherry would be like befriending a hippopotamus. She'd eat me for dinner.*

"I see. You're probably wondering just who I am and what I'm doing here. Usually, the Major Crimes Team for southern Iowa would be in charge of this investigation, but their detective for this case got sent home with the flu this morning, and the rest of the team is stretched thin, due to your other murder in Chaldea."

"Oh yes, Chaldea doesn't have murders and now we have two. I was quite upset to hear about Charlene's death." Charlene Addicks was the wife of the minister of the Methodist Church. "I went to school with her but hadn't seen her in years. I couldn't believe it when she was reported missing." Karen's eyes watered, and she looked away for a second, remembering the day she heard the news that the police found her body under the garage floor. "And now we have the murder, at least it appears to be murder, of our elementary school principal. Students, parents, staff, everybody is going to get hysterical. I'm not looking forward to that."

"Yes, hard for the town, and it will be difficult to keep everyone calm. I lived here as a child but haven't been around in years, so I'll need your help with parents and staff. I'm recovering from an injury and on leave from the Chicago Police Department. It seems they're a bit short on detectives for this case, so the Chaldea Chief of Police asked my Captain for permission to borrow me, provided I continue to make all my physical therapy appointments."

Brian started walking toward the door. "In most murder investigations, I would have been called earlier and taken charge of examining the body and checking the scene, but that's all been done. It feels a little strange to be picking up the investigation now, but I'd like to talk to your superintendent, nail down who was on-site at the time of the murder, release a statement to the press, and get some background information about the school and the community from you."

When Brian entered the school building, he sniffed and said, "That odor certainly hasn't changed in thirty years. It's pine-sol, old cafeteria food, stale sweat, and something new I can't identify."

"That's the pungent smell of dry erase marker." Karen opened the door to the office. Chloe was huddled at her desk, typing away on something.

Dr. Nash was yelling at someone on the phone. "We need that statement now." He glared at Chloe and snarled, "Hurry up with that," and walked toward the principal's office. The presence of yellow tape across the entrance stopped him in his tracks. Irritably, he swung around, catching sight of Brian near the office door. "No press allowed right now."

"Let me introduce myself. I'm Detective Kerns," said Brian, showing his badge.

Working to recover from his visible anger, the man responded, "I'm superintendent of the Chaldea School District, Dr. Nash. How can we help you, detective?"

"Perhaps we should talk somewhere, privately. We need to discuss the situation and set up interviews," Brian responded.

The superintendent glanced around and shrugged. Turning to Karen, Superintendent Nash snapped, "Where can we meet?"

"Since the entire school got evacuated to Lincoln, you have a lot of choices of places to meet," Karen snapped back. Looking at the superintendent's red face, she quickly suggested, "You could meet in the social worker's office."

Dr. Nash nodded and started down a narrow walkway, past the photocopy machine, around a large worktable with a lethal-looking cutting board, and around the corner. There, tucked in an out of the way spot, was a small office, recently renovated from a storage closet. The superintendent threw open the door with a flourish, marched in, and sat behind the desk. Brian looked at the only other chair in the room and tried to fit his long, angular body into the child-sized chair.

With nowhere to sit, Karen stood by the door. *If the superintendent meant to be intimidating, he's done a nice job of reposing behind a large desk with the detective squatting on the other side. One point for Nash.*

"Sorry, you don't look particularly comfortable, but this will have to do for now," Dr. Nash said. "Well, let's get on with it. I'm a busy man and there's a lot to do." Leaning back in the chair, he fired off questions at Brian. "Who are your suspects, how and when was she killed, how many of you are working this case, and when are we going to get some answers?"

Brian, who had been taking his notebook and pencil from his pocket, stopped and stared at the superintendent. "No one and everyone, with a knife late last night or early this morning, you're looking at the detective for this case, and the answers will come when the police work is done. Now, let's just back up and resolve some of the background work." Tipping back in his chair, he licked his pencil point. "Tell me about the victim."

Dr. Nash fidgeted in his chair, glanced out the window, and stared back at the detective. "I'm not sure what you want. Sherry Trandon was a very competent principal who had been here for fifteen years. Before that, she was a teacher for ten years at Lincoln Elementary, downtown." Sounding a bit uncertain, his voice wound down, "Perhaps I should have my secretary fax over her personnel file. That might tell you more. Karen, fill this detective in on Sherry's background."

As Karen began to speak, Detective Kerns interrupted. "Yes, I'll be asking Mrs. Fowler for details later. Right now I'd like to hear your ideas. But by all means, fax Ms. Trandon's file to me. Now, tell me more about her."

Irritated, the superintendent snapped, "Like what? What is there to tell?"

The detective tapped his pencil against his notebook. "I'm sorry; somehow I thought you'd been in the district for twenty-five to thirty years. I assumed you knew all the staff, especially administrative staff, well."

"I have been in the district for twenty-seven years and I've seen us all through some rough times. Of course, I knew Sherry as a colleague. I don't know any details about her life." The superintendent was beginning to sound downright peevish.

"Listen, help me out here. Tell me everything you know and I'll be the judge of whether it's useful to the investigation or not."

Karen looked at the superintendent's turned-down mouth and angry frown. Nash was seething. If the detective's goal was to make the superintendent really pissed, he was definitely winning.

Dr. Nash leaned back in his chair, crossed his arms, and glared at the detective. "As I said—she was competent, a very hard worker, efficient. Nobody got away with sloppiness with Sherry around. She was always very calm and businesslike. Never one to joke at Board meetings or tell funny stories, Sherry was always all work and no play. Is that enough?"

"Keep going, you've got a good start."

Dr. Nash gave the detective an exasperated look. "Her teaching staff respected her, but they certainly didn't invite her out for a drink at Pinky's after work. Right, Karen?"

When there was no response from Karen, he continued, "Parents sometimes complained about her lack of compassion, but frankly, I never paid attention to it. She ran a tight ship. Any superintendent would want her on his team. Never a moment's trouble! Well, until today, that is." He paused. "Well, I didn't mean it like that. Sherry couldn't help what happened today, but I'm going to have frantic parents, staff, and students on my hands."

Brian looked up from his note-taking. "Who were her friends? And what about family? The Police Chief will be notifying the next of kin or her emergency contact. Won't you want to follow up?"

Dr. Nash sighed long and hard. "Yes, we'll contact her relatives, if she has any. Or her emergency contact. As for friends, she doesn't have any that I know about. As I said, all she does is work." Shaking his head, he said, "Family? What family? She never mentioned family, never showed pictures of kids or anything. She never even showed pictures from vacation. I'll have to check the personnel file for her emergency contact. God, I wish you'd just ask Karen. She's right here."

Karen looked down so she wouldn't make eye contact with Dr. Nash. *What a turd! What about her brother out in Last Chance? Everybody knows about him.*

Brian looked annoyed and said, "I will, later. Now I want your impressions. Who would most likely know something about her?" He continued to stare at the superintendent, who was starting to look agitated.

"Talk to the staff here. They ought to know something. This is a waste of my time." Glancing at his watch, he abruptly brought his chair upward. "We're finished for now. I have got to meet with staff, get a statement to the parents, and talk to the school board about what we do for a principal." His voice trailed off as he rose from his chair.

"Just a minute. Whoa—we're not quite finished yet."

The superintendent halted and stared in astonishment at the detective. Nobody ever told him what to do. Standing beside the desk, he tapped his foot impatiently and waited for Brian to speak.

"Here's the plan for today," Brian stated flatly.

"Stop right there, Detective Kerns. I don't need to know your plans. Mrs. Fowler will be your contact person for this investigation. She has my full authority to assist you with talking to staff, parents, children, or whatever it is you do in a murder investigation. I'm in the middle of a huge financial project for the district, so I don't have time for all the little details. Karen will keep me apprised of what is happening." The superintendent scowled at Brian and attempted to walk out of the office.

Brian stood in his way. Very mildly, he said, "I can see you're under a lot of pressure, Dr. Nash, and I'm happy to work with Mrs. Fowler on details. However, do keep in mind that a murder investigation takes precedence over anything else going on in the district. Now, there is one more thing. I'd like to see the statement you're sending to parents. Also, we should collaborate on the statement you're making to the students and staff waiting at Lincoln School."

Nash barked, "Everyone is waiting for your announcement. I will have a very short statement, and then you can provide the details. After that, we'll start dismissing students." Brian looked properly horrified at the idea of talking to a gym full of students and teachers. The superintendent brushed past Brian and charged out of the social worker's office.

Karen could hear Brian muttering as they left the office, "What a supreme jackass, all puffed up with importance. School administrators were idiots back when I was in school and they still are today."

Chloe was in the process of retrieving a paper from her printer. Without pause, she handed it to the superintendent. "Here's the statement from the district office, prepared by Mr. Watson," she said. "The lawyer still needs to approve it." Chloe's eyes were puffy, and she sniffed as she sat dejectedly at her desk. "I wish Kat was here." The mere physical presence of Kat was always reassuring to everyone, but especially Chloe. It wasn't that she was particularly easy to work with, but Kat was efficient and always knew what to do.

The superintendent read the statement and handed it to Brian. "It's a draft. We may change the wording some and the lawyer's got to get his two cents in, but basically, this is it."

Karen and Brian began discussing the logistics of finding a quiet place for him to interview. "At Kennedy, we could cancel the reading specialist tomorrow, and you could use that room. We could move some adult chairs in from the lounge. I'll contact the principal at Lincoln as soon as we get over there today. Space is tight at Lincoln, but I think we can find you something."

Dr. Nash was staring out the window and appeared not to be paying any attention to anything transpiring in the office. His shoulders were slumped, and he turned and looked tiredly at everyone in the office. "This is an abominable mess. Principals aren't supposed to get murdered. Poor Sherry, somebody had it in for her." With that, he announced he was going back to the district office. All the tension in the office seemed to melt away as the superintendent walked out the door.

"Any chance you have coffee here?" Brian asked hopefully.

"Of course, let's go to the teacher's lounge. We should have met there in the first place. I wish I'd thought of it. You looked so uncomfortable in that tiny chair. There was hardly any room for your legs. I'm sorry about that."

"That's okay. It was just an opportunity for that patoot of a superintendent to throw his weight around." Karen laughed.

"So, you're not impressed with our superintendent?"

"A most emphatic no."

As Karen and Brian sat, sipping coffee, she took notes for scheduling staff interviews, contacting the two night custodians for interviews, and locating children who'd been on the playground before school. "We'd better get over to Lincoln for your announcement to staff and students."

"Before we go, I want to look at the crime scene." Brian stepped into the hallway and beckoned an officer forward. "Officer Danzy, the first responders are gone, so I need you to help me. You viewed the crime scene, and I want you to describe exactly what you saw. A first-hand account is extremely important. Mrs. Fowler, it would be really helpful if you could take a look at Ms. Trandon's office. You are probably the one most familiar with it, correct?"

"Kat, the office manager, and Chloe, our office assistant, and I all know the office well." After taking a quick look at Chloe's pale face, Karen said, "Yes, I can do that."

Chloe watched as Brian and Officer Danzy carefully moved the crime scene tape and opened Sherry's office door. Both men pulled on latex gloves and booties. Brian handed some to Karen, and she dutifully put them on. Gingerly stepping inside, Brian gently closed the door behind all three of them.

In front of them was a large, utilitarian desk with one folder sitting askew on it and two blue pens. A high-backed rolling desk chair was pushed back from the desk. There was a cabinet directly behind the desk. Three very old beat-up gray metal filing cabinets were against the far wall, and one rather lopsided bookcase resided under the window. There were no pictures of any kind and no personal knickknacks. One uncomfortable office chair was placed in front of the desk and two matching office chairs were pushed up against the wall.

As Brian gazed around, Karen said, "It's a very depressing office, even more so with all the blood. I don't think Sherry was into decorating." Karen's face was pale, and she leaned against the wall.

Brian continued to look around. Blood was splattered on the desk, the chair, and there was a large puddle on the floor next to the chair. Glancing down at the folder, he saw that it was labeled "School supplies, October." Taking a pen from his pocket, Brian flipped it open and took a look. It appeared to be a list of ordered school supplies, some with checkmarks, and some with question marks. He was not at all sure what it meant, but he made a note to examine it.

Carefully, pulling open the two side drawers of the desk, he turned to Officer Danzy and said, "I want the contents of this desk put into evidence bags and taken to the station. Okay, Danzy, describe the scene."

The officer flipped open his notebook. "When I entered, Ms. Trandon was sitting in the office chair with the upper half of her body sprawled across the top of the desk. She was face-down. The right arm was at an awkward angle as if she had tried to catch herself. The left arm was at her side. There was a knife sticking out of her back. The knife looked like an ordinary kitchen knife. You can see where the blood splattered and pooled. When the coroner turned her face to the side, her expression was shocked. You should look at the photos, sir."

"I will, Officer Danzy. But I want a visual of this from you because you were on the scene before things got disturbed."

"Are you okay, Mrs. Fowler?" Brian's voice was concerned. Karen nodded. "Are any large items missing from the office? Is anything in a different place?"

Karen forced herself to look around. "It looks exactly the way I remember, even her desk. The only changed thing is she seldom kept a chair for visitors next to her desk. She said it invited people to sit down and business was more focused if the person had to stand. If a staff member or parent used a chair, they were always asked to put it back. Strangely, the chair is still pulled up to the desk. As for paperwork, Sherry kept all her paperwork filed in drawers or behind the desk in that cabinet. There was seldom anything out on her desk. That's why it looks so bare."

"Is this folder about school supplies significant?"

"Perhaps I could take a look at it when we go out to the main office."

"Of course, I'm sorry. The scene must be very disturbing for you." Karen nodded and concentrated on not throwing up. That would be embarrassing. Brian strode out of the office with Officer Danzy and Karen Fowler following him. Brian placed the crime tape back in place and told Karen to sit down.

"You'll feel better in a minute. I'm sorry to have done that to you, but your observations are very useful." He handed the folder to Karen.

Brian took a new pair of gloves out of his bag and handed them to Chloe who took the file. She studied it for a few minutes and handed it back. "You should have Chloe look at this too because, for some reason, the school was short on supplies this year. We'd keep ordering items, but the district held them up. This list looks like a copy of a requisition for supplies and the checkmarks are items that never arrived. I'm not sure what the question marks are for. Chloe, what do you think?"

Karen took off her gloves and handed them to Chloe to wear while she examined the file. After all, she was the one who ordered the supplies for the school. After studying the list for several minutes, Chloe went to her desk and pulled out a folder. "Yep, this is our original order." She handed it to Brian. "As you can see, Ms. Trandon created a list of supplies that never arrived. I don't get the question marks. Those supplies were never ordered. And frankly, they aren't for things we would order. Why would we need dishes or clothes?" She pointed to several items. "I don't get it." She handed the list back to Brian. "Anyway, Superintendent Nash called to remind you to get over to Lincoln right away."

"We'll take my car." Brian opened the passenger door for Karen. "Tell me a little bit about Chaldea and Kennedy School. I haven't spent much time here in years."

Karen thought about the question. Kennedy Elementary was located in the center of a lower-middle-class residential neighborhood, but it was probably like that when he attended it. Instead, she explained, "The staff at Kennedy includes twenty-five teachers and specialists, three aides, two office staff, three custodians, and three hundred eighty students. That makes us a small elementary school these days."

"That's going to be a lot of people to interview."

"The district built a new early childhood center that includes the primary grades, so we now have four elementary schools, plus the junior high and high school. What's changed is that all the tiny little towns that we used to play for football and basketball years ago have lost their schools, so everyone comes into Chaldea. Moscow, Zero, No Name, Endroad, the kids are all bused in from there. I guess it was good that the school was built on the far south side to accommodate the rural kids." They were practically out in a cornfield.

Karen paused for a minute. "The city council had hoped that the whole south end would get developed with new companies and small factories. That development just didn't happen, except for one large, ugly Walmart. Have you been there?" Brian shook his head no.

"Taxpayers' antipathy toward spending money has not been kind to any of the schools as most of them need serious remodeling, and teachers are still unhappy with their salaries and benefits. I wasn't teaching in the district three years ago, but the entire district went out on strike. That is highly unusual for a school district in a small rural town. Although the school board and the teachers eventually settled, feelings are still somewhat hostile. Some teachers are leaving the district for higher salaries elsewhere, supply budgets have been cut, and extra-curricular programs are nonexistent."

"I've heard my sister, Natalie, complain many times about being nickel-and-dimed to death by the school," said

Brian. "Just last week, I was asked to buy wrapping paper from my nephew to raise money for new gym equipment."

"Does your nephew attend Kennedy?"

"Oh, yeah. His name is Josh Siddle."

"I know Josh; nice child, a bit rambunctious. I'm pretty sure I went to high school with your sister. Natalie Kerns?"

"That's her. I'll tell her you said hi. I've been eating a lot of my meals at Natalie's. She's such a good cook, but her house is so small I rented an apartment from an interesting family. They're a bit noisy, but I'll survive for a few more weeks."

Brian drove for a few seconds in silence. "I met your late principal, Sherry Trandon, at a school open house. My sister likes to drag me to school functions to serve as a substitute dad for Josh. Ms. Trandon was introduced to me outside the gym." Brian winced.

Karen chuckled, "Sherry Trandon took a bit of getting used to. She was so tall, almost six feet, and she towered over students and many parents. You add in those piercing gray eyes, bad haircut, and forceful personality, and she was a force to reckon with."

"I so agree. She boomed out a loud hello and proceeded to describe my nephew as an overactive little boy who needed to learn the rules. It was all rather distressing, particularly to my sister."

Brian turned the corner onto Chaldea's famous city square. Karen saw Brian glance at the courthouse with appreciation. It was a lovely structure, built more than 100 years ago, with jutting buttresses and a beautiful oval window over the main entrance. It did the city proud.

"It is beautiful, isn't it?" said Karen.

"Yes, it is, but the rest of the square is rather discouraging. Look, there's Browns Shoe Store, where everyone used to be outfitted with back-to-school shoes, and it's gone. Now there's a weird, eclectic resale shop in its place. Oh no, William's Drug Store has a 'Going out of Business' sign in the window. I had been hoping to get a chocolate phosphate at the soda fountain later."

"There's been a lot of changes, Brian. The city council is trying to make Chaldea a tourist destination." *Which is an absolutely crazy idea, but I'm gonna be loyal and talk the place up.*

"For real?" Brian looked startled. "I would never think of visiting Chaldea for its tourist delights."

"We do have three lakes that can be used for outdoor recreation. The plans for the square are to have antique stores and interesting boutiques to attract shoppers from Missouri and the rest of Iowa."

"What is that next to the resale shop? It looks like the recruiting office for the local community college, good old Iowa Southern Central Community College. Gosh, half of my friends from high school attended that college. Prospective students can't just go out to the campus to get information? I guess the town council is on a roll to fill every store on the square."

"You have to give them some credit for trying."

"You're right, I'm not trying to be critical. I'm just surprised about how much Chaldea has changed. I did hear a rumor from my sister that a graduate of Chaldea High School left a sizable chunk of money to the city." He smiled at Karen. "Do you think they might buy some paint? Every building and house in this town seems to need paint."

"Well, that's true enough. Every house on the street where I live needs to be painted. Don't be too disappointed, but they decided to upgrade the city park and refurbish the community swimming pool with the money."

Arriving at Lincoln School, Karen could see Brian staring at yet another dreary school. Only this school looked like it had been built at the turn of the 20th century and never updated. He was shaking his head and gazing at the metal tube extending from the third-floor stairwell window and going down the exterior of the building. "I wonder if they still use that tube for fire drills."

"Oh goodness, I don't think so. That would be a nightmare, getting kids to slide down that dark tube." Karen looked horrified at the thought.

"Yeah, I don't have fond memories of Susan Starkley giving me a vicious push in second grade because I froze in place at the top of the tube during the fire drill. I can still remember her shrieking in my ear, 'Do you want us to burn?' Fortunately, I never had to see her again. The next year I was transferred to Kennedy School to receive special reading help." Walking in the front door, Brian stopped Karen, and they both looked at the cement block at the entrance. "Hey, Mrs. Fowler, 1906. Guess they're getting their money's worth out of this school."

Brian and Karen walked into the gym, abuzz with loud whispers. Teachers were gathered near the far end, all talking, and various aides were scattered about the gym, keeping an eye on the students. Dr. Nash walked purposely to the front, picked up the microphone that someone had put out on the table, and addressed the group. His speech was short, brusque, and lacked information. He simply told everyone that the principal had passed away and the police were looking into it. Several students started to cry and various teachers consoled them. Most of the children seemed shocked as if they didn't quite take it all in.

Dr. Nash proceeded to say that the students who were on the playground before the supervisor arrived would need to speak to the police. All students would be dismissed today, but there would be school tomorrow. Several of the older students cheered at the mention of early dismissal, but Nash's icy glare stopped them mid-cheer.

Karen walked around, checking in with teachers, and talking in a comforting voice to the students. She stopped when Nash handed the microphone to Brian, who attempted to reassure the students and staff that the person responsible for Ms. Trandon's death would be caught. In the meantime, a police officer would be stationed at the school's entrance, and other outside doors would be locked.

Karen could overhear some of the rumors starting up from where she stood. One boy was describing how terrorists had gotten into the school, and several girls were loudly whispering about a thief who stole jewels from the teachers. Karen held up her hand and spoke firmly, "I can hear some of you making guesses about what happened. That is not okay. The only information Detective Kerns has shared is that Ms. Trandon has passed away and we are keeping you and your school safe."

Brian asked Karen to announce that any student who had seen anything unusual in the last few days should come forward and talk to Detective Kerns. *Oh boy, I hope he knows what students like to do, how they love to exaggerate.* Once she announced it to the students, a line formed, and Brian listened patiently to each of the student's stories.

Afterward, Brian laughed with Karen. "You get what you ask for." Three second graders had seen a stranger hanging out by a classroom window yesterday, one third grade girl was adamant that Ms. Trandon was killed by drug dealers, and one creative kindergartener was certain a vampire had bitten her neck. Police Officer Speck, who had shown up to take notes, diligently wrote down all the ideas. Only once did Karen see her lips crinkle up in a slight smile. It was during a kindergartener's lurid telling of the vampire.

Karen was present when Brian talked to three students who had been dropped off before the playground supervisors arrived at school. One very small boy called Ricky Rump said he'd seen a blue—*no*, gray, or maybe it was a brown car in the back of the school, near the trees where cars weren't supposed to be. He'd only seen it because Anthony had kicked the ball back there. Karen hastily explained that Ricky had difficulties with color recognition, due to some color blindness issues. Shaking his head, Brian whispered to Karen, "I'd not want an unfortunate name like Ricky Rump. Must be hard on the kid."

Another child, Travis, was positive that bad guys from Missouri had robbed their school of valuables while he was out on the swings before school. He told Brian, with an air of great importance, that the bad guys from Missouri had been to Chaldea a long time ago and had robbed the bank on the square. The posse, riding in pick-up trucks, had chased the bad guys and caught them when they ran into several cows. The boy's eyes widened in admiration when he told Brian all the cows had been deputized.

Karen leaned over and said, "Travis's story is actually based on a real bank robbery that happened in 1925."

Karen turned to the front of the gym and picked up the microphone. "Detective Kerns needs to meet with all the teachers and staff today. Officer Trausch will be dividing you into various staff groups."

Brian raised his voice and said, "This is going to be a bit of a process due to the large number of people who need to be interviewed. I ask you all to be patient. Mrs. Fowler, come with me to start these interviews."

Brian and Karen strode out of the gym and followed the aides to the reading specialist's room. The custodian shuffled along behind them. *They all look scared to death and guilty, and I know they're not. I guess they're in shock over this whole situation. Who wouldn't be?* Karen moved forward and put her arm around Mary Nash. "It's okay, Mary, this has been hard on everyone."

When they reached the reading specialist's room, Karen gave a short wave to Brian and said, "I'll give you some space to interview, and then please come find me, and we'll get you some lunch."

Karen walked back down the hall, entered the gym, and checked with the Lincoln aides doing dismissal. Everything seemed to be clicking along. She stopped by Rhonda's third-grade class where the students were bombarding her with questions.

"Mrs. Burgess, Harvey told me a poisonous snake from the zoo is loose in the girl's bathroom." Several girls started shrieking.

"Is someone hurt at the school? Where was the doctor?" said Kenny, with a puzzled frown.

"If it's an accident, why didn't we see an ambulance with its siren going?" asked Emily, who was known as a logical thinker. The kids' heads swiveled to look at Emily.

"Yeah, where was the ambulance?" asked several other children.

Karen looked at Rhonda and put up her hand for silence. "Listen, group, we don't know anything other than what Dr. Nash and Detective Kerns told us. When we do, Mrs. Burgess will fill you in." She patted Rhonda's arm. "Good luck with this bunch. I hope you're feeling a little better; you still look very pale." *Come on, Rhonda. Get a grip.*

"I'm all right, I guess. The police want to talk to me after dismissal." Rhonda bent down to answer yet another question from a child.

Karen entered the main office at Lincoln and thanked the staff and principal for being so accommodating on short notice. Then she sat down in the conference room and started writing out a list of things that had to get done.

Ten minutes later, Mary Nash had found her and was complaining at the top of her lungs about that Detective Kerns. Karen shut the door to the conference room. "I don't think I understand why you're upset." Mary's bun was still neatly gathered at the nape of her neck and her black pants and blue shirt still looked fresh and crisp, but she was definitely rattled, and her face was red.

"That detective interrogated me like I was a common criminal, asking me when I arrived and who I saw."

"We're all upset, Mary, but that's his job, to ask questions."

"Well, I told him I arrived about 7:15 and I went to the teacher's lounge like I always do and read the paper. Those other teachers in there are always so noisy. I just keep to myself. I was looking for that new first-grade teacher because I was supposed to work with her this morning when I saw the new reading aide sidling down the stairs from the second floor." She sniffed. "He had no business being on the second floor and was definitely up to no good. I've told you before, Karen, he's too jolly with the students, always goofing around. He acts like he's still in high school. He looked shifty, like he didn't belong up there, and he doesn't. His students are on the first floor."

"Did you ask him what he was doing?"

"No, why would I do that? I don't like talking to him. He makes me feel uncomfortable."

"Mary, you've had a rough day. Go ask Kat if she still needs help, and if she doesn't, take the rest of the day off." *How could this woman be married to Dr. Nash? He was an arrogant SOB, and she was some kind of namby, pamby prude who was nervous and scared of everything.*

Just as Karen was realizing how hungry she was, Brian tapped on the door and came in and sat down. "My interviews are finished, and I have a few questions for you. Brandon Leary, your reading aide, was on the second floor before school. Is that unusual behavior?"

"Not particularly. He works with the younger students, but there could be all kinds of reasons he might be seen on the second floor."

"Your other aide, Mary, was very suspicious of him, but when I asked Brandon what he was doing, he said he was trying to borrow a book from the fifth-grade teacher. He seems like a friendly guy, very relaxed. He did smell odd though."

"Really? I've never noticed that."

"It was like he was trying to cover up an odor by wearing a lot of body spray and cologne. I don't know, maybe he was smoking cigarettes up on the second floor."

"There's absolutely no smoking allowed in the building and I have no idea why he'd go to the second floor to smoke."

"Brandon also mentioned that he saw a man going into one of the classrooms. When pushed, he said it was the classroom of the snarky teacher that no one liked. Who's the snarky teacher?"

"My guess is it's Bobbi Nelson. She's an older woman, not particularly friendly, and she often makes snide comments about everybody and everything."

"He saw a tall man dressed for business with dark pants and a white shirt. Brandon says he wouldn't recognize him if he saw him again. He only saw him for a moment and didn't see his face. Do you have any idea who that might be?"

"A man visiting Bobbi? Before school? How strange. No, I have absolutely no idea." *No, no, there's no way. Can't be. Is Bobbi nuts enough to resume her affair with Dr. Nash again? But he wasn't at school early, was he? It's got to be someone else.*

"I guess I'll have to ask this Bobbi Nelson about it. My other interesting interview was with your daytime custodian. For someone who has worked at the school for thirty years, Jorge is remarkably uninformed and unobservant. He didn't notice anything, everything was as normal as could be this morning, and he assured me he doesn't know anything. He was keeping information back, but I have no idea what or how it might relate to the murder. He did make one interesting statement about a loud discussion between Rhonda Burgess and Sherry Trandon that happened last week. Jorge couldn't remember which day. He didn't seem to know anything about what was said. Do you know anything about that?"

"I'm sorry I'm so unhelpful. Rhonda is a friend of mine, and she never mentioned an argument with Sherry. And if it was regarding a parent or student, I would have thought Sherry would have included me in the discussion." Karen sat and looked at Brian. "I seem to know less about what goes on at the school than I thought."

"Maybe, maybe not. Murder investigations bring out all sorts of strange things. I'll be doing more interviews this afternoon. But you suggested lunch and I'm really hungry."

"Oh, I have such a treat for you. Have you had Chaldea's famous tenderloin sandwich yet?"

"I didn't know the town had a famous tenderloin sandwich. I don't remember one from when I grew up in Chaldea."

"See, another reason we can become a tourist destination." Karen smiled. "Anyway, I took the liberty of ordering from the Over Easy Diner and we're getting tenderloin sandwiches, fries, and coleslaw. The office assistant just made a fresh pot of coffee, so we're all set. I'll go get the food."

Chapter Three
Tuesday Afternoon

Brian stepped into the hall with Karen just as a line of children was passing to get water, carefully supervised by a teacher's aide. "Oh... is that the killer?" one little boy, with very eager eyes, whispered loudly to his classmate. Detective Kerns saw several fingers being pointed at him.

"Nah," said the other boy. "The killer wouldn't stay around. He's the helper; he helps the real policeman. That guy standing at the door with the gun—that is the REAL policeman." He pointed at Officer Danzy who had just entered the school with a bundle of paperwork. Officer Danzy had the physical appearance of the perfect stereotypic police officer: buzz-cut hair, muscular body build, military posture, and a shiny, pressed uniform.

"Well, there goes years of police training, grueling detective work, exams," said Brian wryly. "The guy with the uniform and visible gun is more important."

"You've got to admit, uniforms are impressive," said Karen. "Come on, let's get you a list of staff members and their availability. Kat, our ever-efficient office manager from Kennedy, will have one for you."

Kat did indeed have a list, and she had starred the staff who arrived before 7:30 a.m. Glancing at her watch, Kat stated crisply that Rhonda Burgess was waiting in the reading specialist's room. "She's very nervous and upset as she's the one who discovered Ms. Trandon. She's going home right after the interview."

Brian walked down the hall and into the reading specialist's office to discover four solemn children sitting at a round table and Rhonda Burgess sitting in a chair, crying quietly. Her face was splotchy with reddened eyes, her graying hair was leaking out of the bun at the back of her head, and her patterned dress looked wrinkled as if she'd worn it for several days.

Taken aback, Brian stared at the children. "What are you children doing here?"

A tiny head covered with blond curls peeked out from behind a large picture book. "We is here for the teacher."

"The reading teacher isn't working here today. You need to go back to your classroom." Three children got up and scampered out the door, but the little curly-hair blond girl just sat and stared at Brian. "Well, you read to me," she stated in a formal tone.

"No, I really can't. I am here to talk to Ms. Burgess."

"Oh," responded the little blonde girl. "I will read to myself." She proceeded to pick up her book.

Brian looked at Rhonda helplessly. "Perhaps you could explain it to her," he asked.

Rhonda looked up from her chair. "Celia, you heard the detective. Take the book and return to your teacher, right now."

The little girl got up from her chair and started out the door. Turning, she stuck her tongue out at Brian. "The teacher doesn't want to talk to you. I heard her tell the other teacher. And you should go home. My teacher wants her room back." With that, the child pranced out the door.

Brian turned back to Rhonda and began the interview. He asked Officer Speck to take notes and asked Rhonda to tell him everything she'd done that morning since getting up.

"Oh." Rhonda stared down at her lap. "Well, I got up, fixed my husband his breakfast early, and got him settled for the day. He isn't working right now. Then I fixed my daughter's lunch and left her a note to watch for the bus from the front window. Usually, I wait for her bus, but I wanted to get to school early."

Brian raised his eyebrows and look inquiringly at Rhonda. "Umm, Sherry was evaluating me today and I was so, so nervous. So I left about 6:30, I think. I drove straight to school, got out my bags and poster board, and headed upstairs to my room. I didn't see anyone."

Brian looked at her thoughtfully. "Were there any cars in the parking lot?"

"Uh no, not where I parked, on the side of the school. I never looked in the back."

"And who did you see when you arrived?"

Rhonda shook her head. "No one. It was completely quiet, completely quiet." She stared down and twisted her ring on her hand.

"So—did you like the principal?" Brian suddenly asked.

"Oh, yes, I guess so," Rhonda stuttered.

"Really?" Brian remarked, "From what I've heard, you'd be one of the first."

"Well, Sherry was very particular, and it was important to do things her way," Rhonda murmured.

"Did you ever disagree with Sherry Trandon?" Brian looked down at his notebook and thought about taking better notes. Not his strong suit, taking notes. Good thing Officer Speck took copious notes. Rhonda stared down at her lap. "Well, everyone did at some point."

"And you?" Brian poised his pen over his notepad.

"I guess I did. Oh, little things. We disagreed about how to handle a student or a parent. Just school stuff. I'm not feeling well. Could I go home?"

"Hmm," Brian responded. "In a few minutes. I heard you had a rather upsetting disagreement with Ms. Trandon just last week. What was that about?"

"Who told you that?" Rhonda's face turned a deep red and she started twisting her hands in her lap in earnest.

"Did you?" Brian asked again.

"Well, yes, Sherry and I had a discussion, but it was nothing."

"Yes, but the principal is dead. So why don't you just tell me what the disagreement was about?"

"Oh." Two large tears rolled down Rhonda's cheek. "It really was nothing."

"It's not nothing. In fact, it's important to the investigation."

Rhonda continued to cry, and Brian started tapping his pen on the desk. The woman did look ill. She was sweating, and her face had turned a pale gray.

"I suppose we could do this formally down at the station later this afternoon."

"Oh no." Rhonda looked up completely horrified. "I couldn't do that. Okay, okay. Sherry found out that I'd—I'd sort of misrepresented my teaching experience on my resume."

Brian stopped tapping his pen and stared at Rhonda. "Tell me exactly what that means."

"Well I—I—I didn't really have enough experience for the teaching job here. So I put down experience I didn't have."

"And?" Brian looked at Rhonda expectantly.

"And—I said I had five years teaching at a private school, but Sherry couldn't check it because I chose a school out East that had gone under—I mean, it was out of business." In a rush, Rhonda blurted, "And all the teaching I'd done was a long term sub position that ended up lasting three years in a large school district in Trenton, New

Jersey. I knew if Sherry checked, they'd just say yes, as the records weren't really clear that I was a substitute teacher and not a full-time hire." She paused to breathe. "I felt so horrible, but I needed the job here. Sean, my husband, hasn't worked in several years and I—I have to support him and my daughter. And there was a teacher shortage, so Sherry needed a teacher." Rhonda hung her head and looked as if she was going to puke.

"Mrs. Burgess, do you need water?" Brian asked. Rhonda shook her head.

"So—what was Ms. Trandon's reaction to all this? Describe your meeting."

Rhonda just moaned and shook her head. Brian and Rhonda sat in complete silence for a minute, and then she started to speak hesitantly.

"She—Sherry sent a note up to the classroom, asking me to come by the office before I went home. I didn't think anything of it. I figured some parent had a concern or there was some school activity she wanted me to do." Rhonda shrugged. "So, after I tidied up my room, I stopped by the office.

"Sherry was very formal and told me to shut the door. I knew then there was a major problem. There was an edge to her voice and she was all puffed up like she gets when she goes off on someone. She asked if there was something I wanted to tell her. I denied, but I knew there was something and that Sherry was going to rake me over the coals for it. I just started shaking. Sherry reached into a file on her desk, slid a paper across the desk at me, and then just sat back and smirked. I glanced at the paper, saw it was my resume, and knew I was in for it. I knew I needed to come back at her strong—Sherry hates weakness—but instead, I just started to sob.

"I told her how much the job meant to me, how much I loved the kids and teaching, how badly I needed to support my family, and she just let me run on and on. Then she stood up and self-righteously announced how I could never get anything past her, that she knew I was a bad, inexperienced teacher, and that I would be fired at the end of the semester. I was devastated, shocked; I didn't know what to do. I just sat there and cried. Sherry walked around the desk, told me to close the door when I was ready to leave, and walked out of the office. I don't even know how I got to my car. I don't remember driving home. I don't remember anything about the evening."

Brian looked up at Rhonda kindly and said, "That must have been quite a shock. How did your husband react? And what did the teachers, especially your friends, say?"

Rhonda spoke in a low, tired voice. "I didn't tell Sean, I didn't tell Noreen or Karen, I didn't tell anyone. No one knew. I got up the next morning, went to school, and taught the third- graders as if nothing had happened. No one acted strangely, and Sherry never approached me. It was bizarre. Two days later I got an official note in my mailbox that I would be evaluated today. Frankly, I just didn't understand it. If Sherry was going to fire me, why bother to come observe me?" The question hung in the air.

"So a few more questions for you, Mrs. Burgess, and then we'll be done for now. I know you talked to the police officer this morning, but I want you to describe again, in as much detail as you can, how you found the body."

Rhonda's face drained of what color was left, and she looked as if she might fall off the chair. Officer Speck leaned over and patted her shoulder. Tall and stately, with beautiful almond eyes, Officer Speck exuded compassion and confidence.

"Let me see. I got my plans ready for the day and put the worksheets for math on the students' desks. Then I thought about how awkward it was going to be with Sherry there. So I thought I'd clear the air just a bit and mention how excited I was about teaching this new math lesson. I mean, Sherry was the one who really pushed to get the math program adopted, so—" Rhonda's voice wound down to almost a whisper.

"But I really—I really—kinda hoped that if she saw what an effective teacher I was, Sherry would reconsider and let me stay. So I walked down to the office. Kat wasn't there and the office lights were off. Sherry's door was closed, so I listened to make sure there wasn't a conference. Then I knocked and walked in and and—and—Sherry was bent over her desk, kinda like she'd been reaching for something—maybe, I don't know. And there was blood, lots of blood."

Rhonda paused again and then continued.

"I think I said—'Oh Sherry, are you okay?' She didn't respond and then the knife registered with me. It was like I hadn't seen it before. I mean, it was sticking out of her back. I just stood there—I think my mouth was open. Anyway, I realized I needed to check if she was alive, but I didn't know what to do—I'd never seen a dead body before, or, well—a body with a knife. I leaned over and felt for her artery, but I didn't know what I was doing. She felt warm to the touch. I think, I think—I'm pretty sure I backed out of her office and then I used the phone in the main office to call 911. I told the operator there had been an accident. I just didn't comprehend at the time that it must be a murder because of the knife.

"I think I staggered over to Kat's desk and threw up in the trashcan. Then I just sat on the bench in the office, the one where the kids sit to see Sherry for behavior problems. Then Kat came bustling in and she started putting things away, noticed I was there, and thought I was sick. I told her something was wrong with Sherry and I had called 911. Kat walked as far as the door, gasped, grabbed the counter, and sat down. I don't remember what she said. Then the office started to fill with people, but I was faint and had to put my head down. The paramedics and the police came, and then it got so loud and busy and... they told everyone to go outside." Rhonda wound down like an old-fashioned alarm clock giving out its last tick.

"Weren't you afraid there was a murderer loose in the building after you saw Ms. Trandon? Why didn't you run out of the school?" asked Brian.

"I—I think I thought it was some kind of accident. I think Kat did too. We just saw Sherry and blood and I don't know... I must have been in shock."

"Thank you. That must have been difficult to experience and to retell. Just a few questions about time. You said you left home about 6:30, right?" Rhonda nodded. "How long does it take to get to school?"

"Oh, maybe ten minutes. I live down the street a bit."

"Okay," said Brian. "What time did you get to your classroom and how long did you take getting ready?"

"Uh, maybe 6:40 or 6:45, and I spent quite a while getting ready. And then I went to the office to photocopy my science sheets. The machine is in the main office so Kat can keep an eye on who photocopies and how much we use. But if you photocopy before Kat arrives—well, you can see how that works. So, I got down to the office about—I don't know, maybe 7:25." Rhonda sounded peevish. "I didn't know I'd have to recount my time. You know, I don't look at my watch all the time."

Brian ignored the peevish tone. "That sounds about right. The call went out to 911 at precisely 7:28. Well, that's all for now. I might have some more questions later."

Rhonda stood up, and without saying a word, started walking out of the room. Just as she got to the door, Brian called out, "Did you kill her? Were you scared enough and mad enough?"

Rhonda turned around and her legs started to wobble. Taking a deep breath, she glowered at Detective Brian Kerns and said in a low, angry tone, "I simply didn't have the nerve. She was a truly despicable woman, and I'm not a bit sorry she's dead." With that, Rhonda Burgess lurched down the hall and out the door of the school.

Karen Fowler's name had been added to his list of interviews because she was supposed to meet with Sherry Trandon that morning but had been late. The interview was perfectly normal until she mentioned that a teacher, Mrs. Hart, and her student teacher, Jessamyn Babcock, were supposed to be present at the meeting with the parents.

"Student teacher, what?" Brian sat up in his chair. "I know about the teacher, Mrs. Hart, who was waiting for you in the teacher's lounge for the meeting. She was there until the building was evacuated. But what about this student teacher? When did she enter the building? And where is she now? Why wasn't she on the interview schedule?"

"I'm sorry, I guess she got overlooked in all the chaos. Jessamyn is such a total ding-a-ling that no one takes her seriously. I'm so glad she's not my student teacher. I would have stuffed a teacher's manual in her mouth by now. Perhaps she did see or hear something. According to her, a policeman looked into the classroom but didn't see her because she was completely hidden behind the reading loft. She peeked out and saw him but never questioned how odd it was that a policeman was in the school." The detective couldn't believe someone would see a police officer and then just go about her business as if nothing was going on.

Brian made a note to check this out. He testily told Karen that he would need to interview this student teacher right away. She agreed to send Ms. Babcock to him as soon as possible. She added that Brian was welcome to keep her a long time, a very long time, as she was driving the regular staff, stuck in the gym, crazy with questions and comments.

Karen then went on to explain that she was late for school. "Yes, I was the one who was supposed to meet Sherry at 7:30, but I was late.

"The meeting was with Sherry, Mrs. Hart, the child's teacher, the student teacher, Ms. Babcock, and the parents, Mr. and Mrs. Watson. In the chaos of the morning, I never ran into the Watsons. I expected to see them with the rest of the teachers in the parking lot. It's so unusual for them to miss a meeting, especially an important one that involved Sherry because the Watsons are very concerned about their son. We were going to ask the Watsons to take their son, Preston, back to the family doctor to discuss medication. He had already been diagnosed with Attention Deficit Disorder, but without medication, the child was having a difficult time in school. I haven't heard from them, and with all the events of the day, I haven't had a chance to call them."

Brian stood up and stretched his legs. "Let's go find this student teacher, shall we?

Jessamyn was sitting in the gym, huddled over her phone, but quickly stuck it in her purse when she saw Mrs. Fowler. Detective Kerns stopped a few feet back from them to talk to a police officer. He could hear Karen talking to the student teacher.

"Detective Kerns would like to interview you now," said Karen.

"Oh cool, I'm so bored. Getting interviewed by that cute detective will at least be interesting. Is he the one who's kinda thin and has curly brown hair?"

Karen nodded. "He's right there, so keep your voice down."

Jessamyn said, "He's kinda old, but he's got such a cute butt, kinda like Liam Hemsworth from, you know, *The*

Hunger Games. Too bad he doesn't have a mustache. That would make him look so distinguished."

Detective Kerns turned around and gave Karen an appalled look. The officer he was talking to started shaking his shoulder; he was trying to hold his laughter. Karen frowned at Jessamyn.

In a firm voice, she said, "Maybe you had better think about your movements this morning for the interview and quit thinking about Detective Kerns."

Jessamyn said, "Well, I won't have to think about fashion, that's for sure. His clothes are disastrous. Brown corduroy pants and a white shirt? Does the man have no imagination? Old men always dress like drudges."

By now the officer was openly laughing, and Detective Kerns' face had turned a bright red. He re-joined Karen and Jessamyn, and they walked silently toward the reading specialist's room.

Breaking the silence, Jessamyn said, "Why are you people all so crabby today, anyway? Most of the kids have gone home and there's not much to do."

Karen stopped walking. "Look, this is a difficult day of many to come. The principal has been murdered. People are going to be upset and there are lots of things to do. My own list is a mile long. Check with Mrs. Hart about the substitute plans for tomorrow. She's going to be at a conference."

"Okay, okay, don't get all bent out of shape."

Jessamyn entered the room, looking disgruntled and chewing a large wad of gum. She plopped down in a chair. Detective Kerns gave Karen one more embarrassed look, walked in, and slammed the door.

"I understand you're the student teacher, working with Mrs. Hart."

"Yeah," she replied, unenthusiastically. "I am."

"How do you like it?" Brian asked.

Jessamyn looked up at Brian with interest. "You're the first person to ask me that. Everyone else just tells me what to do."

The detective paused and looked at the student teacher expectantly. "Well, I hate it. I don't like kids, I don't like this school, and I don't really like Mrs. Hart. She's one of those people that does everything right, you know, someone with a stick up her rear end. She reminds me of my fifth-grade teacher, always giving me a hard time."

Brian sighed. "I have a piece of advice for you, Ms. Babcock. You may want to choose a different profession."

"You don't say," responded Jessamyn gloomily. "My parents insist I get my teacher's degree. My Mom said the courses would be easy, but they were hard. I almost flunked *Introduction to Teaching*. My dad said I'd have a secure job. Like, what the f—, who wants an old person's job? I want to travel the world." She slid down in her chair and blew a huge bubble with her gum.

"So, about this morning. Tell me everything about when you arrived at school and exactly what you did with your time. Particularly, I want to know who you might have seen."

"Oh, the mystery, the murder," Jessamyn said. "This is interesting. I can hardly wait to text my friends. Like, none of the other student teachers have had a murder in their school."

Brian looked at Jessamyn with a droll expression. "Try not to get too excited. The principal lost her life."

"Oh, um, right." She attempted to make a sad face. "Um—I arrived at about 6:45. That's early for me, but, like, Mrs. Hart wanted me to teach this stupid language lesson and I told her all the grading for the math tests was done. And, well, like, crap, that wasn't exactly so. I—ah—um—hadn't graded anything 'cause I've just been so busy."

Brian nodded encouragingly. "What happened after you arrived?"

"I saw that frumpy teacher going into the building, Mrs. Fowler's friend. She always looks so worried and her clothes—gross, they must be right out of her grandmother's closet. I mean, she was wearing this long, lumpy, gray sweater over a faded flowered dress; her shoes were chunky type loafers. And the lining of her dress was showing. Her hair, even first thing in the morning, was like all tangled up in a weird bun she'd made at the back of her head. Like, disgusting, who dresses like that?"

"And her name?" Brian inquired.

"Uh, Mrs. —Mrs. Bugeye—no, Burgess, I think. She was in a fricking hurry or I'd have helped her with all her stuff. I followed her in, and she went up the stairs and I turned to go to Mrs. Hart's room. Oh yeah, I went right past the office and, like, it was dark. Creepy, right? The murderer could have been in there. Then I turned on the lights in the classroom and started grading. So... boring!"

"Did you see anyone or notice anything out of the ordinary? Anything?"

"Oh, yeah, I did. I saw that strange new aide sneaking up to the second floor. I mean, why sneak? WTF! Who cares if he's up there?"

"Why do you say he was sneaking?"

"He kept looking back, and kinda sliding sideways up the stairs."

Brian was puzzled. "When did you see that?"

"Oh, I went down to the office to photocopy my lesson."

The detective bolted upright and tried not to look excited. "You went to the office?"

"Oh, yeah." Her eyes popped. "Oh, I was there—oh, I feel sick. Oh my God! The murder!"

"Ms. Babcock, tell me exactly what you saw, did, and heard."

"Okay, okay. Whatever! I walked into the office to photocopy and I heard loud voices in Sherry's office. I figured it was the Watsons. I was supposed to be at that meeting, but I decided to skip it, too much work to do, you know. Now that I think about it, it really didn't sound like them. It was Sherry and someone, yeah, one person's voice, I think, and he or she was really mad."

Brian interjected. "Was it male or female?"

"I don't know—it was a lower sounding voice and angry—but male or female?" Jessamyn shrugged. "Like, I was kinda excited about the yelling because, you know, cool, Ms. Trandon is getting yelled at when usually it's her doing the yelling. So, like, you know, then I did my photocopying and left." She raised her hand toward Brian, palm first. "Now wait, I can tell you. I didn't meet or see anyone on the way back to Mrs. Hart's classroom."

Brian looked at the student teacher very carefully. "I want you to think about this, Ms. Babcock. What time do you think you went down to the office?"

Jessamyn rolled her eyes. "Huh, you're kidding, right? Who pays attention to time? You know, only old people wear watches and the school has all these rules about cell phones. Mrs. Hart gets mad when I get mine out. So time?" She shrugged hopelessly.

"Yes, but there's a clock on the classroom wall, right? And probably one in the office, right? And you were trying to get lots of things done before school? You said you graded papers right away."

Jessamyn looked put out. "Yeah, but like, who looks at clocks?"

Brian tried again. "How many papers did you grade before you went to the office?"

"Oh, like, maybe three. I'm a slow grader and, like, I was also texting my friend. And no, I didn't look at the time on my phone." She looked at Brian helplessly. "I really, really don't pay attention to time."

The detective sighed, "Okay, I'm going to have you work with a police officer to reconstruct everything you did from the time you entered the building, and I want you to think more about the voice and what it sounded like. You and the police officer need to look at your phone and see what time you were texting."

"WTF? I already told you what I did, and you can look at my phone now," Jessamyn whined. "I just want to go home."

"Ms. Babcock, this is a police investigation of a murder. I need your cooperation," Brian reminded her sternly.

"Okay," she muttered. "Okay, okay."

Brian turned Jessamyn over to a police officer with instructions to reconstruct the morning with her and to examine the times she was texting.

Brian walked back down to his new office in the reading specialist's classroom, sat behind the desk, put his feet up, and placed a call to the coroner in an attempt to clarify how Trandon was murdered and the time of death.

The coroner's oral report was short and curt. Stab wound in the back, which punctured the lung. Time of death: sometime between 6:30 and 7:30 AM, approximately. Could be a bit before. The body had been warm when the first paramedic arrived. Death would not have been instantaneous but would have happened within a few minutes. He asked about the murder weapon and was told it was a common kitchen knife, brand yet to be determined.

Brian doodled on the notepad and thought about the information he had so far. *Fairly short time for the murder, wouldn't take much force to push the knife in the principal's back between the ribs, the murder weapon was a kitchen knife readily available, Trandon's door was accessible, the*

*school was wide open to anyone who wanted to enter once
the custodian opened up at 6 a.m.*

*No one seemed to like the principal—in other words,
just about anyone could have done it. Well, maybe not the
young students, but everyone else seemed suspect. But why
was she killed? What was the motive? The night custodians
and the rest of the teachers who'd arrived before 7:30 a.m.
needed to be interviewed. How tedious.* There wasn't much
hope on narrowing down the time that Jessamyn was in the
office or whether she heard a male or female voice. That
student teacher was a real ding-a-ling, just as Karen Fowler
had said.

The afternoon passed with a succession of interviews.
The night custodians were also less than helpful. They
cleaned the school and saw absolutely nothing. They left at
midnight and locked the school. It seemed as if the aide and
the daytime custodian were up to something, but he'd have
to pry further to figure out what. Officer Speck had taken
copious notes of interviews with teachers and staff arriving
before 7:30 a.m. and had started constructing a chart
showing where teachers and staff were between 6:00 AM
and 7:27 AM.

Interestingly enough, no one, not the teachers, office
staff, aides, or students seemed at all sad at Ms. Trandon's
passing. Concerned, yes, curious about who would be the
temporary principal, and certainly disturbed by the death.
The students were intrigued and a bit upset by the murder,
but not sad about the death. Some were terrified a killer
was loose in the community and about to break into their
homes, but kids liked to dramatize.

Brian strolled up and down the hall, deep in thought.
The staff, when prodded, shared a common dislike of the
principal. She was opinionated, strong-willed, and
remarkably nasty. It seemed that everyone on the staff had
been the victim of the principal's biting comments.

Sherry Trandon enjoyed putting people down, not a particularly good quality to have as a principal. The principal had devoted her life to Kennedy Elementary School, but it appeared no one was going to really miss her.

Brian retreated to the reading specialist's room to gather his notes and make plans for the evening and the next day. Sitting at the desk, looking grim, was a woman. She was petite, with a pixie-like face, her braided hair circled her head like a wreath, and she was dressed in a tailored skirt, with a matching blazer. A silver chain hung from her neck. Everything about her looked expensive, which seemed unusual for a teacher.

"How long will you be using this room?" she asked. "I have children to teach."

"Hi, I'm Brian Kerns, lead detective for this investigation. I know it was inconvenient, but I'm moving back over to Kennedy tomorrow. I'll be in the reading specialist's room there."

She scowled at Brian, and he asked, "And you are?"

"I'm Milly Landon, reading specialist for the elementary schools. I was without a room today and it appears I won't have one tomorrow, either." Milly turned and marched out the door.

Brian called out, "Why didn't we interview you with the rest of the staff?" But Milly Landon had zoomed down the hall and out the front door. He made a note to interview her tomorrow. He was beginning to wonder who else he had missed.

"A friendly place." Brian sighed as he sat down behind the desk. Officer Speck entered the room, and Detective Kerns suggested they develop a plan. He would talk to the business manager for the district, Vince Watson, and Mary and Phillip Nash tonight.

Looking through their notes and schedule, both Brian and Sergeant Speck realized that Kat had not put herself on the list to be interviewed. Interesting! It was an oversight by the superbly efficient office manager. Also, one of the teachers had gone home sick—a Bobbi Nelson. Brian was pretty sure that was the teacher Brandon Leary, the aide, had described as having a visitor. They would need to interview her tomorrow, plus the reading specialist who had raced out of the room. He told Speck to set up the interviews with the Nashes and the Watsons and text him the times. He was going to stop by the evidence room at the police station and view the knife. Then he would do the two interviews.

Chapter Four

Late Tuesday afternoon and evening

Brian heaved a sigh and hoisted himself out of the rather uncomfortable desk chair. He gathered his papers, shoved them in his leather bag, and started down the hallway. He passed Kat scurrying into the office with an armful of papers and a laptop computer. Brian called out, "All the kids get home okay?"

"I think so; I haven't heard any complaints or calls of alarm. It's been an exhausting day." Kat shook her head. "I guess we'll see you at Kennedy tomorrow."

"Yes, definitely, and I need to interview you. How did you miss being on the list?"

"I wasn't on the list?" Kat sounded surprised. "I guess I was just so rushed, I forgot to put my own name on it. I had so many things going on—upset staff, crying children, hysterical parents. I just grabbed the staff list from the office, made a few adjustments, and handed it off to you. I'm sorry if I made a mistake."

Kat didn't sound sorry. She sounded exhausted. Brian shrugged. "Oh well, we caught it, and we caught Milly Landon too. She was missing from the list."

"Oh, I did forget odd Milly. She just started working at Kennedy recently, so she wasn't on the staff list, and she's just kinda forgettable. Well, I'm glad you caught it." Kat jerked the office door open and let it slam behind her.

Brian looked around for Karen Fowler before he left and found her upstairs talking to some crabby-looking teachers. "Hi, Mrs. Fowler. I just wanted to let you know I've finished the staff interviews for today. I'll see you over at Kennedy tomorrow."

"Yes, that's fine. Are there any updates I can pass on to our superintendent?"

Brian knitted his brows. "No, nothing. I don't release information until the investigation is done or unless we need help from the public. The superintendent could check with the Chaldea Police Chief for official information."

As Brian left the school, he acknowledged he was a bit disappointed by Karen Fowler's professional but distant demeanor. She'd been so much friendlier earlier in the day. She probably wasn't pleased about her friend Rhonda being interviewed so intensely. *Oh well, that's how police investigations go. The thing is, I like Karen. She's pretty, intelligent, fun—wait, I can't get involved with someone who's connected to my investigation. No, no, no—*

Brian pulled out his phone and started texting his sister as he walked across the parking lot to his car. It was great to be around Natalie again. She was always reassuring and positive, which is what made her such an excellent nurse. Natalie had always done better in school than he had. It was too bad she'd gotten married so young and settled down in Chaldea. But he was never going to mention anything about her choices.

Brian:
Hey Natalie, can I stop by and have a quick bite to eat?

Natalie:
Sure, if I can hear all about the investigation.

Brian:
No, but you can tell me about the school and the teachers as background information.

Natalie:
All right, it's sloppy joes and Josh will be delighted.

Brian:
*Tell Josh I can't play tonight but we're on for Saturday.
I'm betting on the Cubs to beat the Brewers in the playoff.*

Natalie:
In your dreams.

Natalie and Brian were longtime Cubs fans, but Natalie's ex-husband had corrupted her into thinking the White Sox could actually play baseball. Brian and Josh, Natalie's ten-year-old son, were scheduled to watch the Cubs game at his apartment while eating as much junk food as possible.

He soon pulled up in front of Natalie's small house on West Jackson Street. Brian noticed that even more repairs were needed. He'd need to clean out the gutters, the shutters were loose again on the front windows, and the porch railing needed painting.

Sometimes Brian wished Natalie had never divorced her loser husband. At least he had kept the house in good repair. Now the tasks had fallen to him, and he didn't have time for it. But he loved his sister and his nephew, Josh, and he'd do anything to help them out. Money was tight and Natalie was barely making a decent salary as a nurse at the Chaldea Community Hospital, so Brian had become the inexpensive repairman.

He hopped out of his car and waved at Mr. Dorsey next door, who was lumbering down the steps toward him, probably to interrogate him about the recent murder. Dashing into the house, he ran straight into his sister, who was laughing at his quick getaway.

"An escape from my nosey neighbor." She laughed. "You're lucky. John Dorsey would have had you out there jawing for half an hour if he could. He's so lonely since his wife died. You look bushed. Here, sit down." Natalie kicked a chair out from the dining room table. "Give me a sec and I'll have your sloppy joe ready. Here, drink some coffee." She slid a cup and the carafe of coffee toward Brian.

As he was pouring his coffee, Josh bounded into the room, wide-eyed. Always moving, freckle-faced Josh dashed around the table, bouncing a basketball. "Uncle Brian," he shouted, "tell me all about the murder. It's so exciting. Poor old Trandon, I bet she wasn't expecting to be—" Josh slid his finger across his throat.

Natalie held the sloppy joe pan in her hand in the dining room doorway and stamped her foot for Josh's attention. "Josh, inside voice, no bouncing balls, and sit down and talk to your uncle quietly." She waited until Josh set down the ball and fell into a chair next to Brian.

Brian made a face at Josh and said, "That's pretty much exactly what your Grandma used to say to me, Josh. You know a detective can't talk about his case, so as exciting as it is, mum's the word."

"Darn." Josh looked dejected. "I was going to tell the guys all about it tomorrow. You know, because I'd have inside knowledge."

"Sorry, no can do," responded Brian. "But why don't you tell me about Ms. Trandon so I can start to understand her."

Josh stared at the table, scratched his head, and said, "Will I get in trouble if I tell you she was an awful old lady?" Brian shook his head. "Well, I don't know why she wanted to be a principal because she really hated kids, she was always yelling at us, telling us to line up, don't do this, don't do that, and be quiet, blah, blah, blah. Did you know she used to walk the halls after we were in class, and line up our boots, shut locker doors, and pick up paper off the floor? She was a freak."

"Was there anyone she was particularly mean to?" Brian asked.

"Nah, she was mean to everyone, even the teachers."

"Really, what'd she do to the teachers?"

"Oh, she was really mean." Josh looked up at Uncle Brian tentatively. "I saw her make a teacher cry."

"Tell me about it."

"Well, I had to stay in for recess one time last year and I was sitting in the corner by the bookcase doing math, and Ms. Trandon sorta stomped into the room. She started yelling at my teacher that she was stupid, and she kept saying, 'We could have been seen.' She said it several times. It was really wacko. Then she left and the teacher sat down in the reading chair and started to cry. I just kept quiet in the corner. I think Mrs. Burgess forgot I was there."

"Mrs. Burgess was your teacher last year?"

Josh nodded. "Yep, she was okay, although she had trouble getting us to do our work. Mom said she needed to be stricter. I wish I had the other third-grade teacher, Mrs. Hart. She's much nicer and some of the boys say she's really hot." Josh made a face. "I don't get it; she looks normal to me."

Natalie pushed the swinging door between the dining room and kitchen and brought out a plate with two sloppy joes on it and a huge helping of coleslaw. In her other hand, she carried a small plate bearing a large piece of cherry pie.

"Oh, that looks delicious. I didn't realize how hungry I am." Brian picked up his fork and started to dig into the coleslaw.

"Josh, give your uncle a break and let him eat his dinner in peace. Besides, you have homework, so up to your room. I'll check on you in a little while." Natalie looked sternly at Josh. "I expect all the math to be finished, and then there's one half-hour of reading to do."

Josh looked crestfallen but got up from his chair. "See you Saturday, Uncle Brian. I can tell Mom wants to find out all about the murder, and she doesn't want me listening. Too bad for you, Mom, because a detective can't tell. Mum's the word." Josh ran out of the room and up the stairs. Brian, who had just taken a huge bite of sloppy joe, nodded and waved goodbye.

Natalie laughed and said, "Hard to get anything past that kid." Turning to her brother, she asked, "Background information, huh? What would be helpful to know?"

"Great meal!" Brian swallowed. "Start with this Mrs. Burgess. Josh says he had her last year for his teacher."

Brian whipped out his notebook and made a few notes as Natalie proceeded to give him the low down on some of the teachers and staff. When she had finished, Brian sat and stared at his notebook. "Do people know everything about each other's business? I guess that's the price you pay for living in a small town," he said. He looked at Natalie. "Why do you live here?"

Natalie glared at Brian. "Look, big city boy. There are some good things about Chaldea. People are friendly and willing to help you out. My neighbors keep a lookout for Josh after school. I know the family when I hire a babysitter. The schools are okay. I mean, they worked for you and me. So, people are nosey and sometimes gossip. So what?"

"I'm sorry, Natalie. I asked you for the background and that's what you gave me. It's just a bit different than gathering information in Chicago from neighbors who usually know nothing about the murder victim. Well, let me review what you've told me."

Brian looked down at his notes and began to star the new information. Mrs. Burgess attended a church out near Last Chance, a town that had gone belly-up after coal mining fizzled out. The church was conservative, evangelical, and downright crazy, according to Natalie. There had been rumors that parishioners walked on hot coals. Her husband didn't work and the neighbors were vocal about not liking him because he didn't help out around the house. Rhonda Burgess appeared to do all the work. It was time to find out more about the Burgesses.

There was nothing new about Sherry Trandon, except more reports that she was quite an offensive person, but this was tolerated because she ran the school so smoothly. Natalie had told him that Ms. Trandon was Director of Christian Education at the Presbyterian Church, so the pastor might have information about her. He made a note to interview him or her.

Bobbi Nelson appeared to be a colorful teacher. Not only had she been in the district for a long time, but she'd also known the principal for a long time. She seemed to be good at angering people with unpleasant comments (a bit like Trandon) and she had been involved with Dr. Nash off and on for years.

Mary Nash, the superintendent's wife and aide at the school, had unexpectedly developed quite a temper when Dr. Nash told his wife he was divorcing her. It was quite a surprise to everyone in Chaldea since most people considered her to be spineless. Mary had thrown all Nash's possessions out the window and onto the front lawn. That included underwear, condoms, a valuable antique rifle collection, and a wild assortment of other belongings. Then she'd stood at the second-floor window and poured wine and beer over everything she could reach.

The pair had reconciled as they were both living in the same house again. However, the rumor was that the affair with Bobbi Nelson had rekindled. Brian wasn't at all sure if this affected the murder, but he made a note to check it out.

Natalie knew very little new information about Jorge, the custodian. He'd been in the district forever, so Brian remembered him. She and Brian recalled attending his citizenship ceremony at Lincoln School as children.

Kat was efficient, but she hadn't gotten along very well with Ms. Trandon. Parents were quick to report on arguments between Kat and the principal and there had been a few juicy ones. Brian planned to interview Kat tomorrow, and this would be a good topic.

Of course, he'd asked about Karen Fowler, and Natalie had smirked at him. "She's single," were the first words out of her mouth. Karen had also grown up in Chaldea and had been three years behind him in school. Natalie went on to tell him she had married a handsome dude right out of college who'd joined the military. He'd been killed in Iraq and had left Karen with an infant daughter.

Karen had moved back to Chaldea two years ago to care for her elderly mother. Her mother had passed away and left her the family mansion; at least it was a mansion by Chaldea's definition. It was the one a block over on Garfield Street. It had been in a state of disrepair. People thought Karen should marry, preferably someone who was handy with tools and could help restore it. Gabby, her daughter, was now a teenager who made it clear to everyone how much she disliked their small, boring town. Gabby had babysat for Josh several times and done an excellent job. Natalie liked her.

Brian snapped his notebook shut, told Natalie the information had been great, and headed out the door to his car. Glancing at his watch, Brian realized he'd have to get to the coroner right away or the guy would be gone for the day. *Maybe small towns are good*, he thought. It was a ten-minute drive at most to the coroner at the hospital. In Chicago, it'd take him forty-five minutes at least.

Sometimes, Brian missed his old job with the Chicago police force. But he'd needed a leave of absence after getting shot during a domestic dispute, and then his divorce had been devastating. It had been too much. When Natalie had suggested taking a respite in Chaldea and getting to know his nephew better, Brian had agreed. It would be dull and peaceful. Two murders later, he wondered if Chaldea was as peaceful and safe as its citizens seemed to think. Driving once more around the square, Brian noticed how everything looked so closed up. There was definitely no bustle in Chaldea. *How do these merchants make a living?*

He headed out highway five and pulled into the brand new Chaldea Community Hospital. It was certainly an improvement over the old hospital on Harding Street. That building had been falling down since he was a boy and was known for harboring ghosts. It was very popular on Halloween. Brian hopped out of his car, rushed into the new lobby, and headed to the basement. He met the coroner on the stairs.

"It's about time you got here. I was about to give up on you," said the coroner. He turned and went back down the stairs and walked toward the lab. Brian followed. "The autopsy's been completed and I'll have a final report for you by 10 a.m. tomorrow."

"Anything of interest?" Brian asked.

The coroner grunted. "Not really. She was a healthy woman, organs were sound. I already told you about the wound. It really wouldn't take much force. A woman or a man could have done it. Due to the angle of the knife and the resulting wound, Ms. Trandon must have leaned over her desk when the knife was plunged in. She did try to have some tattoos removed a really long time ago, but it was a botched job. Some body piercings had completely closed up— bellybutton, nose, and three on each ear."

"Really," responded Brian. "Where were the tattoos? Could you determine an image?"

"Hard to say about the images. There was a tattoo on her right buttock, one on her outer left thigh, and one in the lower crotch area." The coroner wrinkled his nose. "Doesn't exactly fit the image she had here in Chaldea." He chuckled. "Must have had a wild youth. Well, as I said, you'll have the report tomorrow. You should take a look in the evidence box at the police station. There's a nice surprise in there for you."

"Oh," Brian said with interest. "Give me a head start on that surprise."

"The forensics team found a bloody lab jacket near the body. The murderer must have been wearing it when he/she murdered the victim. It's got blood splatter on it from the victim, but no fingerprints. The murderer must have worn gloves."

Brian looked at the coroner. "A lab jacket?"

"Yup, it even says Science Teacher, Kennedy Elementary School on it. Ms. Trandon had all the teachers wear white lab jackets when they taught science to," he scratched his head, "look more like a scientist, I guess. You'd have to ask the teachers about that."

"Thanks for the interesting details. I'll look forward to the report." Brian turned and headed up the stairs. As he did, his phone beeped with a text. The lab jacket would have to wait.

Officer Speck:
Interview with the Nashes at 7:30 and the Watsons at 8:15. Nashes were quite irritated that you needed to interview them again. The Watsons were rather forceful about saying they didn't know anything. Good luck! Am sending you addresses now. You wouldn't want to get lost in Chaldea.

Brian glanced at the first address, 223 Roosevelt Street. What is it with Chaldea and dead presidents? The schools were all named after presidents who died in office and the streets were named after past presidents. Funny, he hadn't noticed or paid attention to any of it when he was growing up.

Brian soon pulled up in front of Nash's stately home. It was a stunning house, with a wide front porch, an old-fashioned porch swing, and two columns on either side of the front door. The front yard was huge and contained two massive oak trees, one on each side of the front walk. Two large bay windows graced each side of the front door. He rang the doorbell and could hear the chimes inside.

Mrs. Nash came to the door. Her hair, which had been twisted into a ponytail at school, was now down, curly around her face. She was dressed in a long, flowing red skirt, and a flowered, almost translucent blouse. Holding a cocktail glass in her hand, Mrs. Nash held the door open. "We've been expecting you."

Brian followed her into a long, elegant hallway with plaster moldings on the ceiling and a long antique table running down one side of the hall. He glimpsed a formal living room on the left, complete with matching leather sofa pieces, a grand piano, and oil paintings on the walls that reminded him of an art gallery. To the right was a formal dining room lit by an exquisite chandelier. Was this how superintendents in small rural towns lived?

Brian recalled his tiny apartment in Chicago with its minuscule kitchen, a tiny bathroom that got flooded from the tenant above him, and the bedroom with no closet. *Crap,* he thought, *I'm ready to become a superintendent. It can't be that hard.*

Mrs. Nash wobbled down the hallway on high heeled silver sandals, turned left in front of him, and entered a large family room that seemed to extend across the back of the house. One wall was all windows looking out on the back yard where Brian could glimpse a large deck, barbeque area, and what appeared to be an in-ground swimming pool. Dr. Nash was sitting on the couch watching a football game. He too had a drink in his hand, and a pitcher, which he picked up to refill his glass, was on the coffee table.

"Drink?" he asked Brian.

"Thank you, but no," responded Brian. "I'm on the job right now." Gingerly, he sat down on the easy chair next to the sofa. Mrs. Nash settled herself on the couch, next to her husband.

Reluctantly, Dr. Nash muted the TV and turned toward Brian. "Well, it's been a hell of a day, don't you agree?" The detective nodded, reached into his pocket, and got out his notebook. "I have a few questions. First, when and how were you notified this morning that there had been an incident at Kennedy School?"

"Well, let's see." He turned to Mary. "We were up early, weren't we, honey?" Mary took a long sip from her cocktail and nodded. "About 6 a.m., I think. I wanted to get to work early because I had so much to do. It's been an unusually busy few weeks and the board meeting is tomorrow. So I slipped out the door much earlier than usual, and I actually entered the administration offices through the back door and went straight to my office. I just didn't want to be disturbed. Randy notified me about 7:35 or so that he was at the school and Sherry Trandon was dead. I was horrified and got ready to rush right over."

"Randy?" Brian looked confused.

"Oh, I forgot, you just don't know people around here," Nash chucked. "Randy Daniels, Chief of Police."

"And who did you meet or see on your way to the administration offices or at the office?"

"Oh, no one. It's too early for administrative staff and people aren't out and about at 6:30 in the morning."

"So no one can vouch for you?" Brian asked.

Dr. Nash huffed, "What am I, a suspect? You're way off your mark here, detective. Why would I kill the most efficient principal I have? Have you any idea how hard she will be to replace?" Nash looked at his wife and started chuckling. "She's one of the last people I'd kill. Not that I have a list," he hastily uttered. "Just, you know..."

Ignoring him, Brian turned to Mary and inquired, "Do you have anything to add to the statement you made at the school?" Mary took another long sip of her drink and shook her head no. She turned and looked disdainfully at her husband.

Nash spoke up. "I'm appointing Mrs. Fowler as an interim principal. She's got the administrator's certificate, she's quite capable and so much easier to look at than Sherry Trandon." He gave a guilty laugh.

"Oh, she's accepted the position?" Brian asked.

"No, but she will. It's a big boost in salary and she needs all the money she can get to fix up that monstrosity of a house that her mother left her."

Brian asked a few more perfunctory questions about the school district and funding. Then he stood up. "Well, thank you. I'll let you get back to your game." Dr. Nash stood up to walk the detective to the door.

"I'll see myself out. I know you're anxious to return to your game."

"Okay, thanks." Dr. Nash turned on the TV.

Brian stood outside the door for a minute. He could hear talking. Was that Nash telling his wife that the interview seemed to go okay? It was hard to hear. Brian leaned closer to the door. Mary was talking.

"Why, dear, you owe me big time. Don't you forget it. Lovely story you just told. Where were you really? And, by the way, you wouldn't want me to share what I know about you and Watson with the school board. I think I'll go check that Caribbean Cruise I mentioned." With that, she strutted through the door and straight into Brian.

"What the f—are you still doing here? Listening at doors? You're disgusting." Mary pushed past him and ran clumsily up the stairs.

Dr. Nash rushed to the door and watched his wife disappear up the stairs. "Don't pay attention to my wife, Detective. She's been under a lot of stress. Mary's always been fragile, if you know what I mean, and she's in one of her bad periods right now, not quite in touch with reality. Here, let me walk you to the door." Dr. Nash put his hand behind Brian's arm and practically pushed him down the hall.

"Please let me know if you need anything. Remember, your contact person is Mrs. Fowler." He opened the front door with a flourish and slammed it shut as Brian started down the porch steps. Brian could hear the deadbolt turn in the lock.

Brian sighed. *That interview will have to be repeated. All I got were lies. What's up with the Nashes?*

The interview with the business manager, Vince Watson, and his wife was uneventful. They lived in a much smaller house. Neither of them was particularly helpful nor insightful. They'd forgotten the meeting with the principal. So sorry! They had nothing to say about Kennedy Elementary, except that Mrs. Fowler and Ms. Trandon were pushy about their son getting medicine.

And as for finances? The district was doing okay, although resources were tight. It was looking as if they'd have to go for a tax referendum soon to raise money for the district. It would not be popular with the citizens of Chaldea. As for Sherry Trandon, she got upset about every little thing. Dr. Nash had told him that Sherry was reading the financials incorrectly. Brian climbed back in his car and drove toward the Chaldea police department.

It was a sad little building that was supposed to be a temporary home for the department, but after 10 years of occupancy, it had taken on an air of permanency. There was no one around but the night police officer. Brian sat at a temporary desk with the evidence box and examined the crime scene photos. They were less than enlightening and matched what Officer Danzy had described.

Brian leaned back in his chair and examined the blood splatter. Whoever had murdered the victim certainly would have gotten blood on him or her. He carefully looked at the lab jacket in the plastic wrapper. Then he picked up the bag with the knife in it. It looked as if it was from a set of knives. He noted that the forensics guy had left a report saying it had yellow crumbs and white frosting on it. So it had been used recently. They were tracing the model. Brian quickly snapped pictures of the knife and lab jacket for future reference. It was beginning to look as if the murder was planned, since the murderer had brought both a knife and a lab jacket. He returned the evidence box to the locker and made note of three boxes labeled "Trandon's desk files." He'd have Officer Speck examine those tomorrow.

Chapter Five
Late Tuesday Afternoon and Evening

Karen stumbled out of her car, bone-tired, and started up the front walk of her house. It was depressing to look at the front of her childhood home. The front steps were broken, the front porch needed painting, and the Venetian blinds had seen better days. She kicked off her shoes in the vestibule, threw her jacket over a hook, and proceeded into the large double living room. Two large rooms were joined together and spread out over the entire width of the house. The mahogany doors with glass panes which led to the kitchen, the formal dining room, and the solarium had been the pride and joy of her mother. Sometime soon, Karen thought, she'd have to remove the carpeting and expose the hardwood floors. *What to do first? Get rid of the Venetian blinds or pull up the carpeting and refinish the floors?*

Karen tossed her book bag in the direction of the magnificent old oak desk in the corner of the room and proceeded into the kitchen. Thank goodness her mother had remodeled the kitchen, as well as the bathroom. The floor had been tiled, and more granite counters and wooden cabinets had been added. The built-in shelves were still in place, and her mother's wedding china and crystal were displayed.

Sitting at the kitchen table, her feet propped up on a kitchen chair, was Gabby finishing off a bowl of ice cream. Gabby looked up from her iPad. "You're finally home. The entire town is excited about the murder of old Trandon. What gives? What do you know?"

Karen sat down heavily in a chair. "Honestly, I haven't had time to think about it yet. I've been so busy getting children sent off with the right adult, calming down teachers, and dealing with Mrs. Hart's student teacher. And it's Ms. Trandon, Gabby."

"Really, Mom, you can even make murder sound dull. Tell me what you know."

Karen proceeded to tell Gabby about her day; she listened with rapt attention.

"Huh, who could have killed her? The internet says people kill for passion or money. Ms. Trandon has no money to speak of, does she? And passion?" Gabby snorted. "Yuck, that's too gross to even think about. Of course, according to you, she was hot on the trail of missing supplies or a messed up supply budget. Maybe there's a motive there." Gabby grinned ruefully at her Mom. "It sure sounds as if your friend Rhonda had a terrible, horrible, no good, very bad day. Discovering the body, sick."

"I never expected part of the title of one of my favorite children's books to be used to refer to murder," responded Karen.

"By the way," Gabby continued, "Rhonda called you on our home phone about an hour ago. She sounded awful and some guy was yelling at her in the background. He took the phone from her and said you didn't need to call back. It was so rude."

"That was probably her husband. I don't like him. He controls Rhonda and bosses her around all the time. If he wasn't such a lazy SOB, he'd undoubtedly try to come to school and push her around in the classroom. I wish she would dump the lousy crap head."

Gabby was staring at her in astonishment. "Wow, name calling. It's a good thing we're alone or you'd lose your reputation for always being sweet and kind. But we both know the irreverent comments you make in private." She winked and gave her mom her special lopsided smile. "I've heard you call Rhonda a doormat, Ms. Trandon, a J. Edna Hoover, and Dr. Nash, a witless wonder. Tsk, tsk."

"Okay, that's enough; don't remind me of that now, especially on the day Sherry Trandon got murdered. Once in a while my sarcastic thoughts get the better of me. But I do feel sorry for Rhonda. She's such a kindhearted person. She deserves something better. I'm kind of curious about what she wanted, but I don't dare incur the wrath of Sean. I guess I'll talk to her tomorrow." Standing up, Karen said, "I'm way too tired to cook tonight. Let's go out to the Over Easy Diner. They expanded their menu to include supper."

"Can't." Gabby looked down at her bowl. "I'm meeting Logan at school." Karen made a face. "I know you don't like him. You have been super clear about that, but you'll like that Logan convinced me to try out for the annual musical production. Can you believe they're doing *Brigadoon*? Who puts on an ancient musical like that? This town is an antique."

"Okay, but eat some nutritious supper." Karen glanced meaningfully at what was left of the ice cream in Gabby's bowl. "I'm glad you're starting to finally get involved with activities, Gabby, and you do have a beautiful singing voice."

With that said, Karen turned and climbed up the stairs. She called back down, "Be home by 10 p.m. It's a school night, you know." She continued up the stairs and into the master bedroom. She loved this room. It was large, airy, and bright. The alcove with six windows which led to a second-floor balcony was one of her favorite places to read. The rotten wood on the balcony had been expensive to repair. She wished some fairy would drop gold nuggets down the chimney, as the house regularly ate up money.

Karen threw herself down on the bed and called her neighbor, Lucy. They had been friends all through school and had rekindled their friendship when she moved back to Chaldea. Lucy was witty, easy to talk to, divorced, and raising two kids on her own. She was constantly on a diet, although she didn't need to with her short petite figure. With her hair pulled back in her usual ponytail, she looked like a teenager. "Want to go out to eat at Over Easy?" she asked her friend. "Gabby's meeting despicable Logan tonight, but at least she's trying out for the school musical."

"Gabby turned you down, so I'll do, huh?" Lucy snickered. "Sure, let's go. The word is the food's gotten much better since their cook went to culinary school in Plain View. And, you know... you can tell me all about school and the murder."

"According to Gabby, my recounting of the day is boring, even though it involves a murder. I'll try to liven it up for you with garish details. Come on over around 6:30 or so and we can walk up to the square." Karen hung up the phone and set her alarm for 6 p.m. A power nap is just what she needed.

Karen met Lucy outside her house, and they chatted as they walked slowly up the street. It was one of those crisp autumn nights, and the moon hung in the sky like a big round platter. Walking down Garfield Street, she admired all the old houses and huge trees in everyone's yard. "This used to be such a wonderful neighborhood," Karen said. "Now the houses just look old and rundown, and we're missing all the elm trees. Sometimes I wish I would win Mega Millions, and then we could revitalize the entire neighborhood."

Lucy chuckled. "I think if I won, I'd keep all the money and move someplace warm. Who would want to stay in a crummy old house and put up with Iowa's winters of snow and ice and summers of hot, humid heat? Not me, thank you very much."

Opening the door of the diner, Karen looked in at a horde of people. "Oh my, it's crowded. I think the murder has everyone out and talking tonight. I'm not sure I should have come. I really don't want to talk to anyone, and God help me, I don't want to meet any parents."

Taking her friend's arm, Lucy guided Karen around to the back door. "I used to work here eons ago. We'll go in through the kitchen and sit in the back booth that's usually reserved for staff. They're so short-handed right now that none of them will need the booth tonight. Leave it to me. I'll even put our order in with the kitchen staff so the waitresses won't have to bother with us."

Slipping through the kitchen, Lucy called out hello to the kitchen staff. They both slid into the booth clear at the back of the restaurant. "This is perfect," Karen said. They were far from the prying eyes of parents. Sitting in the back booth, framed by a variety of discarded artificial plants, they were almost impossible to see. Karen examined the new menu and finally chose her favorite sandwich anyway. "What I want is a breaded tenderloin sandwich with the works and an order of French fries. Ever since the Dairy Bar went out of business, I've been craving a good old-fashioned tenderloin sandwich. The Dairy Bar made the best tenderloins, so I hope the Over Easy can compete. They didn't have the faintest idea how to make tenderloin sandwiches in North Carolina."

"Is that all you missed when you lived in North Carolina?" Lucy asked.

Karen looked a little forlorn. "I'm adjusting back to life in a small town. But I do miss the choices of restaurants, movie theaters, shopping. And I miss my good friends. And well, I think I miss my old school at times. Sherry was not easy to work for. Gabby misses her friends and all the things she had access to in a bigger suburban environment, like her dance class, music lessons, and if you ask her, the list goes on and on."

"They do make really good tenderloin sandwiches here. I'm having one too. The hell with diets." Lucy got up and bustled into the kitchen. When Lucy returned to the booth, she sat down and gazed at Karen attentively. "Now spill the goods about what happened. I'm dying to know what's going on."

Karen dutifully retold her day again, this time to Lucy, a good friend, and the current president of the PTA. When she finished, Lucy said, "Sherry did have a thing about not getting supplies like she used to. She even complained to me. But I do agree with Gabby. No one would kill Sherry for the money. I think her sister would inherit anything she has."

"Sister—she has a sister?" Karen asked.

"Oh yes, I met her at the PTA conference in Kansas City. You remember, Sherry and I went together." Lucy grimaced. "Sherry is no fun at a conference. The bright spot was that her sister lived there and took us out to dinner. She's a bit like Sherry, bossy, but she's nicer and a lot more fun. I'm sure she'll rush to Chaldea as soon as she knows about Sherry. Does she know?"

Karen shrugged, so Lucy continued, "As for passion," and she giggled, "I agree with Gabby, I just don't see it. I can't imagine Sherry with a lover. That would be just too weird. You know, I always thought of Sherry as sort of sexless. Well, I don't want to speak ill of the dead, but Sherry and passion? All she had a passion for was Kennedy School and that's just sad. One needs more to life than that." Karen and Lucy bent over their tenderloin sandwiches and proceeded to munch.

After a while, Lucy said, "We need to plan a memorial service for Sherry for the students and parents. I'll call a meeting of the PTA Board and we'll start planning. You'll have enough to do. I'm betting our good friend Dr. Nash will ask you to be acting principal."

"Me?" Karen squeaked. "Why me?"

"Well," Lucy drawled, "you're already assistant principal, you're respected and efficient."

"Oh my God, Lucy. You're describing Sherry."

"You're no Sherry," answered Lucy. "Let me finish. I know you have an administrator's credential, you're well-liked, you'll listen to people, and you've got more common sense than half the people in this town. And there's going to be a lot of rumors and hysteria. You'll do great." She patted Karen on the arm. "And no offense, there's nobody at the district office who could take over. Can you imagine Watson or Nash doing it? What you need right now is a drink at Pinky's. Yep, the next principal of Kennedy School needs a drink."

"Lucy, I shouldn't. It's a school night. There might be parents there."

Lucy looked at her friend. "Quit worrying. They're going to see Mrs. Fowler having a drink after a very tough day at school at," Lucy paused dramatically, "7:45 p.m."

After paying the bill, Lucy and Karen walked past Lester's Hardware, which had every small tool in stock displayed in the window. Then they crossed Harrison Street, went past the pool hall, and turned down the side street. Pinky's was lit up with a new sign, sporting a pink martini glass. Pushing open the door, Karen gazed in amazement at the new décor. Pinky had outdone himself. There was the original, oak bar with the huge mirror behind it, outlined with pink fluorescent lights. The place had new pink and purple tables with matching padded chairs, a jukebox that was working, and what looked like three new pool tables.

"Wait until you see the ladies' room," Lucy whispered. "Pinky put up stalls around the toilets, which is a vast improvement. Everything in the lady's room is pink—the walls, the floor, the toilets." She started to giggle. "It is *vomitrocious.*"

"Whatever possessed him?" Karen whispered back.

Lucy smiled. "He says it was a mid-life crisis. Let's not analyze that, okay?"

Karen walked toward one of the wooden booths. Thank goodness it had not been painted pink but had retained its natural wood color. Lucy followed. Karen looked around. Pinky's seemed pretty quiet despite the two murders that had taken place in town. There were a few young-looking guys playing pool, a scattering of what looked like regulars sitting at the bar, and a few groups gathered around the tables.

Pinky showed up at their booth, decked out in a pink apron. "I haven't seen you in here for a long time, Lucy, my girl. Heard you broke up with that fella. And you," turning toward Karen, "it's been a very long time. It's good to see you, Mrs. Fowler. Big happenings over at the school today, for sure. You'll be needin' a *Pinky's Special* to get you through this mess. And you'll want your usual Sex in the City." He pointed a manicured finger at Lucy, who nodded.

"Nice to see you too, Pinky. The *Pinky Special* sounds intriguing, but I think I'll just settle for a Sidecar. It's become my favorite drink."

Lucy and Karen chatted about this and that, both attempting to forget about the events of the day for a while. Nursing their drinks, they talked about Lucy's ex-boyfriend, Max. According to Lucy, he was a real jerk who left her always paying for entertainment when they went out, and he didn't even like kids. She was still trying to figure out why she had dated him. Then they discussed Karen's lack of a man in her life and the fact that she hadn't dated anyone seriously since Cliff died. Lucy suggested several Chaldea eligibles, to which Karen made a face.

Gabby's new boyfriend, Logan, was thoroughly analyzed, and both agreed Gabby was far too good for him. They acknowledged he was cute: the blond hair, blue eyes, and engaging smile made all the teenagers swoon, which was a good reason for Gabby to stay away from him. Those good looks spelled trouble.

They couldn't resist digressing into the Methodist pastor's wife's murder. Nothing like it had ever happened in Chaldea. Lucy described the pastor's wife as the kindest, sweetest person ever, just as she'd been when both of them had gone through school with her.

"I couldn't believe her husband would do that to Charlene, but I heard he'd had an affair with the church secretary, a Mrs. Trotter, and they were planning to escape to Venice, of all places," said Lucy. "I did a Google search on that Mrs. Trotter, and she's divorced and used to live in Cedar Trees."

The time flew by quickly.

"Lucy, I'm so glad you talked me into going to Pinky's. I really needed some down time. You know me, I spend the day being polite and saying the right thing, but inside I'm trying to hide my cynicism. It's been a bad habit I've had forever."

Lucy giggled. "I'll never forget the time you told the social studies teacher she was a boring old cow. And you were her favorite student. I knew you hadn't meant to voice it out loud, but nobody else understood that, especially the principal. Two weeks of detention. You broke that teacher's heart."

"Oh, don't make me remember. My Mom made me do the supper dishes for a month. I think it cured me of blurting out my thoughts."

Gazing across the room, Lucy leaned over toward Karen. "Some cute guy is looking your way," she confided. "My, but he is a looker. Tall, lean, with brown curly hair. He's coming this way, Karen."

"Hi, Mrs. Fowler." Detective Brian Kerns was standing at their booth, beer in his hand. "It's nice to see you again."

Turning to Lucy, he said, "I don't believe we've met. I'm Brian Kerns. I'm working for the Chaldea Police Department, looking into the murder of Sherry Trandon. Mrs. Fowler and I met at school today. She's been helping me organize my interviews and tracking down employees, including a most interesting student teacher."

"Jessamyn Babcock, yes, indeed—I've been listening to stories about that young woman for two months. I sincerely hope she never teaches one of my children, ever. By the way, I'm Lucy Calkins, Karen's neighbor. I was just telling Karen that I'll gather the PTA Board together tomorrow, and we'll start working on a memorial for Ms. Trandon. Here, sit down and take a load off. We promise we won't pelt you with questions about the murder." Lucy slid over and Brian sat down.

"Did you attend Chaldea High, Ms. Calkins, at the same time as Mrs. Fowler?"

"Call me Lucy and yes, I did. I was Lucy Melrose then."

Smiling, Brian said, "Okay, please call me Brian outside of the investigation. I—I do remember you. You were friends with my sister Natalie. You did that cheer thing—the Pompom Squad. Karen, too, I think."

Karen grimaced. "Oh my, I haven't thought about the Pompoms for years. G-O Go Reds, R-E-D-S. Yeah, we went to all the games and led cheers. I guess we were quasi- cheerleaders. And you were the oh-so-famous quarterback."

"Oh, I don't think I should have brought up this conversation. You're going to remind me of the state championship we lost due to me being sacked behind the line." Brian looked chagrinned. "I have no fond memories of that game."

"High school was a long time ago," Karen said. She remembered Natalie telling her how proud she was when Brian got a scholarship to Northwestern University after high school, and then a position with the Chicago Police. "I just didn't realize you were Natalie's brother when you first showed up at Kennedy today. She has kept me up to date about you. I'm so sorry about your injury. Are you healing?"

Brian nodded. "There's some stiffness in my shoulder still, but physical therapy is helping. Thanks for asking. It's been a difficult time, getting shot, and then Natalie probably told you, I got divorced. I came here to rest and see Natalie and Josh, but Chaldea seems to be teeming with murderers at the moment, so I'm helping out the police department."

Lucy's eyes widened. "Oh, do tell us about your murderer in Chicago. We just get absolutely no excitement around here, you know." She laughed.

"You probably read about it in the paper, but basically, my partner and I were called to a domestic dispute. You're always careful with domestics because they're so fricking unpredictable. And this one surely was. The caller, who turned out to be the wife, did not tell the dispatcher that she'd already killed her husband. She called and said he'd gone out of control and she was scared.

"So, anyway, we approached carefully. The wife was sitting behind a desk, and the husband was on the floor in front of her, with a gunshot wound in the chest. I shouted for the woman to raise her hands. She started to do it, but then she shot me in the shoulder right through the desk. It would have been worse, but I was kneeling, with most of my body behind the door. My partner then shot her in the arm. She dropped the weapon and fell to the floor. I was out cold, but my partner told me that when the ambulance was taking the wife away, she said she was tired of always having to make coffee for the bastard. So there you have it. Don't ask your partner or spouse to make coffee all the time." Brian laughed.

"That's quite a story. Normally, I'd say what do you expect from Chicago, but since we have a pastor who just buried his wife in the garage, I guess I'll say bizarre stuff can happen anywhere. You know, the last time we had a murder in Chaldea was Bandy, and that had to be twenty-five years ago. Do you remember it?"

"Yeah," said Brian, "Now that you mention it, I do. I don't remember Bandy's last name, but I do remember he was a vocal and crabby man, always picking fistfights. I had a good high school friend who worked at the local diner where Bandy washed dishes. Unfortunately, the guy developed a crush on her, and she is still livid about how he used to chase her around the kitchen prep table, sometimes holding a butcher knife, while the rest of the kitchen staff laughed."

Karen remembered how upset everyone was when Bandy decided to join the Black Panthers and traveled to Kansas City to do so. It wasn't like there were a lot of black people around Chaldea to join the movement. The problem was, he bragged about his membership and threatened the wrong people. He was found in the alley behind the diner, with several knife wounds. The murder remained unsolved, although it was pretty clear to most people who had been responsible. Karen's mother got really upset over the injustice of it all.

"That is one of the many reasons why I left Chaldea right after I graduated high school. I needed to get away from the sanctimonious bigots. Of course, what I discovered was that there are bigots everywhere. But, by then, I'd fallen in love with Chicago, so to Natalie's disappointment, that's where I call home," he chimed in.

Lucy glanced at her watch and exclaimed, "It's late! I've got to get home. Kids, you know. Homework, bath, bed—it never stops." Standing up, she turned to Karen, "You stay and chat with Brian. Nice meeting you, Brian. Talk to you later, Karen." She scooted out the door.

Karen and Brian continued to sit and talk about high school, mutual friends, and life since Chaldea High. Brian quizzed her about Kennedy Elementary and the staff. There wasn't much to tell Brian. She did mention how pressed for money the district was. It seemed as if things had gotten much tighter, and no one seemed to know why. Dr. Nash kept saying there was no money, but now essential supplies weren't even being purchased. When Brian got up to get another beer, Karen sat back and realized how much she had enjoyed talking to another adult who wasn't a teacher or a parent and happened to be good-looking and interesting. When Brian returned, he asked, "Who's with Mary Nash?"

Karen turned around in her seat and glanced over her shoulder. There was Mary Nash, looking half-smashed, on the arm of some guy. *Is that my mailman?* She squinted and looked again. Turning back around to Brian, she quipped, "Why, that is my mailman, I'm pretty sure. He's new to my route, so I don't know his name." Pausing and looking surreptitiously over her shoulder, she continued, "I'm kind of surprised. It's a bit unlike the Mary I know to show up at the local bar, mostly drunk, and with some guy other than her husband. I wonder what's going on with the Nashes."

"Here I go with the gossip. I heard that Dr. Nash is having an affair with Bobbi Nelson."

"No, not again?" replied Karen. "Bobbi has never said anything to me, but she has seemed happier lately, less caustic."

"Does Bobbi always get to school early?"

"Gosh, I really don't know. She's never around the office or the teacher's lounge. If she arrives early, she must hang out in her room."

Mary stumbled by on her way to the restroom. She half-waved at Karen and stared haughtily at Brian. "I'll just go see if Mary's okay." Karen got up and followed Mary to the bathroom.

Mary was leaning against the sink and examining herself in the mirror.

"Are you okay?" Karen asked. "You seem a little out of it."

"Who, me? Who the frick cares?" Mary grimaced at herself in the mirror. "I'm finished with being the good wife all the time. Phillip can go to hell. He's gonna owe me big time for covering for him with this district thing he's gotten himself into. And I'm sick and tired of his on-again, off-again affair with Bobbi Nelson." Mary practically spit at Karen. "I'm divorcing the bastard and taking the house, the cars, the artwork, and half his pension." She slammed into a bathroom stall, where she proceeded to throw up. "My God, Pinky is crazy," whimpered Mary. "Even these stupid toilets are pink."

"Do you have someone to take you home, Mary?"

A plaintive "Yessss, of course" came from under the stall.

"Okay, if you're sure. I'll see you tomorrow." Karen quietly closed the door of the bathroom and returned to the table. "Mary's had too much to drink, but she says she has someone to take her home. I've got to get going. It's going to be a really difficult day tomorrow. This was fun. I enjoyed talking about old times with you."

"Do you mind staying a few more minutes and telling me about this student teacher at your school?"

Karen looked at him in surprise and settled back down in the seat. "Well, what do you want to know?"

"She's hiding something that happened at school this morning. I can just feel it, but I can't figure out what. She got to school early but only managed to grade three papers. There's just too much time unaccounted for. She was doing some texting. Who is KN? She has some cryptic messages on her phone from KN."

"Hiding something?" Karen sighed. "I'll be so happy when her student teaching stint is up. She's the worst one we've ever had. But—hiding something? KN? That must be the boyfriend, Knowlton. I don't know his last name. Jessamyn talks about him constantly."

"Has he ever been at the school, like maybe before or after classes?"

"I don't think so, but you might want to check with her supervising teacher, Mrs. Hart. Jessamyn usually arrives right before the students, and she literally rockets out the door at the end of the day. The only day she's ever shown up early was today. And that was a bad day to show up early, as you know. Mrs. Hart told me she was worried about the lesson she was going to teach. And this young man certainly hasn't been around during school. I have never met him. What makes you think he was at school?"

"I'm not sure, just wondering," Brian said vaguely. "I interviewed Rhonda Burgess today. She was very upset about finding Ms. Trandon's body. What's she like?"

"What's she like? That's a hard question to be impartial about because she's my good friend. She is kind, generous, helpful... She's also an outstanding teacher with absolutely no confidence."

"Did you ever have suspicions about her teaching credentials?"

Karen stared at Brian, horrified. "What are you saying? She isn't credentialed? Of course she is. I've seen her Iowa teaching credential. She had it transferred from New Jersey. What a strange question to ask."

"Sorry, ignore that. Did she get along with Ms. Trandon?"

"As well as anyone on the staff did. We all had our issues with Sherry. She was difficult to work for. Very demanding, very structured, no sense of humor, never a kind word... My list could go on and on. Rhonda is not a murderer, if that's what you're thinking. She's just too sensitive and well, afraid of her own shadow." She picked up her jacket and purse. "I've got to get home." Karen started walking to the door.

Brian jumped up and followed her. "Did you drive?" he asked.

"Gracious, no. In Chaldea? I live just a few blocks away."

"I'd feel better if you'd let me drive you. It's late, you know."

Karen laughed. "Chaldea is not Chicago, although there have been two murders recently. Okay, I am kind of tired. Sure, you can drive me home."

Brian and Karen climbed into Brian's old rusty Ford Explorer and talked about mundane things all the way to her house on Garfield Street. Just as Karen got out of the car, he said, "I appreciate you answering questions. I hope I haven't put you in an awkward position. It was great running into you tonight. I'd like to ask you out to dinner Saturday, but I think I'd better wait until I have a better handle on this murder."

Karen climbed out of the car. Sticking her head back in the window, she said, "Am I a suspect?"

"Everyone's a suspect at this point in the investigation. Right now it's just one big mash-up. It'll sort itself out sooner or later." Brian smiled. "But no, you're not much of a suspect."

Karen walked up the front walk and stairs and practically ran over Gabby and Logan, who were sitting on the front porch. "New boyfriend, Mom?" Gabby asked.

"No, no. I went out with Lucy to the Over Easy Diner, and then we went to Pinky's for a drink. We met Brian there and he gave me a ride home."

"Brian?" Logan said, excitedly. "That's Brian Kerns, that detective from Chicago that got shot. He's renting the top floor apartment in our house. Nice guy, old car. He should be driving something much sharper since he's a detective."

"Hanging out with the detective, Mom, when you and all the teachers are suspects. Hmm, trying to get in good with him? Did you get any new information?"

"I did not get new information. And how were the tryouts? Did…"

Logan interrupted to say, "You're looking at Fiona, the female lead in *Brigadoon*. Gabby's voice is awesome."

"That's terrific, Gabby!" Karen reached over and hugged her daughter.

Gabby looked both pleased and disgruntled at the same time, no small feat. "I am happy I got the part, but *Brigadoon* was written years and years ago."

Logan almost snapped at her. "Miss Grundy does try, Gabby, but she has no theater budget. The rights to new musicals are more expensive than the rights to old ones. And Miss Grundy has the old costumes. We used to have money in the budget, but now there's almost nothing." Karen was looking at him with a startled frown. "Oh, I'm the theater manager and I've been doing it for three years now. That's how I know."

Karen tried to hide her surprise. She headed towards the front door. "School tomorrow, kids. I'm off to bed, and you need to come too, Gabby."

"Okay, in a minute."

Karen turned on the light in the vestibule and flicked on the light switch for the front porch. If Gabby and Logan were going to make out, they'd be doing it in the light. She wished she liked Logan more. He did seem supportive of Gabby's singing. But why couldn't he keep his saggy pants pulled up? She hated whatever statement the boys were making by wearing their pants down around their hips.

Karen wondered if part of her dislike stemmed from Logan's younger brother who attended Kennedy. He'd been an absolute terror last year, and she'd had to tangle with the mother about his behavior at least ten times. The mom knew curse words she'd never heard. She hoped it was a short high school romance that would disappear in time.

Chapter Six
Wednesday morning

Brian stumbled out of bed when the alarm sounded. Blindly, he reached for his Keurig machine and punched the power button. What a great idea to put the machine right next to his bed. Waiting for his coffee, he quickly checked for messages on his phone. Two texts from the Chief of Police telling him to check in with an update and a text from the coroner with the autopsy report attached. Glancing through his emails, he tagged a few to read. Most of them were junk, but he probably should read the one from his landlord in Chicago and his partner on the Chicago Police Force.

Right now, his life in Chicago seemed so far away. He hoped his cranky, elderly cat, Sibelius, was okay. The cat hated travel so much that he'd left Sibelius with his neighbor next door, who professed to love cats. Brian hoped she had the patience for Sibelius. His ex-wife had said the cat was crazy. As a musician, she'd been the one to name the cat after the Finnish composer, and then she'd complained about the cat constantly. He did admit the cat was a bit weird. Sibelius was the only cat he knew who dragged a white security blanket around with him and cried when he couldn't find it. The cat appeared to love music. Whenever Brian played his guitar, Sibelius would sit under his chair and purr. He wrote himself a reminder to call his neighbor and see how the cat was doing.

Drinking his coffee, he skimmed the coroner's report. There wasn't anything different than what the coroner had told him last night. Where and when did Trandon get those tattoos and piercings? This had to be a piece of the puzzle that was Sherry Trandon. He'd have to find out.

As Brian showered, he reviewed what he needed to do. Arrange to speak to the Presbyterian pastor about Trandon and take another good look at which staff had been at school before 7:27 a.m. yesterday. He sighed. Another interview with the student teacher was warranted, plus he needed to interview that odd reading specialist, Mindy or Milly something, and also the office manager. Oops, he almost forgot. He needed to interview Bobbi Nelson. And what about the daytime custodian, Jorge, and that teacher's aide? Something strange was going on there. There were so many pieces of the puzzle. Brian hardly knew where to start.

Well, as his old mentor at the Chicago Police Department had always said, just keep pulling at the threads, and eventually, everything will unravel. He'd have Officer Speck look through employee personnel files and see if there was anything that looked unusual. She seemed to have a real instinct for things like that. After that, he'd have her comb through Trandon's desk files.

Brian stood in front of his closet and viewed with dismay what was available to wear. He hadn't exactly done laundry for quite a while. When he left Chicago, he'd been so anxious to get out of the city; he'd just thrown a few clothes in his car and taken off. There was no way he could wear jeans, so Brian pulled his good suit pants from a hanger, chose a dark green dress shirt, and decided that would do.

His outfit wouldn't please Jessamyn Babcock. All that girl seemed to think about was how people were dressed. He was sure she had some snarky comments about his clothes. He didn't care about the spacey student teacher, but Brian admitted he did care what Karen Fowler thought. He smiled as he thought about their conversation last night. Detective work paid off with unexpected dividends, sometimes. Deducing that she'd been at Pinky's was no accident. He'd been hoping to run into Karen. With that in mind, he ran a comb through his hair and straightened the collar of his shirt.

Pulling up in front of the Chaldea police station, Brian noticed an unusual bustle of activity. The parking lot appeared to be almost full. He walked into the lobby and looked back into the interior of the department. The Chief of Police was sitting in his office, phone in hand, looking frustrated. He gestured the detective in, hung up the phone, and swung around in his seat to face Brian. "The mayor wants to make sure we're protecting everyone. I never hear from him unless there's some crisis. Then all I get is his whining in my ear. Politics, you know." Brian nodded.

"You've noticed we have everyone on duty plus some extras for today. We've got to cover all three elementary schools, the middle school, and the high school. Everyone's gone crazy thinking a murderer is loose in town. So, no pressure," the Chief grimaced, "but where are you in the investigation?"

Brian paused. "I've got several leads to pursue but no, there's no clear cut answer to Sherry Trandon's murder. I do think it was premeditated due to the lack of fingerprints and the use of the lab jacket. I think Trandon knew the person, or you'd think she would have raised some sort of ruckus. The murderer was standing behind her, so she must have trusted the person. Exactly why Trandon wasn't alarmed, we may never know. I have a lot of people to talk to today. I'd better get going."

"Okay, but let me know if there's anything I can do to speed things along. You've got Officer Speck and I'm also assigning Officer Danzy. Remember, Officer Speck is about to take the detective exam. She's eager to prove herself and she's tough, has to be to get along in an all-male department. I'll expect a full report from you on Speck at the end of the investigation. And any of the officers can do the grunt work for you. This is top priority.

"Oh, and we've notified the next of kin. We notified her brother, John Trandon. He says he and Sherry weren't on speaking terms and to let his sister handle everything. So we contacted the sister, Brenda. She was pretty upset about it all. She'll be arriving in town tomorrow sometime and will probably want an update on the investigation. You know, soothe her but don't tell her a thing."

The Chief chuckled. "Oh, one more thing, we've parked Trandon's car in her garage and the keys to her house are in the evidence box. The warrant allows you to remove whatever you need from the house, files, computer, or whatever, anything that helps you with the investigation."

The Chief looked at Brian over the top of his glasses. "I had a nice chat with your Captain in Chicago to sort out compensation and insurance. I left the paperwork on your desk. He said to remind you that everyone's a suspect in a murder case. And I'm suggesting that small towns have ears and you need to be careful."

"What exactly are you saying, sir?"

"I'm saying Mrs. Fowler is a suspect just like everyone else. So don't get too friendly. You were observed and overheard at Pinky's last night." The phone rang, and the Chief swiveled in his chair and waved Brian out the door.

Jackass, I know everyone's a suspect. But Karen Fowler is an excellent source of information. Small towns, crap! They're full of busybodies who need to pay attention to their own damn business. Now I remember why I moved to Chicago. Small towns are cesspools.

Brian got himself a cup of coffee, and then walked over to his cubicle to find Officer Danzy examining the spreadsheet that had been developed yesterday. It showed where all the staff had been before and after the 911 call. Speck had a stack of personnel files and was laboriously going through each one, examining the details, and making notes.

Brian brought both officers up to date, told Speck to continue with the personnel files and that she should examine Trandon's desk files. He told Danzy to look for discrepancies in interview statements gathered from the staff yesterday. He was going over to Kennedy Elementary to finish up a few interviews and they should meet him there when they were done. As he left, he called over his shoulder, "Danzy, start researching the make and brand of that knife. It had to come from somewhere."

There was definitely increased police activity around town. Brian spotted two state trooper cars on the square. When he arrived at Kennedy Elementary, a policeman was stationed at the front door, and another one was patrolling the halls.

Kat looked exhausted and flustered when Brian entered the office. Looking up from a pile of papers on her desk, she handed the detective a list. "Here are the absentees from yesterday, and I took the liberty of notifying them they'd be interviewed today. Should I contact Bobbi Nelson and tell her to be in the reading specialist's room in five minutes?"

Brian nodded. Looking around, he commented, "You've got some extra help, I see."

"Yes, the PTA has come to the rescue. It seems as though every parent is calling to see if we have school today. Why they can't just pay attention to announcements is beyond me. But I am grateful I've got some help answering the phone and calming down children."

Glancing toward the back of the main office, Brian saw Karen talking earnestly to a parent in the corner. Turning back to Kat, he asked, "So, Karen Fowler got promoted to principal?"

"Oh, yes," Kat responded distractedly. "Dr. Nash announced it to the staff this morning before school. Karen will be good. She knows the school and the parents and she has a calming presence."

Kat pointed Brian in the direction of the reading specialist's room. Brian was grateful that someone had moved in an adult-sized table and chairs and had left a computer on the desk with the password on a sticky note. Not that they'd want to use a school computer. He hoped Officers Speck and Danzy had laptops to bring with them, but perhaps not. The Chaldea police force, as well as the school district, seemed to be woefully underfunded.

Bobbi Nelson stalked into the room and slouched down in a chair. She was a bit taller than Brian. With her long black hair flowing behind her and big watchful brown eyes staring out at the world, she had a striking presence. "Take your time interviewing me. The kids are hell on wheels today. They're all wound up about the murder and none of my usual threats are working. I've got a substitute teacher in there right now; she can handle the little monsters for a while."

"Um, well, I wasn't planning on this taking very long, but let's get started." Looking at his copy of the spreadsheet, Brian said, "I see that you got to school around 7 a.m. Is that right?"

"Yes, I like to get here early, have a cup of coffee, and read the paper on my iPad. It's quiet and peaceful in my room."

"So, who did you see from 7 a.m. to 7:35 when the school was evacuated?"

"No one. I was in my room reading the paper."

"So you didn't see Jorge sweeping the floor or the first-grade reading aide, Brandon, getting books from the fifth-grade-grade teacher's room?"

Bobbi shook her head. "It's quiet up there, detective, and my door was closed."

"So how long have you known Dr. Nash?"

"Why, what an odd question, detective. Do you ask everyone that? I've known Phillip Nash for years. We've both been in the school district for ages." Bobbi smiled sweetly at Brian. "But then, you're not asking that, are you? Shame on you, detective, you're into our Chaldea gossip. Well, I'll let you be the first to know. Phillip is finally leaving his wife and we're both going to retire and move out of this dusty little corn town. How this gossip affects your investigation of our dear principal's murder, I don't know." Glancing at her watch, Bobbi spoke, "Oh, I do need to get going. I want a cup of coffee before I go back to the classroom." Bobbi got up and started to slide out of the room.

"Hold it, Ms. Nelson, I'm not done yet." Brian rose out of his chair. "Sit down."

Sulkily, Bobbi returned to her chair. "Sorry, I thought you were." Glaring across the table at the detective, she testily said, "Get on with it, then. I do need that cup of coffee in the lounge and our new principal won't like it if I'm out of the room for a long time."

Suspicious of her sudden change of heart, Brian changed topics. "I'd like to know what your thoughts are about Sherry Trandon. How well did you know her?"

"Oh, good God, Sherry! I don't want to speak ill of the dead, but Sherry was a lousy principal. Fussy, loud, bossy! Anyone on the staff will tell you that we fought constantly. She had a whole set of stupid rules and they mostly disagreed with me. But I have tenure. You've surely heard of public school tenure, job security for teachers. So she couldn't touch me. I only knew Sherry in a professional capacity. We never, ever socialized and I have no ideas about who killed her. There, is that enough?"

"No, not really. The teacher's aide saw someone going into your room at approximately 7:10 or 7:15. A tall man, according to Brandon Leary. Who was that?"

At first, Bobbi looked dismayed, but she quickly collected herself. "That was Dr. Nash, stopping by for a cup of coffee, and it was more like 7 a.m. because I followed him into the school. And he left right when the announcement to evacuate was made."

"Interesting, so I guess you did see someone then. And you weren't alone in your room as you said. I'll remind you that it's not a good idea to lie to the police," Brian stated. He made a note in his notebook to ask Nash about being at school. It certainly conflicted with his story from last night. Why would he lie?

"Am I dismissed?" Bobbi asked with a snap to her voice.

"For now," Brian replied.

The next interview was with Milly Landon. She was unusually surly and uncooperative, giving one or two-word answers. Brian couldn't decide if Milly was always unpleasant or if she had issues with the police interviewing her. He put a question mark next to her name and decided to ask around about her.

Kat's interview didn't provide any useful information either. Kat admitted that Sherry was very difficult to work for and there had been many disagreements. Sherry had not liked the way Kat dressed, was outspoken in her dislike of Kat's boyfriend, and basically picked apart everything she did. Sherry was so negative that Kat had been actively looking for a different job for the past two months. But new jobs were hard to come by in Chaldea.

Officer Danzy arrived just as Brian was preparing to interview Jorge again. The detective told him to have a go at the interview this time. Danzy attempted to get Jorge to relax a bit by talking about sports. Jorge loved the Iowa City Gold Sox of all teams. Brian had never heard of them, but he patiently listened as they discussed the team's standing.

Once again, Brian heard about how difficult Ms. Sherry Trandon was to work for and what a stickler she was for cleanliness. When asked about the teacher's aide, Brandon, Jorge seemed to fumble about and look uncomfortable. Jorge looked at the floor, twisted his hands in his lap, and finally muttered that they'd been smoking. Next, Jorge wanted to know if he was going to be deported. Danzy looked confused for a moment and asked what they'd been smoking. Jorge confessed it was marijuana and started sobbing that he'd lose his job and for sure would be deported.

After a confusing explanation of how years ago his uncle was deported for driving over the speed limit, Jorge stopped speaking. With great patience, Danzy explained that his uncle was not a U.S. citizen. Danzy, whose dad was a police officer at the time, remembered the hullabaloo when it was determined that Jorge's uncle was undocumented. He reminded Jorge that he was a U.S. citizen. Danzy remembered his citizenship ceremony at Lincoln School years ago; it had left a huge impression on him. So Jorge would be in trouble for breaking the law but wouldn't be deported.

Once Jorge had calmed down, Brian told him he'd let the new principal know. He was sure there'd be consequences, but perhaps because he'd always been a loyal employee, both the judge and the school board would put him on probation. He couldn't promise anything.

Brian put his head in his hands. He was finding out more about the staff than he'd like to know, but none of it seemed to be related to the murder. He groaned aloud at the thought of once again interviewing Jessamyn Babcock. He glanced at his watch and his list of interviews. Where was she?

He wandered down the hall toward Mrs. Hart's classroom and stood outside the door. Jessamyn was inside arguing with an older woman. Brian peeked in the window. The student teacher's face was bright red. Brian's eyebrows rose as he took note of how she was dressed. Today she was wearing what looked like 4-inch heels, thin tights, and a tunic that touched just below her rear end. The older woman wasn't shouting, but she was holding several papers in her hand, which she periodically shook at the student teacher.

Banging the door open, Jessamyn hurled through it. "I don't give an eff—" she snarled. "I don't care if you hated my lesson, you old goat. I quit!" She ran straight into Brian. "Oh, it's you. It's been a fu—frick of a day and I hate this job."

"Slow down, Ms. Babcock. It seems like feelings are running high. Let's walk down to the reading specialist's room and you can cool off before you blow your teaching career before it's started."

Jessamyn tottered alongside Brian, tears streaming down her face. Several teachers glanced out their doors and gave Brian sympathetic looks. It looked as if the student teacher's dramas were well known by the staff. He steered her into the reading specialist's room and into a chair.

"Tough day?" he inquired.

"Oh yeah, a real f...ing day. I thought Mrs. Hart was mean. But this decrepit substitute they've gotten out of the old age home is ten times worse. God, I wish Mrs. Hart was back from her stupid conference in Des Moines. She wasn't even going to attend because of the murder, but Mrs. Fowler told her to go." She slid down in her chair, put her head down on the table, and started to sob.

"I'll go and get you a cup of coffee from the teacher's lounge." Brian stood up and prepared to leave the room. He nodded at Officer Danzy to stay. "Just keep an eye on things."

Jessamyn looked up in horror. "Regular coffee? I don't drink regular coffee," she snorted. "There's a shelf next to the refrigerator that holds a sack with my name on it. You'll find my herbal tea in there. Make me a cup of that and remember to ice it." She put her head back down on the table.

Brian sighed loudly as he set off down the hall looking for the teacher's lounge. He felt like an errand boy. If it calmed the young lady down so that he could interview her, it would be worth it. Five minutes later, he was carrying a cup of herbal tea down the hall to her, properly iced. Turning the corner, he ran straight into Karen Fowler. She stopped, stared at him, and began to laugh.

"Uh oh, only Jessamyn drinks that stuff and it's usually after a complete meltdown. Did she get upset during your interview?"

"I haven't even gotten to the interview yet," Brian complained. "She melted down at the substitute, flung herself out the door with curse words, and proceeded to sob on the reading specialist's table. I'm hoping this calms her down so that I can interview her."

"Oh no, I'm going to hear it from the sub. We talked Mrs. Gumper out of retirement to help us out. She's an excellent teacher, but a bit old-fashioned. She'll never be able to tolerate Jessamyn while Anita Hart is at her conference." With an enormous sigh, Karen said, "Yet another problem to solve."

Brian nodded sympathetically. "You've got a lot to deal with and I have yet another problem for you, this one with Jorge and the new teacher's aide, Brandon. Let's plan a time to talk later."

"Okay, end of the day, I guess. Let's say around 5 a.m. in my office." Karen laughed morosely. "I don't exactly have an office. Meet me in the corner of the main office." She hurried off down the hallway.

Brian returned to Jessamyn and handed her the drink. She smiled and said, "Thank you, you're so sweet."

"Ms. Babcock, I need you to pull yourself together. I have a murder to investigate and I need some honest answers from you."

Jessamyn nodded sweetly and sipped her drink.

"So tell me what you were really up to between 6:45 and 7:40 when the police found you wandering the halls. You say you graded just a few papers. An officer checked the texts from your phone. Who is KN?" Brian glanced down at his notepad. "You texted him at 6:30 and 6:42."

"Well, like, you know, he's a friend." Brian continued to watch her closely. "So like, he's kind of a boyfriend. We hang together sometimes."

"Uh-huh, and so has this boyfriend ever been at Kennedy?"

Jessamyn's face turned bright red. "How did you know?" she gasped.

"Ms. Babcock, I'm going to remind you again that this is a murder investigation. You need to be forthright and tell me the truth. When was this boyfriend at Kennedy?"

She began to cry again. Looking up, she asked, "Am I in trouble?"

"You will be if you don't tell me exactly what you were doing yesterday morning. Now, out with it."

"You old people get angry so fast. I invited Knowlton to come visit before school yesterday. There was nobody here and I was bored."

"Knowlton? Knowlton who?"

"Why, Knowlton Nash. He is so cute." She practically smacked her lips.

"Knowlton Nash. Is he related to Dr. Nash?"

"Oh, I think so. I don't really pay attention to that sort of thing. I think Dr. Nash is his uncle or something."

"When did Knowlton arrive, what door did he come through, and how long was he here?" Brian barked.

Jessamyn wiped her eyes with a tissue and blew her nose. "You people always want to know details, details, details. I'm not sure exactly when, but I think it was around 6:45. I let Knowlton in through the side door, near Mrs. Hart's room. We went in the classroom for a while, and then he left around 7:05 or maybe it was 7:15." She threw up her hands. "You and time, like, who pays attention?" Her voice ran down, and she looked embarrassed.

"Okay, let me see. So this boyfriend was there for approximately 30 minutes, and you two were just talking?"

"Yeah, sorta."

"Ms. Babcock, what do you mean? Describe to me exactly what was going on."

Jessamyn's face turned an even brighter red. "Old people, always wanting to know what's going on. We were having sex. I was nervous about teaching the language lesson and it relaxes me. Do you want more details? We did it behind the reading loft. Then I walked Knowlton to the side door," she practically spit at Brian, "we kissed with lots of tongue, and then I went to do the photocopying."

"Oh," said Brian dryly. "That would explain your use of time. Did you see anyone when you let Knowlton in or when he left?"

"No, no, no. I saw no one. No one at all."

"Ms. Babcock, you should've told me about Knowlton yesterday when you were asked. He was at Kennedy during a murder and you lied during a murder investigation. That's serious."

"Whatever." Jessamyn turned up a pouty mouth toward Brian. "My dad's a lawyer. I didn't see anything yesterday that means anything for your stupid murder. My dad won't like you hassling me."

"Your dad won't like that you withheld evidence," retorted Brian. "So let's both calm down because I want to hear about the voice you heard in Ms. Trandon's office. You've had some time to think about it, so tell me more about that voice. What did it sound like?"

"I don't know anything about that voice," Jessamyn wept. "I know nothing. I just want you to stop questioning me." Brian sat and coolly observed her. Finally, she continued, "I'm not sure, but the voice was not as deep as my dad's. It was a little bit higher pitched, I think. It could have been a man or a woman. I just don't know. And the person was angry, really angry. She or he kept shouting stuff like 'No, you said you would,' and 'I won't.' It didn't make any sense. Ms. Trandon kept saying, 'Get it together, stop it,' several times. She laughed once but it was an unkind laugh. I hurried with the photocopier because I didn't want her to come out and accuse me of eavesdropping. That's all I remember." She crossed her arms defiantly.

"That's been helpful, Ms. Babcock. It's 9:30 right now and I want you to leave your phone in the office with Kat." Jessamyn opened her mouth to protest. "Let me finish. I do not want you talking to Knowlton, so please do not borrow someone else's phone. You will be in severe trouble if you contact him before the end of the teaching day."

"How about I keep the phone and just not contact him?"

"No, it's better if it's left in the office. I can't make you, but I think it would be for the best."

"Whatever." She slammed her phone down on the table. "I suppose you're going to tattle to Mrs. Fowler and Mrs. Hart about Knowlton and me."

"No," responded Brian mildly. "I won't say anything unless it becomes necessary, although I wouldn't advise any more trysts with Knowlton at school."

"Trysts, what's that?"

Brian looked at Jessamyn with resignation. "It's a rendezvous between lovers."

"Oh, why don't you just say 'hooking up.'" She rolled her eyes. "I'm out of here." Jessamyn got up and struggled to walk gracefully out the door on her heels.

Brian leaned back in his chair and rubbed his forehead. Knowlton Nash needed to be tracked down and questioned about what he knew. Did he leave the school as Jessamyn said or did he stay around? What was the real story of Dr. Nash's whereabouts? He could hardly be at his office and in Bobbi Nelson's room at the same time. It was time to find out more information about Sherry Trandon. He'd stop by the teacher's lounge, and then he'd go find the Presbyterian minister. He glanced over at Danzy who'd been taking notes. "Murder investigations get messy, and this one is headed that direction."

After dropping off Jessamyn's phone with instructions that Kat keep it until the end of the school day, Brian, with Danzy in tow, wandered into the teacher's lounge. Mrs. Fowler and a teacher were arranging massive amounts of food on a large table. Bagels, cream cheese, fruit plate, vegetable plate, cookies, and small sandwiches. Above the table was a sign, "Happy Birthday, Michael."

"I hope people don't think this is tacky so soon after, you know, the murder," said Sue, the second-grade teacher, as she labored to put a gigantic cake in the middle of the table. "It's just that Michael is so particular about having his birthday celebrated on the right date, and he's so annoying when we forget or have it late. Where's the knife for the cake?"

Karen was rummaging through the drawers in the mini-kitchen. "It was here, I know it was. It was right here. Remember, we used it for Tina's bridal shower. God, I can't believe she's getting married after all these years. Oh, I meant that nicely, I really did. I mean, good for her. Where is that stupid knife?"

Brian had been standing near the door, watching, and then stepped forward. "Mrs. Fowler, hello again. So, you're missing a knife?"

"Hi, Detective Kerns. We're looking for a missing knife. It's always here, so it's a bit disconcerting not to find it."

Sue started rummaging through the other drawers. "Well, someone probably borrowed it. But really, it shouldn't be in a classroom. That's a bit dangerous. Sherry would—not—like—that! Oh, oh my. Oh gosh, I forgot. It just seems like Sherry, oh poor Sherry, should be in her office. It's hard to get used to. This has been the hardest week." Sue sat down abruptly in a chair.

"Why don't you describe the knife to me? Use as much detail as possible," Brian probed.

Sue looked at the detective suspiciously. "You don't think it was stolen, do you?"

Brian patiently repeated, "Just describe the knife."

Sue looked at Karen.

Karen thought for a moment. "It was old, kind of beat up. The handle was brown—no, it was black, I'm pretty sure. I do know that the knife had three silver dots on the handle." She looked at Brian and asked, "Does that help you?"

Brian took out his phone and scrolled through to the picture he'd taken of the knife when he'd been examining the evidence. Putting the phone in front of Karen, he asked, "Does that look like the knife?"

"Why yes, it does."

Sue came over and looked at the picture. "Oh that's it," she replied, "or it's a replica. What's that brown stuff on it? Why do you have a picture of our knife on your phone?" Sue suddenly looked sick. Clutching Brian's arm, she gasped, "Oh my God, oh my God, that's the knife that was used on Sherry, isn't it? Oh, that's awful, awful, oh my, that's just awful. I feel sick. That's her blood on the knife. Oh no, I really feel sick now."

"Here, put your head down," Brian said kindly. "It's a shock. You'll feel better soon." Glancing at Karen, who seemed much calmer, he suggested she should get Sue a glass of water.

As Karen did so, Brian said, "Now, let me get this straight. You used this knife last week for a bridal shower and it's a knife that's kept here in the teacher's kitchen."

"Yes, that's right," Karen said. "Tina's shower was last Wednesday. Gracious, that seems like ages ago. We've had that knife forever. It was kind of dull, so Michael took it home before the shower to sharpen it. Apparently, he has a fancy knife sharpening kit. Anyway, he brought it back and it worked well on the cake. It's sickening to think about how it was used." Karen sat down too.

Brian told Danzy to take out his notebook and start taking notes. Karen and Sue watched them in dismay.

"So someone took the knife from the kitchen drawer and murdered Sherry. That's truly awful," whispered Sue. "That means it probably was someone who knew the knife was there and that means," she looked up in horror, "that it was someone from the staff who knew that we had it laying around in the kitchen. This just gets worse and worse. They probably even knew Michael had sharpened it. He announced it to everyone. It's a nightmare, a total nightmare." She laid her head back down on the table. Karen patted Sue on the back and looked apprehensively at Brian.

"I'm going to have Officer Danzy take your complete statement." Brian looked at Karen with compassion. "I'm sorry; I think I put a damper on your birthday celebration."

"We'll get over it. I think we're all just trying to adjust to Sherry's death. It's going to take time," Karen said.

Brian pulled out his phone, called Officer Speck, and gave her the news about the knife. He then asked if she had learned anything from the personnel files. He could sense the disappointment in Speck's voice as she related that she'd taken notes, but nothing had popped up that seemed to relate to the murder. Officer Danzy hadn't found any inconsistencies in the teacher's interviews, and she'd sent him over to Kennedy to help out.

"Did you get that interview with the minister at the Presbyterian Church?"

Officer Speck sounded frustrated. "I tried, sir, but the minister is reluctant to talk to a detective, something about confidential information. I have an idea that might help, though: you should take Karen Fowler with you. She's known the minister for years and he really likes her. Last year she settled some kerfuffle between the organist and the choir director. Practically saved the church since people were taking sides."

"Okay, I'll try to take Mrs. Fowler. Set up the interview for this morning, if you can."

Brian asked Speck to track down Knowlton Nash's address and phone number. He explained the circumstances and suggested that both she and Danzy interview Knowlton about the time he spent at the school. He proposed they meet for lunch at the Over Easy Diner and they could discuss some details and plan what to do next.

Chapter Seven
Late Wednesday Morning

Karen was upstairs in the library chastising a tow-headed young boy for jumping off the top of the bookshelves when Brian found her. She grinned at him. "Remind you of old times?"

Brian chuckled, "Why, yes it does, although I would have chosen a higher bookcase. More challenging. I hope you and Sue have recovered from viewing the knife. It was a bit gruesome, but the information I got is important."

"Yes, I sent her back to class and told her not to think about it. She said she had no plans to use large cake knives for a long time." *I almost told Sue to quit having hysterics and suck it up. That would have been a typical Sherry comment. So glad I swallowed it. We've got to get out from under Trandon's cloud of nastiness.*

"I know you're very busy with the school, but I need a favor. The minister of the Presbyterian Church knows Sherry Trandon quite well, from what I've been told, and I want to interview him. However, he doesn't know me, and he told my officer he was reluctant to speak to a detective. I thought if you attended the interview with me, the minister might be more forthcoming."

"I do know Reverend Wilmot pretty well. He is an older, traditional minister. Sure, if you think it will help. When is the interview?"

Brian glanced at his watch. "I just checked with my officer and it looks like the minister is available right now."

"Okay, here's the deal. We've been searching for the manual for the Iowa State Tests and can't find it anywhere. I'm thinking Sherry must have taken it home. Can you get me into her house to look for it?" Karen looked up at Brian, hopefully. "We can't administer the tests without it." *If I have to tell the state office we've lost it, I'll go down in Iowa history as the principal who lost the TEST DIRECTIONS. Damn Sherry. She shouldn't have taken it home.*

"Sure, it's a deal. I need to go over to the house anyway. We'll do it after the interview."

"Give me a few minutes to finish some things here, and I'll meet you at the church."

When Karen drove up to the church in her red sports coupe, she found Brian admiring the stunning exterior of the Presbyterian Church. "Chaldea does have some beautiful old buildings and this church is an architectural wonder. Just look at those stained glass windows. I don't know who replaced those old oak doors with ugly, white, metal ones. That was a mistake," said Brian.

"You should have been there for the six months of committee meetings. It was a drawn-out, bitter debate, beauty versus money, and the tight budget won." *No Christian charity shown at those committee meetings. Ugly!*

"Do you remember the chimes that used to play every evening at 5 p.m.? So peaceful." Brian looked downright wistful.

"Hey, just because you moved away doesn't mean we don't have chimes. They still play every evening."

"Oh, I thought they broke. Do you remember when a chime got stuck and the same note pealed over and over?"

"Oh, gosh, yes. Everybody went crazy. It seemed like every adult in town, including my father, climbed up to the tower to take a look and attempt to fix them. The minister of the church finally saved the day and got them turned off.

The chimes were broken for a long time, but we have Sherry Trandon to thank for organizing a fundraiser to get them fixed. She truly was a formidable force in this town, serving on various committees, handling fundraisers, and generally solving problems. And that was in addition to her work with the school."

Brian's eyebrows raised. "So she does wonderful things for the community, is extremely efficient at running a school, and appears to have no friends."

"Yes, I guess so. It's sad. Sherry and I were all business. I knew nothing about her private life." Karen really didn't; she couldn't stand the woman and didn't want to know anything about her.

Karen and Brian stepped through the door and into the inner gloom of the narthex. Seeing a sign pointing to the pastor's study, Brian led the way across what appeared to be a large meeting room and tapped on the minister's study. A tall, thin man with greying hair opened the door and welcomed them.

"I'm Reverend Wilmot. You must be Detective Kerns. How nice to meet you. Karen, it's lovely to see you. What tragic circumstances." His voice was soft, deep, and melodious. "How are things at school?"

"Rather hectic. Everyone is sad about Sherry's death and distraught about her murder. But the teachers are holding it together for the kids." The Reverend gestured to two comfortable chairs and sat down in the chair opposite. It had a pile of books next to it, some face down and some marked with a bookmark. The Reverend clearly spent a lot of time reading.

Karen looked around at the study that she dearly loved. Floor to ceiling books, mostly thick leather-bound, lined all four walls. There was an old roll-top desk in the corner, probably some antique from years past. A fireplace was against one wall that looked as if it hadn't been used this century. Several padded chairs and a cushy couch were placed in a conversation circle. Two large rag rugs, sewn by the Mother's Club, completed the study.

"I see you're both admiring my books," the Reverend chuckled. "I wish I could say they were all mine, but I inherited them from the last pastor, who inherited them from the previous and so on. It's quite a collection. You're welcome to examine them."

"Perhaps another time. Karen has limited time and I'm here on business," said Brian.

The pastor nodded solemnly. "Yes, you'd like information about Sherry Trandon."

"I would. Various staff members at the school and administrative staff have tried to describe her, but no one seems able to tell me about Sherry as a person. I need to understand her. How well did you know her?"

Reverend Wilmot placed the palms of his hands together and tapped his fingers. "I've been thinking about what to tell you and I've been praying. Although much of what I know is private, I think Sherry would want you to know if it will help bring her murderer to justice. When your Officer Speck called, I was quite distressed about confidentiality, but now that I've prayed about it, I'm ready to talk. Of course, you understand that everything I say is confidential."

Brian and Karen nodded solemnly. He took out his notebook. "Thank you for speaking to me. How long have you known Sherry Trandon and what can you tell me about her?"

"I've known Sherry most of her life. She lived in Chaldea as a young girl. Her family moved to St. Louis when she was in high school; the move was very hard on her. As a youngster, Sherry was a responsible young lady who looked after her two younger siblings regularly. She didn't have many friends. She was just too bossy and adult-like. Other children found her unapproachable then, just as adults found her intimidating when she was a teacher, and then a principal."

"Do you know anything about her time in St. Louis?"

"I know that she was desperately unhappy. Her father was very stern, and her mother was always sick. Sherry had to take care of the family. But she had no friends or acquaintances in St. Louis, so it was hard, very hard. She was a smart girl, though, and when she finished high school, she insisted on going to college. There were many arguments with her father, who wanted her to stay home and take care of the younger children."

"But her father allowed her to go?"

"Well, no. Her aunt on her mother's side, darn, I don't remember her name, she intervened. Sherry wrote to me about it or I wouldn't have known. Anyway, her aunt offered to pay her way through the University of Iowa, so off she went. I didn't hear from her for some time. And then one day, she just showed up at my study door. I hardly recognized her. She had tattoos and piercings, a spiked hairdo, lots and lots of makeup, and she was wearing old ratty jeans and a torn t-shirt. She was a very different looking Sherry than the one who had moved to St. Louis."

"I was startled, but I work hard to be non-judgmental. I invited her in and we talked awhile. I must say, I think Sherry was on drugs. She rambled, she looked sweaty, and the pupils of her eyes—I'll never forget it—they were tiny pinpricks. She was mighty stirred up. She kept talking about the love of her life, but I could never figure out who or what she meant." The Reverend shook his head.

"I tried to convince her to stay at the house. I was hoping she could pull herself together. But she said she had a lover outside, and they were off to explore the world. I asked about college, and she said she was taking some time off. I walked her to the door, said good-bye, and watched her take off on a motorcycle, hanging on to a wild-eyed girl with long blond hair, who revved the motor. I didn't quite know what to make of it.

"But, as I said, I try to not be judgmental and I never told anyone until now. I consider her past life highly confidential." Brian and Karen nodded. "I didn't see her again until she was hired to teach fourth-grade at Lincoln School. We never spoke of the incident, and it was as if it had never happened."

Brian continued to jot some notes in his notebook. Looking up, he asked, "What about her time living in Chaldea as an adult? Did you have contact with Sherry?"

"Yes, I did. Not the kind of contact I'd had with her as a child when she confided in me, but Sherry was active in the church. She sang in the choir, taught Sunday School for a while, and she recently became the Director of Christian Education. She'll be missed. Sherry always helped with programs and fundraisers. You could count on her."

Brian started to ask about personal conversations or confidences when the Reverend shook his head. "Sherry was very private about her personal life. I was not allowed in. She remained single, and I never heard of her dating anyone. She was a very efficient teacher and principal, but I never got the idea she longed to have any children of her own."

Brian asked, "What can you tell me about her sister Brenda? She's coming to town tomorrow."

"Ah, Brenda." The Reverend smiled. "She was a happy-go-lucky child, always smiling and laughing. She's three years younger than Sherry. I haven't been around her for years. I did hear she got a divorce a few years ago. As for other siblings, I don't think you'll hear from Louise. According to Sherry, Louise split from the family as soon as she turned eighteen and wanted nothing to do with her father, John, Sherry, or Brenda.

"John is the pastor out at a little church in Last Chance. He didn't move to St. Louis with the family but stayed in Chaldea and lived with a devout Christian family. He finished high school, and then went to Moody Bible College on a scholarship. Sherry did see him occasionally because she told me about their fights over religion. The mother has passed away. It's sad what families do to each other." He sighed. Sitting back in his seat, the Reverend looked inquiringly at Brian. "Is there anything else?"

Brian said, "You've been so helpful. I'm beginning to get a glimpse of Sherry as a person. Will you be the pastor for the funeral?"

"Oh yes, I'll wait for Brenda to arrive and we'll plan it together. I've already been in touch with the PTA about the memorial service they'll have at the school." He took Karen's hand. "We'll talk later about the details, dear."

Once more Brian thanked Reverend Wilmot for his insightful comments and left him to his reading. When they got outside, Brian thanked Karen for accompanying him.

"I think you were a calming presence, Karen. Thanks for coming."

"I didn't really do anything, just sat there. But if it helped, that's great." *Sherry took drugs? Rode a motorcycle? Had a lover? Holy Mackerel, that's a very different Sherry than the J. Edna Hoover I knew*—A loud ring interrupted her thoughts. "Darn, there goes my phone. It's Kat." Karen listened for a few moments, then stopped and spoke to Brian.

"I'll meet you at Sherry's house. This will take a few minutes." She turned away and started speaking rapidly into her phone.

Brian climbed into his car, inserted the key, and attempted to start the car. Dead silence greeted him. "No, not now." He hit the dashboard with his fist. "This stupid rust bucket!" He popped the hood, climbed out of the car, and stared miserably at the engine. "What do I know about cars? Damn!" He kicked the front bumper.

Karen walked over and stood next to Brian. "Do you need a mechanic?"

"I need a new car. But yes, a mechanic would be helpful."

"When I finish here, I'll call Joe's Garage and have them come take a look at it. They'll tow it to their garage on Polk and I'll drop you there before returning to school. Why don't you walk over to Sherry's house and I'll meet you there? Just go left at the square, then walk as far as Jackson Street. Her house is in the second block, a smallish white house with a wrought iron fence. Chrysanthemums are lining the walkway and baskets of mums hang from the porch."

"Thanks, I have the address. I need to get 15,000 steps a day on my new fitness step counter, so a nice stroll will help."

Karen watched as Brian strode purposely toward the square. *The student teacher was right—cute butt.* Five minutes later, she had averted yet another crisis at school and was on her way to Sherry's house. *Funny, I've never been inside Sherry's house. If it's like her office, it's gonna be downright boring.*

Quickly, Karen got out of her car at Sherry's house when she saw an elderly lady brandishing a cane at Brian. She hurried up the walk and stood beside the detective.

"Thief, thief, I've called the police. Now, you stay away from Miss Sherry's house, you hear? I've got the police on speed dial and they'll be here any minute." The woman was shaking an ancient phone receiver at him. The cord was extended across the yard and it looked as if it went through the front door of the house next door.

"Madam, I'm so sorry I startled you. I'm Detective Kerns and I'm working with the police. Allow me to get out my identification." Brian slowly reached into his pocket and pulled out his badge.

He showed it to the woman. She handed him the phone to hold while she bent closer to examine the badge. The elderly lady pushed her glasses down on her face, took ahold of Brian's hand and held the badge up close. "This is so hard to read, but I can tell it says Chicago. This is not Chicago, sonny."

"No, it certainly isn't. I'm working with the Chaldea police temporarily on the murder investigation of Sherry Trandon."

Karen smiled at the elderly lady. "I can vouch for him, Miss Brown. He truly is the detective on the murder investigation."

The elderly lady squinted and peered more closely at Brian. "Why little Brian, you've grown up. I hope you've learned to sit still and listen."

Brian looked again at the woman. "Miss Brown, I didn't recognize you. You're looking wonderful."

"Flattery didn't work for you in fourth-grade when you didn't have your homework and it won't work now," said Miss Brown, tartly. "I'm old, and not looking all that wonderful. A policeman, really, and a detective! Who would have thought? I heard you went to college. That must have been hard for you with no money to speak of. I know you didn't cheat on tests. You were always an honest little boy. So I'm thinking you worked hard to get to where you are now." By now, several adults were out on their porches gazing across the street.

"I did work hard, Miss Brown, and I have you to thank for teaching me to read so well." Miss Brown lowered her cane just as a Chaldea police car pulled up. Two policemen walked up the steps. Brian could tell they were working hard to keep the grins off their faces.

"Miss Brown, I see you've caught another burglar." The first policeman grinned at Brian and Karen.

Miss Brown pulled herself up to her full height of five feet, one inch, and stared at the police with a frigid look, one that she acquired through years of teaching. "I did not know that little Brian Kerns was helping you all find Sherry Trandon's murderer." Handing the badge back to Brian, she took the phone from his hand. "It was lovely seeing you, Brian Kerns. Good luck with your investigation. The Chaldea police need all the help they can get." Miss Brown turned and haughtily walked back across the yard, dragging the long extension cord behind her.

Both policemen allowed themselves to guffaw once Miss Brown had left. One policeman said, "I see you've met the neighborhood crime-stopper. Miss Brown takes her job very seriously, and I guess we have to give her credit for this one. You're not in uniform and you even got a cardboard box for the loot, even if it is labeled evidence box. And you've got an assistant in crime." He winked at Karen. "I suppose you did look suspicious, little Brian Kerns." Both policemen started laughing.

Brian laughed along with them. "I guess I deserved that one." He took another long, hard look at the first policeman. "But I'm thinking you have a few old elementary teachers around that might call you little Jimmy Sterling. It's good to see you again, Jimmy. How are the wife and kids?"

"Good," responded Jimmy. "It's hard keeping track of eight kids, but we're doing okay. I heard you were in town, eating up your sister Natalie's good cooking." Looking at the front door, Jimmy said, "I'll let you get on with your business. It's an awful thing that happened and everyone is shocked. Sherry Trandon was such a presence in this town. It's hard to imagine someone got the better of her and stuck a knife in her back." He turned to Karen. "Mrs. Fowler, it's a tough time at Kennedy right now, but the wife and I are happy that you're in charge."

"Thank you, Officer. We're managing."

Brian unlocked the front door, and they walked silently into the house. It felt closed up and it'd only been a day. Walking into the brightly lit living room, Karen noticed that it was certainly more cheerful than Sherry's office, but the room lacked personality. It could have been copied out of a magazine. An expensive-looking couch and matching chairs were placed around the fireplace. The coffee table held no mementos and the two bookcases next to the fireplace were filled with a variety of fiction and nonfiction books. Brian was looking around with interest.

"I've never been in Sherry's house," said Karen. "It feels like an invasion of her privacy. I need to look around for this manual. It might be out in plain sight or tucked away somewhere. Sherry sometimes used a briefcase and it's not at work, so maybe it's here with the manual in it."

"We'll look around together. Stick close to me and don't go wandering off. The house is not the scene of the crime, but it could hold useful information."

A small dining room held an antique table, four chairs, and a buffet. Brian took a minute to quickly go through all three drawers of the buffet. He held up neatly folded cloth napkins, some placemats from San Francisco, and a handful of silverware. Karen stood close by, watching Brian go through drawers. "It all looks so impersonal," she commented. "Doesn't she have mail and bills and such? Where are her photo albums? There's no junk drawer."

Walking down the hall together, Brian came across a small table with a landline phone and address book. "Finally, something of interest." He scooped up the address/phone book and placed it in the small cardboard box he'd brought with him. He'd have Officer Speck go through it later.

The kitchen held nothing of interest. A cup, saucer, and bowl were sitting on the drain board. "I guess she had breakfast yesterday. She was extraordinarily tidy. Nothing is out of place. I really hate going through her house." Karen moved away from the door. There were no bills in the kitchen and no junk drawer there, either. Continuing into the bedroom, Brian and Karen stopped in their tracks.

"Wow," Brian said out loud. Karen just stood there with her mouth open. The room was painted a stark white. The king-size bed was covered with what looked like a very expensive black duvet and the bed had a variety of black striped pillows against the headboard.

"Could we take a look in the nightstand for the manual?" Karen asked. Brian nodded. She carefully opened the drawer and they gazed at the contents. "Oh my," was all Karen could blurt out.

"Very interesting," was Brian's response. The night table drawer was filled with a variety of sex toys. He carefully closed the drawer and said, "I'll have someone inventory these later."

Against the far wall was a huge flat-screen TV, with a Blu-ray player, stereo system, and speakers. The carpeting was white shag and Karen could tell it was soft, even with her shoes on. Against the other wall was a long dresser with a massive mirror.

Karen quickly looked for the manual or missing briefcase that might be propped up against the dresser or bed but found nothing. Brian opened a door and walked into an enormous walk-in closet; Karen followed him. One wall was filled with racks of pantsuits, shirts, and trousers. Below were sensible loafers and comfortable looking dress boots. Those looked like the clothes she wore to school. Against the other wall were jeans, leather pants, dressy corsets, and sheer blouses. In one back corner, there had to be twenty tight looking shimmery dresses with baubles, beads, and glitter. Below were high heels of every color. Brian shook his head. "This is a Jekyll and Hyde closet, for sure. What kind of double life has Sherry Trandon been living?"

Karen was standing in the closet, staring at the sparkly dresses. "I don't think I knew Sherry at all. I never even thought of her as having a private life. Certainly not one where she would wear these dresses. What you don't know about people always amazes me." *Good heavens, and she gave me a hard time about how I dressed. 'Wear a suit, show those teachers you're in charge.'*

Brian bent down to examine the heels and said, "My ex-wife, Vivienne, would have loved this shoe collection." Picking up a bright orange heel, Karen tried to imagine how Sherry Trandon would have looked in one of those skinny dresses with orange heels. It was beyond her imagination. Karen continued to bob her head back and forth from the rack of business clothes to the more recreational clothes. "This is not the Sherry I knew."

Looking around for papers or junk boxes, Karen noticed a small cupboard right above the shoe rack of heels. Turning the knob and yanking on the cupboard door, she looked in at two small boxes. Opening up one box, she found herself staring at piles of photos of naked women. *Someone was an excellent photographer.* Taking several out and laying them on the closet floor, she realized that one of them was a picture of Sherry Trandon from many years ago. She was lounging on a sofa, completely naked, and looking up at the camera shyly. Her body had intricate tattoos and several piercings. A somewhat wild Sherry Trandon leading a very different life for a period of her young adulthood was becoming much clearer.

Suddenly Brian was there beside Karen and quickly scooped up the pictures and put the two boxes of photos in his evidence box.

He turned to Karen, who was still staring at the boxes, and said, "Anything you see here is absolutely private. You mustn't say a word to anyone." He frowned at Karen.

"Absolutely, I won't say a word."

The bathroom was rather dull after seeing the bedroom and closet. It had been recently remodeled and did hold a huge Jacuzzi tub and a walk-in shower with six nozzles in various locations. The medicine cabinet and drawers held the usual over-the-counter medicines and lotions and so on.

Across from the bedroom was another door that led to a study/guestroom. There was a sleeper sofa, a large desk filled with papers, files of information, and a safe in the closet. Karen started toward the papers. "Just a minute, you stay here. I'll look for the manual," Brian quickly said. After looking through the piles of papers on the desk, he triumphantly held up a manual. "This is it, I think. It says Iowa State Testing for Elementary Schools."

"Oh, wonderful. I'm so glad we found it. I wasn't sure what I was going to do if I had to tell the state it was missing."

"Mission accomplished." Brian smiled at Karen. "I know I've already reminded you, but it almost goes without asking that you keep everything you've seen today to yourself for now. I've probably shared a few things I shouldn't have."

"No problem," replied Karen. "I hate gossip and I've got enough on my plate with running the school to have time to chatter about Sherry Trandon. I'll wait for you in the car and give you a lift to Joe's garage."

"One question. I'm not much of a judge of furnishings, but doesn't everything in here feel expensive to you?"

"Oh my, yes. Principals are paid more than teachers, but I'm surprised Sherry could afford all this on her salary. Have you seen her car? It's a Mercedes Benz." Karen tucked the test manual under her arm and let herself out the front door.

Chapter Eight
Wednesday Afternoon

Brian stood on Sherry Trandon's porch, pulled his phone from his pocket and dialed the Chief. "I need the Major Crimes Team to go through the house this afternoon before the sister arrives, box up any papers and files to bring away to examine. Also, I need someone to inventory the house and list the value of the furnishings. I need to look at her bank account because I think she was living beyond her means. I didn't find her phone here and it wasn't at the crime scene, so I want the officers to search for that too. Her home computer will need to be examined by the IT tech. The team needs to be on the lookout for hidden cubbyholes. I already found one in the closet, but there might be more."

"Okay," said the Chief. "I'll get the Major Crimes Team right on it. No phone, huh? That's curious. Let's meet late this afternoon and touch base. I want to know what you found in Trandon's house and where you are with the investigation."

Brian hung up and walked over to Karen's red sports coupe. "Thank you for waiting, but I'll have to get my car later. I'm off to the Over Easy Diner to discuss the investigation with two of the officers who are assisting me. I'd like to invite you along, but it's a business lunch." He made an apologetic face. "How about a rain check? I feel I really owe you a meal for helping me with that Presbyterian minister."

"No problem," said Karen. "I need to get back to school anyway. It's important to be around for lunch and recess. See you later."

Brian glanced at his watch and called Officer Speck. "Let's meet at the Over Easy Diner and see where we are with the investigation. Bring Danzy along." He locked up the house and started walking down the street toward the diner. He waved at Miss Brown, who was standing inside her house, looking out her front window.

Brian walked into the Over Easy Diner and asked for a booth near the back, out of the way. The restaurant was busy, but the waitress put him in the back booth, far from the other customers. He could hardly see the rest of the restaurant, due to the array of artificial plants that were displayed on the ledge behind him. A large fake palm tree was draping itself over the booth. Officers Danzy and Speck soon joined him and all three checked out the menu. Brian leaned across the table. "So, what's good here?" he asked.

The two officers exchanged looks, then Officer Speck said, "Most anything, Detective Kerns. I guess it depends on what you like."

Brian grunted. "Okay, I guess I'll get their blue plate meatloaf special."

"Oh, don't get that," Officer Speck said in an agitated whisper that Brian could hardly hear. "It's Wednesday."

The detective gave her a puzzled look. Officer Speck quickly explained. "On Wednesdays, Marilyn makes the meatloaf and... well, it's pretty awful." She made a face. "Only tourists order it," she chuckled.

"Hmm, okay." Brian scratched his head. "I guess I'll get the green bean casserole with a side of mac and cheese. Is that good?" He looked at Officer Speck.

"Good choice," she replied.

Glancing around, Brian was pleased to see that no one was seated near them. He updated the two officers about what he had learned from Reverend Wilcot, the Presbyterian pastor. Then he backed up and summarized the interviews he had that morning with Bobbi Nelson and Jessamyn Babcock. Last, he described Trandon's house and said the Major Crimes Team would be careful taking it apart this afternoon. Danzy should accompany the team in their examination of the house. But he should also search for Trandon's missing cell phone.

Officer Speck told Brian how she and Danzy found Knowlton at the community college and questioned him about his whereabouts on the morning of the murder. When Speck finished, Brian said it lined up with what Jessamyn had said, except for leaving. She had indicated that Knowlton had left by the side door near Mrs. Hart's classroom. Knowlton, however, said he left by the front door. That would mean he walked right by the office. They would need to go back and question him again.

As they were finishing up their meals, Brian started outlining the afternoon activities. After interviewing Knowlton Nash with him, Speck was to examine the files from Trandon's office desk, with particular attention to her personal finances. Then she should start researching the district finances. She should ask the District Office for anything she needed, and if it was refused, she should make a list so they could subpoena the necessary documents. But who knows, asking might get her what she needed. For help with interpreting finances, Speck should contact Milford Ashton, the city accountant. He'd helped the police department in the past, and the Chief had told him he'd be available for this case.

Brian explained that he had informed Karen Fowler he'd be searching the classrooms at night for lab coats when the building was empty. But she'd told him very few teachers had their names written inside the lab jackets and he'd have a challenging time finding all of them. Some teachers kept their lab jackets in their classroom closets, some in the bottom of their file cabinets, some in their equipment cabinets and some who knows where. The only thing Karen could guarantee was that every classroom teacher had been issued a white lab jacket and they were to wear them while teaching science.

So he now had a new plan to find out which teacher was missing a white lab jacket. Officer Speck was to call Kat near the end of the school day to make an announcement. The teachers were to come to the gym immediately after school. Once gathered, Brian would announce that they needed to return to their classrooms to get their white lab jackets. He wanted to know whose jacket was missing and how that person acted.

Brian reminded Danzy and Speck that he wanted both of them to observe the teachers and look for any unusual behavior. He also wanted a few extra officers at the school roaming the halls while teachers located their lab jackets.

Officer Speck paid the bill at the cash register and waved at Marjorie, who was working behind the counter. Brian watched with interest as Marjorie attempted to extract information from Speck about the investigation. "Stop it, Marjorie. You know I can't talk about an ongoing investigation."

Marjorie turned to Brian. "You know, Rebecca was supposed to be a model, not a police officer; she would have gone far."

"Marjorie, you're embarrassing me. It was actually your dream, not mine. I'm happy as a police officer."

Marjorie shrugged. "All those macho males, I don't know how you stand it." With that, she slammed the cash register drawer shut.

As Officer Speck and Detective Kerns walked out the front door, Brian said, "By the way, we'll need to take your car. Mine died outside the Presbyterian Church and it's been towed to Joe's garage. Let's go there first so I can find out how much it's going to cost me."

They both climbed into Officer Speck's battered, bright red Volkswagen Bug. "What a beauty and what a relic from the past." Brian patted the dashboard. "I've got fond memories of Volkswagen Bugs."

"It belonged to my brother. He lives in Vietnam, of all places, and sends me postcards inquiring about his car, even though he gave up ownership years ago. I'm hoping the Bug will last a few more years."

Soon they pulled up in front of a dilapidated garage surrounded by rusting hulks of vehicles and old tires. "I hope this place is better than it looks," said Brian, as he climbed out of the car.

"Joe's a marvel with cars, Detective Kerns. You're in good hands."

Brian was soon back at the car. "The car's a total wreck. We're talking a new engine, and the car is not worth it. Joe was surprised the car even made it here from Chicago. He suggested that a detective like me should drive a Ford Explorer, and it so happens that Brad Melrose has a used one at his dealership out on highway five. I can't believe this. I'm going to have to buy a car in order to get home."

"I'm sorry about that. But Brad Melrose is a very respectable dealer, so you might find a good deal."

"I'll worry about a car later. Where is Knowlton Nash, out at the college? Or do we have his home address?"

"I've got his home address, but I'm guessing he's not there at this time of day. I'm sure he has a part-time job somewhere. I'm going to call my cousin; she graduated with him. Mary tends to keep tabs on everybody."

Picking up her cell phone, Speck dialed the number and put it on speaker. Just as she was about to hang up, Mary answered, "Hi, Rebecca, what do you want? I just got Anthony down for a nap, thank God. I'm dying to know about the murder. What's happening?"

"Mary, I can't talk about the investigation. But I am curious about where Knowlton Nash works."

"Oooh, is he a suspect? Harmless, handsome Knowlton."

"No, he's not a suspect," Speck answered huffily. "I just need to talk to him."

"Yes, but what about? Is he part of the murder investigation? Hmm, did he have an affair with Sherry Trandon?" Mary laughed.

"Go back to your soap operas, Mary. But first, tell me where Knowlton works."

"Oh, okay. You just have no sense of humor since you've become a police officer. I still can't believe you're a cop. When we were little, all you wanted to be was a beautician. What happened to that dream?"

"Mary, please, do you know where Knowlton works or not?"

"Okay, okay! I'm pretty sure Knowlton still works for Jim Nagly's Best Men's Wear."

"Thanks, Mary. Talk to you later." Rebecca shoved her phone in her purse.

Nagly's Best Men's Wear was located on the square, where it'd been for the last 50 years. Every male in Chaldea bought a suit there, at least once. Usually, it was for a wedding, but sometimes you didn't get a Nagly's suit until your funeral. But every male graduate from Chaldea High School who could afford it bought his suit for senior pictures from the store. It was a cherished institution in Chaldea.

Officer Speck parked her Volkswagen Bug in front of the store, and she and Brian entered the regal old store. The shelving was all oak, the walls were pure plaster, and intricate moldings filled the space where the walls met the ceiling. But the best features were the four crystal chandeliers that hung majestically from the ceiling. It was like entering a museum, rather than a men's clothing store. An older gentleman, dressed in a navy suit, approached them. "And how might I help the police today?" he inquired.

"I'm looking for Knowlton Nash. Is he working this afternoon?" asked Officer Speck.

"Why, yes, he is, young lady. Mr. Nash is back in the storeroom. I'll fetch him for you."

Knowlton soon appeared from the back of the store. "Officer Speck, I'm surprised you're here. And you must be the detective everyone is talking about." Brian, who'd been looking around at the store, nodded.

"I answered your questions this morning." Leaning closer to Officer Speck, he whispered, "You've got old Henry in quite a tizzy. He doesn't think it's proper for the police to be here in the inner sanctum of Nagly's Best Men's Wear." Knowlton winked at Officer Speck.

"Perhaps there is someplace else we could talk?" asked Brian.

"Why don't I take my break and we can step over to John's Garage and have a coffee. That will make it easier for everyone. Just a minute and I'll be right back."

Knowlton soon re-appeared with a black top jacket slung over his arm. He was dressed in a deep blue suit with a thin silver stripe pattern. The shirt was a light blue with a blue patterned tie. He even had a dotted blue pocket square. The classy outfit looked good on his boyish figure, helped out by his boyish grin. Detective Kerns was beginning to understand how Jessamyn might like him.

Knowlton caught Officer Speck looking at him. "Believe me, it's for the job. Dressing up like this every day is not something I'd do if I didn't work at sacred Nagly's."

John's Garage, a new fast-food restaurant, was filled with locals drinking Coca-Colas and eating French fries. Brian looked around at the crowd. *Don't people have to work? It's the middle of the day.* He sat down in the only empty booth while Knowlton and Officer Speck went up to the counter to get coffees. When they returned, Officer Speck flipped open her notebook and said, "I need to clarify some details with you about yesterday morning."

"Okay, shoot."

"This morning you told Officer Danzy and me that you left the school, but you didn't specify which door. Which door did you exit?"

Knowlton looked up from his coffee and frowned. "I went out the front door because I was looking for my Uncle Phil. He'd just announced to the family that he was getting divorced and I wanted to get the low down. I thought he might be visiting Bobbi Newton, his girlfriend, so I was sort of hoping I'd run into him."

"I ask because Jessamyn Babcock told Detective Kerns that you left by the side door."

Knowlton looked annoyed. "That girl—she's two french-fries short of a happy meal." He shrugged. "All she thinks about is fashion and clothes."

Brian leaned forward. "Tell me about when you left. Who was around? What lights were on?"

Knowlton took a sip of his coffee and said, "It was only 7:10 or thereabouts, as I told Officer Speck. No one was there. I didn't see anyone walking down the hall and all the classrooms were dark. So was the hall for that matter. And you know, the office area was completely dark too."

Knowlton stopped talking for a few seconds and then said, "But I do remember seeing someone outside the school. As I was walking around the front of the school, I saw a kid in the bushes. He was there and then suddenly he wasn't. The kid must have scrunched down when he saw me."

Officer Speck looked up from her notebook. "This is important information, Mr. Nash. Exactly where did you see him?"

Knowlton rubbed his forehead. "I turned right out of the door and it was the bushes under the second window. Yeah, that's right—the second window. I really didn't see much of the kid. It was just a blur of the back of the head. Brown hair, I think."

Officer Speck snapped her notebook closed. "You've been very helpful, Mr. Nash. We'll be in touch if we have any additional questions." She started to rise from her seat when Knowlton put his hand on her arm.

"I've got a few questions for you. I've been thinking about becoming a police officer. What's it like?"

Officer Speck stared at Knowlton, open-mouthed. "Uh, that was not a question I was expecting." Brian sat back and looked from one to the other.

"What's the matter? Do you think I can't handle it? I mean, if you can do it, I certainly can." Knowlton flexed his arm muscles. "Besides, it's pretty easy. You ride around in a police car all day, right? What's the pay like? It's got to be better than Nagly's." Brian snorted softly. Knowlton glanced in his direction but then turned back to Officer Speck.

"I hadn't considered whether you can handle it, Mr. Nash." Officer Speck's voice was curt and short. "I just know it's a lot of hard work, requires more schooling than you think, and the hours can sometimes be really brutal. Like now, when we're working nonstop. I'm not prepared for career day questions today. I suggest you ask someone else." Officer Speck got up abruptly and walked out the door.

Brian rose to follow her. "I think you really pissed off the officer, Knowlton, insinuating that anyone can do the job."

Brian climbed into the car and saw that Officer Speck was seething with anger. "How dare Knowlton Nash ask about becoming a police officer? My cousin says Knowlton is a lazy student and a goof-around who brags about breaking minor laws."

"He's a bit of a jackass, but you handled him well."

"I guess. It's just that I worked so hard to become a police officer, and there's been so much harassment. It's hard being the only woman on the force." She leaned exhaustedly against the steering wheel. "It just seems that every jerk in the county thinks being a police officer is just flexing muscles and riding around in a police car."

"I really admire you, Officer Speck, for being the only female in the Chaldea Police Department. It must be a rather lonely position. In my experience, male police officers can often be unbelievably sexist. We need female role models like you. Stay with it."

Officer Speck shot Brian a grateful look. "Thank you. Not to change the subject, but we have a possible witness, and a kid, no less. It's a bit weird, though. This kid was at school well before children were permitted to be there."

"Good point, Speck. I interviewed all the kids who were on the playground early, but I'm almost positive this kid wasn't included. And he would have been in the bushes at 7:15 or so when Knowlton Nash left. The question is how long was he there and what did he see or hear? Who could this kid be?"

Brian pumped his fist and hit the dashboard. "Finally, a breakthrough! We need to identify this kid, but we'll have to be careful. We'll start with teachers and staff, and find out what kid might have gotten dropped off that early. And I want you to ask the custodian, Jorge, too. Custodians always know what's going on in schools. Be very careful about how you do it. I don't want the murderer alerted."

"Yes sir, I'm on it," responded Speck.

"Let's drive back to the station. I want to talk to the Chief, and you need to call Kat Davies at Kennedy and let her know she should make an all-school announcement for all teachers to report to the gym after bus duty."

Back at the station, Brian got out of the car. "Officer Speck, organize Trandon's desk files by putting the most useful information on top. I'll want to take a look at important papers after talking to the Chief. And, oh, if you have time before we go to Kennedy, familiarize yourself with the district finances on their web page. School districts are supposed to be transparent, so there should be some useful information there."

Brian tapped on the Chief's door, walked in and sat down. "Let me update you on the investigation," and he proceeded to detail the interviews he'd conducted that day.

The Chief was mildly displeased that Dr. Nash had not been cleared as a suspect. "Tread carefully with him. He's not a friend, but he would make a powerful enemy. Why haven't we found Sherry Trandon's phone? Everyone has a mobile phone these days."

"There was no phone at her office, in her purse, or in her house. We'll just have to keep searching, sir."

When Brian was finished, he went looking for Officer Speck. She had pulled up the district website and was looking at the financial information.

"Just as I thought, there's a lot of information on the site." He leaned over Officer Speck's shoulder. "Look, an annual budget, monthly reports to the board, and a detailed accounting of large purchases are all there. Be sure you contact the city accountant to walk you through all this."

"I will. Even with my degree in accounting, school district finances are a challenge to untangle. There are so many rules. I organized Trandon's files. Policies are in one pile, bills paid and unpaid in another, and here, I found her will. Most of her estate goes to her sister, a Brenda Sousa. But a Douglas Vanderhoot receives $300,000, whoever that is. Where would Trandon get $300,000? I'll look into it further. The lawyer listed is William Babcock. Oh, we've got to go; it's almost time for dismissal at Kennedy."

"Vanderhoot? Vanderhoot? Isn't that the last name of your district's congresswoman?"

"That's why the name sounded familiar. Yeah, it is. She was appointed when her husband died two years ago and then she ran for office and won last November. She's the family values woman. Do you think Douglas Vanderhoot is related to her?"

"Not sure. Check that out as soon as possible. Gosh, let's hope not, I hate dealing with politicians. They're squirrely."

Detective Kerns and Officer Speck dashed to the car. When they arrived at Kennedy, they found an enormously long line of cars for pick-up. It looked as if more than half of the Kennedy parents were taking no chances with a murderer on the loose and were picking up their children themselves. The busses were half empty. Teachers were rushing around trying to organize the children and the unusually large car line. Obviously, they'd not been expecting so many parents. Mrs. Fowler was right in the thick of it, directing traffic. She had a bullhorn in her hand and a whistle around her neck. She was using both, frequently.

Teachers were entering the building from the bus and carpool line, and Brian could hear mutterings. "Parents," sniffed one teacher. "Did you see Karen almost get run over by that parent? Just what we need, another incident at this school. It's like we're under a curse."

"Yeah, but at least Karen doesn't take it out on us. Sherry would have been screaming through her bullhorn at all the teachers, making us feel like fools. Oops, I really shouldn't talk like that. I really am sorry Sherry is dead. I just wish she'd gone and been a principal somewhere else. Now we have to go meet in the gym, and I'm so exhausted. What the devil is this stupid meeting about?"

Teachers were now headed to the gym in groups of twos and threes and settling themselves on the bleachers. Kat's voice sounded over the intercom. "Reminder, all teachers need to come to the gym for a mandatory meeting now. No one may leave the school. This is a mandatory meeting." Brian stood at the door and watched the teachers. Most of them looked totally zapped. Officer Speck was across from him, also observing the teachers. Karen entered the gym, and the talking dimmed to a murmur.

Karen smiled at the teachers. "It's been quite a day, but we got through it. You all handled yourselves magnificently. That enormous carpool line was a bit unexpected, but we'll be ready for them tomorrow. Detective Kerns and Officer Speck are here and have something to say." Brian nodded to Speck, and she stepped forward and faced the teachers.

"I would like all teachers to return to their classrooms, get their white science lab jackets and return with them to the gym." The teachers stared at Officer Speck with puzzled looks.

Michael called out, "Why? What's up?"

Speck ignored him. "I need you to go now, and quickly. I want each one of you to be back here in the gym within five minutes. Now, go!" Reluctantly, the teachers stood up and started moving toward the gym door. Most of the teachers looked either mystified or downright irritated.

Officer Speck followed the teachers out and headed down the first-floor hallway, while Brian followed the teachers up to the second floor. He could see teachers moving into their classrooms and could hear the thud of closet doors opening. He spotted another police officer at the end of the hall and nodded. Soon, teachers were reappearing with lab jackets over their arms.

Suddenly, Bobbi Nelson stalked out into the hallway. "Okay, which one of you yoyos has my lab jacket? I had it last week for that experiment with gravity we all did." She glared at the fifth grade teacher. "Did you take it?"

"No," squealed the teacher. "I just have mine." She scurried down the hall toward the stairs.

Seeing Detective Kerns at the top of the stairs, Bobbi marched over. Every inch of her was furious, from her red face to her boots, which were stomping with every step she took. "What the frick is going on here, Detective? What's so important about a lab jacket? Mine was taken from my closet sometime after the gravity experiment last Friday. So what are you going to do about it?" she asked belligerently.

"That's a problem, Ms. Nelson. "We need to find your jacket, so let's go down to the gym and see if any other jackets are missing." Bobbi stomped down the stairs in front of the detective, and together, they entered the gym. Officer Danzy was at the door, checking each teacher. So far, all teachers had a white lab jacket with them. A few straggling teachers entered the gym, each with a lab jacket. Kerns walked over to the officer. "Is every teacher accounted for and does each teacher have a lab jacket?"

"Almost everyone," responded Danzy. "The only teacher missing a lab jacket is the teacher who came in with you." He consulted his list. "A Ms. Bobbi Nelson."

Turning to the teachers, Brian announced, "Okay, thank you, teachers, for cooperating with us. It's been a long day for you." Looking at Karen, he said, "I don't have anything else for you."

"What about an update on the investigation? Are we really safe with a killer on the loose?" Michael bellowed from the back row.

Several other teachers were nodding their heads. "Yeah, what's been happening?" several called out.

"I really can't comment on an ongoing investigation. However, we have taken precautions with the school and there will be a policeman stationed inside at all times, and patrols will drive by regularly. I hear that there will be a memorial service here at the school on Friday. I hope that will give you some closure." Brian walked away from the bleachers and gestured for Bobbi and Officer Speck to follow him. The teachers started talking amongst themselves and wandered out of the gym and toward their classrooms.

"So, my white lab jacket was used somehow by the murderer, is that it? Is that why you're seeing who's missing a lab jacket? What'd he or she do? Wear it during the murder?" asked Bobbi. She paled. "Oh, blood splatter. The murderer did wear it."

"Are there any identifying marks on your lab jacket?"

"Identifying marks? I don't know." Bobbi gave the detective a disgusted look. "How would I know? I wore the stupid thing because Sherry insisted. I never really examined it." Then a funny look crossed Bobbi's face. "Actually, there is an identifying mark. Last year we wore them during this cooking project and Kyle dumped hot grease on the table and some of it got on my sleeve, near the wrist. I never could get it out, although frankly, I didn't try all that hard. Who cares about a stupid lab jacket?"

"Thank you, we'll check out the grease mark."

"Are you going to tell me the murderer wore my lab jacket?" snapped Bobbi.

"It's none of your business," retorted Brian. "I do need you to re-verify that you used the lab jacket last Friday, and where you left it, and that you haven't used it or seen it since." He nodded at Speck who took out her notebook and waited for Bobbi's response.

"Yes, that's it. I used it Friday and left it in my classroom closet on a hook, and I haven't seen it since."

Brian stared at Bobbi Nelson. "And you're telling the truth this time?"

"Yes, I am," said Bobbi. She turned on her heel and charged out of the gym.

Brian turned to Officer Speck. "Get ahold of the tech from the Major Crimes Team and have them check that lab jacket for a grease spot on either sleeve, near the wrist. Meanwhile, I'm going to go ask Mrs. Fowler about that child who was in the bushes at 7:10. Good job today, Speck. Maybe you'll make detective yet." Brian grinned and walked away.

Following Karen Fowler into the main office, Brian asked, "Mrs. Fowler, could I have a minute of your time?"

Karen turned around, smiled, and nodded. "Of course." She started walking back to her desk in the corner, and Brian followed. She sat down behind her desk and motioned for him to take a chair.

Brian flipped open his notebook and said, "Yesterday morning, a Knowlton Nash was visiting with Jessamyn Babcock from approximately 6:50 AM to 7:15." Karen's eyebrows arched and she grunted.

"Really? Before school? That's unusual, I hope."

Brian continued, "He left by the front door and turned right. He saw a child squeeze down in the bushes right below the second window—Ms. Trandon's office window—a child with brown hair."

Karen was now looking at Brian closely. "A child in the bushes at 7:15 outside the principal's office?"

"Do you have any ideas who that might be?"

Karen looked thoughtful. "I really don't. Sherry always had strict rules about children arriving early. Brown hair! That describes a lot of kids. I don't know—let me think about it and ask around. I can let you know what I find out."

Brian frowned. "This child may have witnessed events leading up to the murder or the murder itself. Be careful how you ask around. We don't want anybody wondering about this child."

"How about if I revisit the policy about early arrival with the teachers and remind them children can't be dropped off early? Then, as teachers always do, they'll start talking about what kids might be violating the policy."

"Thanks for your help. Let me know as soon as you know something. I'm anxious to interview this witness." On his way out the door, Brian stopped and asked Kat about children who arrived at school early, before 7:10. Kat reiterated Sherry's policy about early arrivals but couldn't think of anyone who arrived that early.

"Do you know if Dr. Nash is in the building? I need to speak to him."

"He just called and said he's on his way over to talk to Karen. If you wait a few minutes, he'll be here." Brian sat down in an office chair, took out his notebook and started doodling. It helped him think.

Chapter Nine
Wednesday Afternoon and Early Evening

Karen was scowling at her phone. "Mrs. Fitch, Sheldon is waiting for you to pick him up from school."

"Why didn't he walk, the stupid kid? The boy is so fu—lazy. I'll get there when I can." There was a loud slam on the other end of the line as Mrs. Fitch hung up the phone.

Karen walked around her desk and looked at a skinny child who was sitting on the bench, swinging his legs back and forth. "Your mother will get you shortly. She's very upset that you didn't walk home, Sheldon. Why didn't you walk?"

Sheldon continued to swing his legs and scuff his shoes across the floor. "'Cause she said she'd pick me up 'cause it wasn't safe," he muttered. "But she forgets a lot since my dad isn't around, especially when she's drinking beer."

Karen nodded as if she'd heard all this before. "Here, have a candy bar." She reached into her desk, retrieved a Milky Way, and handed it to him.

"Thanks." Sheldon grinned, exposing a very bad set of teeth. He tore the wrapper open and ate the candy bar in three bites. "Did the murder happen over there?" He pointed toward the principal's office where the crime tape was still in place. "Is he still hanging around?"

"No, the murderer is gone and it's quite safe here," responded Karen, "and now you need to be quiet so I can get my work done."

Brian walked over to Karen and said, in a low voice, "I think that's the young kid who lives below my apartment.

He seems to have a tough life. The older brother seems fairly responsible, but the mother is drunk most of the time."

Karen shook her head. "We're constantly contacting the Department of Human Services about Sheldon. It doesn't seem to do any good. The high school does the same for his brother, Logan." She turned back to her computer and Brian stood, gazing out the window.

"Uh-oh. Mary Nash, Dr. Nash, and Bobbi Nelson are all in the parking lot, arguing. They may need a referee soon," said Brian.

Kat got up and looked out the window. "I'd say Bobbi is holding her own. Mary's crying and getting back in her car. Ouch, she's losing some rubber off her wheels with that exit. Now Dr. Nash and Bobbi are talking seriously and Bobbi's doing a lot of arm-waving, not a good sign."

"Really, you two, stop gawking at them. It's like living in a soap opera." Karen returned to her computer and started pecking away. Brian moved over and sat down in a chair, took out his notes, and started making notations.

Ten minutes later, Karen and Brian both jumped when they heard a resounding smack behind them. Mrs. Fitch was standing over Sheldon. She was an enormous woman, with a huge posterior, drooping breasts, and a mean face. The boy was crying and rubbing his face. "But you said you'd pick me up," he cried. "You said the stupid police in this town would never catch the murderer and we'd probably all be killed in our beds."

"Shut up," snarled Mrs. Fitch.

Both Kat and Karen moved toward the woman. In a calm voice, Karen spoke, "You may not hit Sheldon, Mrs. Fitch. Please, just take a step back, and let's all cool off."

"Dontcha tell me what to do, little miss. He's my stupid kid and I'll do what I want."

Brian stepped forward and firmly put his hand on Mrs. Fitch's arm. "Remember me, Mrs. Fitch? I'm the detective who's renting your upstairs apartment. Mrs. Fowler is absolutely correct. You may not hit Sheldon like that. When a child is harmed, we must call the Department of Human Services."

Mrs. Fitch glared at Brian. "He's not hurt. Sheldon's a big crybaby, aren't you, boy? Aren't you?"

Sheldon looked fearfully from his mother to the detective and back to his mother. He nodded. In the smallest voice possible, he whispered, "Yep, I'm a crybaby."

Brian took a step closer to Mrs. Fitch. "You've been drinking, Mrs. Fitch. You should not be driving a car."

"Well, how d'you s'pose I got to this here school? Did ya think I walked? And I'm not walkin' home. Ddidya hear me?" Mrs. Fitch abruptly sat down on the bench.

Brian took a step back, looked at Mrs. Fitch, and said, "The house is less than three blocks from here. You will walk. Leave your keys with me and I'll have an officer drive the car over and leave it in your driveway sometime tonight. And this is your last warning regarding hitting either Sheldon or your older son, Logan. If it happens again, the Department of Human Services will be involved."

Mrs. Fitch huffed, "I shoulda never rented to you. I knew you was trouble from the start. Come on, Sheldon. We're walking home." She turned and pointed a dirty finger at Brian. "There'd better not be a scratch on that car or there'll be trouble." Mrs. Fitch tossed the keys at Brian, who deftly caught them, then grabbed the door handle, pushed Sheldon through it, and slammed it behind her.

"I feel so sorry for that kid." Kat sighed and walked around her desk, turned off her computer, and picked up her purse. "It's been quite a day, Karen. See you tomorrow." She hurried out the door.

"I feel sorry for the kid too. He carries quite a load with an alcoholic mother," said Brian. "The good thing is the older brother seems to have it together. Perhaps he will continue to help his little brother."

Karen looked up from where she had abruptly sat down in the nearest chair. "You know Logan?" she asked.

"I don't know him very well, but we have discussed the disadvantages of my car. He seems like a nice kid. You look worn out, Mrs. Fowler."

"I am," responded Karen. "That woman is exhausting, and I've got a pile of paperwork to do."

At that moment, Dr. Nash strode through the door and over to Karen's desk. "We've got things to discuss."

Brian stepped forward. "Dr. Nash, I need to talk to you."

Dr. Nash turned around and said, "Can't you see I'm busy, Kerns? You can just sit down there and wait." He pointed to a chair across the office.

"Sir, we can do this now at the school or I can have you escorted down to the police station. Which would you prefer?"

Dr. Nash's face turned red and a vein near his temple started throbbing. "Throwing your weight around a bit, aren't you? I am personal friends with the police chief and he's going to hear about this."

"That's fine, you tell him. But right now, I need to interview you. It can be here or down at the station."

Dr. Nash threw the papers he had in his hand down on Karen's desk. "Here will work as I'm extremely busy." He stood and glared at Brian. "Karen can be my witness if you get out of line." He walked briskly over to Kat's chair and sat down. Karen smiled sympathetically at Brian, shrugged, and started working on her computer. *All I need is one more angry person in this office today. Brian has no idea what a jerk he's dealing with. Nash hates having his plans interfered with. What a power trip the a-hole is on.*

Slowly and deliberately, Brian sat back in his chair and took his notebook and pen out of his brown leather bag.

Dr. Nash glared at Brian. "Hurry up, let's get on with it. I have things to do."

Coolly, Brian nodded and began to speak. "I'd like for you to revisit the statement you gave me last night regarding the morning of the murder." He flipped back several pages. "At your house last night, you stated that you got up early, around 6 a.m., drove to the administrative offices where you saw no one. The Police Chief contacted you about 7:35 regarding Trandon's murder. Do you have anything you'd like to add or change about that statement?"

Dr. Nash tapped his fingers against the desk and looked at Brian. "Well yes, I think I do need to amend the statement. Saying I was with Bobbi Nelson in front of my wife would have upset her. So, you're right, I didn't go to the administration offices." Karen bent her head even lower over her files. *Oh God, do I really have to listen to this?* "I went to Kennedy School to meet Bobbi. I'm sure she can vouch for me. I know you're going to ask me the time, but I'm not sure, perhaps it was 6:55 or 7 a.m. or 7:05. I parked around back but went around to the front door and then straight up the stairs to Bobbi's room."

"Who did you see?" asked Brian, impatiently.

"Ah, nobody. It was really quiet and I didn't want to be seen."

"Was Ms. Nelson in her room?"

"Um, no. I got there first."

"Then what happened?"

Dr. Nash was looking embarrassed and his face was flushed. "Bobbi arrived and well, um... well, um...." The superintendent's voice faded away.

"Well, um, what?" Brian sounded disgusted.

Dr. Nash lowered his voice even further and glanced over at Karen. He was practically whispering. "Bobbi and I are both consenting adults. We had sex, what do you think we were doing?" The superintendent's face darkened, and he looked as if he was regretting his insistence on staying in the office.

"After the sex, then what?" said Brian, in a loud voice.

"I left. What do you think I did?" Dr. Nash was downright belligerent now.

Brian stared at the superintendent long and hard. "Look, you're interfering with a murder investigation. I need you to cooperate or we'll just take this down to the station."

"You're a little prick, detective. The Chief of Police and I are hunting buddies from way back. Just how far do you think you'd get by arresting me?"

Brian crossed his arms and counted to ten in his head. "Look, we could have a pissing contest here, waste a lot of time and effort, and get nowhere. Or you could simply tell me what you were doing at Kennedy School, who you saw, and when you left." He sat back in his chair and waited for the superintendent to respond.

Good show, Brian. You are one skilled interviewer. Karen was secretly rooting for Brian.

Dr. Nash glanced over at Karen and slumped back in his chair, rubbed his temples with both hands, and sighed. "I didn't leave until I heard the announcement to evacuate the school. I went down the back stairs and out the emergency fire door. The alarm should have gone off, but it's been broken for some time. Karen can confirm the door is broken." Karen looked up and nodded. "My car was parked in the back. I went down the back alley and started to drive toward the Administrative Offices. I was hoping to get a call about what was going on at Kennedy so that I could legitimately turn around and go back. I was worried.

"Then I got the call from the Police Chief and headed back toward the front of the school." The superintendent sat back in his chair and looked drained. "My wife would be furious if she knew I visited Bobbi yesterday morning. There, is that enough?" Turning and looking directly at Karen, he said, "I'm sorry you had to hear all that. It's very confidential."

Brian looked at his watch. "There may be more questions later. I'm guessing your wife knows all about your affair with Ms. Nelson and probably knows you were at the school yesterday morning. Wives are amazingly perceptive."

Dr. Nash glared at Brian, stood up, and stormed out of the office.

Karen watched as Brian calmly put his notebook in his pocket and answered his phone. Brian's face went red and his side of the phone conversation sounded frustrated.

"Okay, does he understand this is a murder investigation? What's with these pastors? They're all so difficult... What? I didn't know that... Yes, I can ask her. Did he ask for her specifically?" Brian nodded and turned off the phone. He sat down across from Karen. "I need yet another favor."

"Okay," said Karen tentatively.

"I want to interview John Trandon, Sherry's brother." Karen nodded. "Apparently, he's also the pastor for Rhonda Burgess, which is why the pastor has asked for you."

"For me?" Karen gave Brian a perplexed look. "I've only met him a couple of times, and it was always for a church event I was attending for Rhonda."

"Well, he's not comfortable talking to a detective and he specifically asked for you to come along. He says he trusts you."

"Oh, good grief. I don't care much for John Trandon or his church or his beliefs," said Karen in a slightly irritated voice. "I don't know what you'd learn from him. His perspective is very narrow and he refers to a Bible verse for everything he says. It's rather annoying. But gosh, I wouldn't want you to face him by yourself. If he's asked for me, he's certain to stonewall if I don't show up with you."

A few minutes later, they got into Karen's car, and she started to Google the location for Rhonda Burgess's church out near Last Chance.

"Isn't Last Chance west of town?" recalled Brian. "You go out on Highway 2 and then you turn on County 62, and the town is on Sheridan Road. The church has to be near there."

Karen stared at Brian in amazement. "After all these years you remember where the flyspeck town of Last Chance is?"

"I love it when you're impressed, but I had a girlfriend in high school who lived out there. That's why I remember the directions."

Driving with the windows open and the country radio station from Des Moines blasting away, Karen relaxed and started to enjoy the ten-mile ride. Brian was so easy to talk to. They consciously avoided talk about the murder, and instead, discussed movies, books, and marathons. Brian ran in the Chicago Marathon every year and Karen confessed she hated exercise. Coming over the hill on Sheridan Road, Karen saw a small building. "That's it, that's the church."

Brian, who'd just checked his texts, looked up. "It looks a bit like a strip mall store without the strip mall. It doesn't even have a steeple." Karen pulled into the gravel parking lot and got out. The front door was locked, so they walked around the building.

Out back they could see someone on a power lawnmower. The person waved and the power lawnmower started toward them. Pulling up, a man jumped off. He was all skin and bones; Karen was reminded again that he was perhaps one of the thinnest men she had ever seen. "Mrs. Fowler, I'm so glad to see you." He reached out and shook her hand. "You are always welcome at our church. We'd love to have you attend a service."

Brian stepped forward, saving Karen from having to make a reply. "I'm Brian Kerns, the acting detective for the Chaldea Police Department, investigating the murder of Sherry Trandon. Are you John Trandon?"

"Yes, I am."

"I have a few questions I'd like to ask."

The man mopped his brow with a large kerchief he took out of his pocket. "Let's go inside and talk." He led the way into the church through the back door. Inside, the church was simplicity itself. There weren't pews, just rows of folding chairs. There was a podium made of plywood for the pastor and an altar that contained two candlesticks. In the corner was an old upright piano that had probably seen better days.

"This church, The Spirit of The Word, is my home. I don't quite see how the church affects your murder investigation." The pastor folded his hands as if in prayer.

"I don't wish to intrude on your church, pastor, but I would like to ask you a few questions about your sister."

"I have no idea why. Sherry and I seldom saw each other. We did not enjoy each other's company. She was not a godly woman."

"Why do you say that?"

"It is her duty as a woman to get married and bear children. Timothy, Chapter 2, verse 15: 'Yet, she shall be saved in childbearing.'"

"When was the last time you saw your sister?"

"Not for a long time. She was out here last spring arguing about Rhonda Burgess, insisting that I tell her that she could divorce her husband."

"Really, why was she concerned about that?"

"I'm sorry I mentioned that. I don't really want to go into a discussion about Rhonda and Sean Burgess. Information about them is highly confidential."

Brian gave the pastor a determined look. "I'll remind you this is a murder investigation. I'll ask the questions, and if you feel I've gone into a highly confidential area, please say so. Okay?"

"I guess. I'm not particularly comfortable with this." The pastor looked out the window and Brian waited patiently so he could continue.

"So why was Ms. Trandon concerned about the Burgesses?"

"Sherry came bursting into my church and started shouting at me about the Burgesses needing to get a divorce. She seemed to think I was the one standing in the way. I hadn't seen her that upset for years. She bullied my younger sister and me growing up, while our parents just watched. But I hadn't seen that kind of anger in a very long time."

There was a long pause and the pastor looked out the window again. Finally, Brian said, "What happened?"

"I told her divorce was a sin and she needed to respect the Burgess's marriage. I told her that Rhonda was an obedient wife who took her duties seriously."

Brian worked to keep his face neutral at the mention of "obedient wife." "Just what do you mean by obedient wife?" he asked.

The pastor looked at Brian thoughtfully. "You're not a church-going man, I see. 'Wives, submit to your husbands, as to the Lord.' That's Ephesians 5, verse 22. I can provide you with other verses if you want."

"No, that's okay." Brian looked a bit puzzled. "So, Rhonda was an obedient and submissive wife. What does that mean, exactly?"

The pastor pursed his lips and looked at the detective long and hard. "I don't need you criticizing my church, but it means that the husband is the head of the family, and decisions regarding the wife and children are made by him."

"And did that work for Rhonda and Sean Burgess?"

"Yes, for the most part," retorted the pastor. "There were some difficulties due to circumstances..." The pastor paused, and Brian stopped writing and looked at him intently. Sighing, the pastor continued, "Sean was unable to work, which made Rhonda the breadwinner. There were times when Rhonda wanted more of a say in family finances. And then because she worked, it was hard for her to keep up with all her duties as a homemaker. We prayed a great deal over these matters." The pastor bowed his head.

"Were there other difficulties?" asked Brian.

The pastor looked off in the distance and then returned his gaze to Brian. "I don't understand where your questions are leading and what they have to do with the murder investigation. The Burgess's troubles have nothing to do with the murder."

"Let me be the judge of that."

"This information needs to be kept confidential." He looked angrily at both Karen and Brian, who indicated they understood.

Again, the pastor bowed his head. "Sean is a very unhappy man, and at times, he would get physical with Rhonda. That's one of the reasons Sherry was so angry. She said Rhonda had bruises all over her body. Of course, she exaggerated."

"Is there more?" asked Brian.

"Sean would lose his temper and hit her, leaving a few bruises. Once he broke a plate over her head. And once, he put his hands around her neck and tried to choke her. However, we have prayed together over this matter, and I have told both the Burgesses what a terrible effect Sean's temper was having on their dear child, Sophie. It has gotten much better since then."

Karen looked shocked. "I had no idea it got physical. I've seen Sean be condescending and nasty to Rhonda. But physical violence... Oh God, I feel sick about it. Has it stopped?"

The pastor bowed his head. "I have prayed, and Sean and Rhonda have prayed, so I'm sure it has stopped."

Brian gave the pastor a look of disgust. "That's abuse, Pastor John, and it needs to get reported to the police. I really must encourage you to have Mrs. Burgess make a police report, and if the abuse happens again, you should immediately remove Rhonda Burgess and the child from the home, and then contact the police."

The pastor sighed. "I knew you would say that. You only see it from your narrow police perspective. You forget that prayer is powerful. We take care of our own here, Detective Kerns."

"So, let me be sure I understand this. Sherry came to you very upset about Sean Burgess's abuse of his wife. What did you tell her?"

The pastor looked at Brian and then away. His face was flushed. "Our discussion dissolved into a terrible argument where we screamed and shouted at each other. It ended up with me physically pushing her out the church door and locking it behind her. I'm ashamed of my behavior, but Sherry has always known how to make me angry. I never saw or spoke to her again."

Brian took a few more notes and then looked inquiringly at the pastor. "I can understand Ms. Trandon's concern about one of her teachers. But it seems like a very dramatic step to confront you about it?"

"Oh, you didn't know my sister. When she got going on some injustice, she never let up. Although, frankly, I thought her attachment to Rhonda Burgess was overly protective." The pastor stood up. "Is that all? I need to prepare for services this evening."

"Yes, that's all for now. I do want to encourage you to report abuse to the police for the protection of the person or persons being abused. Thank you for your time."

As Brian was opening the back door, the pastor called out to them, "I'm surprised you didn't ask me if church members walk on hot coals. Most nonbelievers ask."

Brian turned and raised his eyebrows, "I had heard some rumors. Do your church members walk over hot coals?"

"You'll just have to come to church and find out." With that, the pastor turned around and went into the next room.

Karen was unusually quiet as she drove down highway two. *Oh my God, poor Rhonda. I had no idea the abuse had gotten physical.* No wonder she always wore long sleeves. She was covering up bruises. She hit the steering wheel with her fist.

Brian looked at Karen's angry face. "I guess you're a bit shocked that Sean Burgess is an abuser."

"I am, and I wish there was something I could do about it. But her church and Sophie are very important to her. I think she's afraid she would lose both if she left Sean. She's spent so much time telling me divorce isn't allowed in her church."

"What was Rhonda's relationship with Sherry?"

Tapping the steering wheel with one hand, Karen glared frostily at Brian. Finally, she said, "She was scared of her, like most of the teachers. But there was a time last year when they were almost friendly. It was as if Rhonda could do no wrong. I thought it was because Sherry finally appreciated what an excellent teacher she was. But then lately, Sherry started picking on her again. I don't know, it's all so confusing."

Karen and Brian stared out the window for a while at the Iowa countryside.

"I'm sorry about Rhonda, Karen. As her friend, encourage her to leave. There are safe houses for victims of domestic abuse. I can tell from experience that it will only get worse."

By now, they had pulled up to the school. Karen sighed and said, "It's been a stressful day. I'm exhausted. You can do me a favor. Let's get some supper, take it back to school to eat, and you can tell me your concern with Jorge."

"Certainly. You know Chaldea better than I do. What's a good place?"

Karen looked at Brian mischievously. "You look... yep, you look like someone who would appreciate a Maid-rite. Remember Maid-rites?"

"Oh geez, I used to love Maid-rites. I haven't had one since I left Chaldea. No one outside of Iowa makes that special ground beef sandwich with, oh, what was on it? Mustard, onion, salt, pepper, and mayonnaise. A loose-meat sandwich like that would be laughed at in Chicago."

When they got to the Maid-Rite, it was like walking back into the fifties. A nondescript, rather colorless counter ran down one side of the room, complete with red plastic bar stools. Four red plastic booths were across from the counter. Brian ordered a maid rite and fries for himself, Karen ordered a chef's salad, and they both ordered coffee. Karen sat on a barstool and idly glanced through the local paper from yesterday, serving Chaldea and environs. The national news was short and terse. The rest of the paper seemed to be devoted to local affairs, marriages, births, and deaths. She showed Brian the bottom of the front page, which had the story of Sherry Trandon's murder.

"I'm surprised Trandon's murder didn't make the headlines. It's not often a principal gets murdered in Chaldea, is it?"

Karen shrugged. "I guess the city council's decision about Pancake Day was more important. I'm glad the pancakes are still free but charging for sausages is going to make everyone mad." *Brian must think we're all nuts in Chaldea. Murder—no big deal, but paying for sausages, how dare they?*

"Look at this." Brian shook the paper. "There are seven errors in four paragraphs about Trandon's murder. This comment disturbs me the most." He pointed at a sentence partway down. "The reporter is implying that a vicious murderer is on the loose and no one in Chaldea is safe. If I'd been interviewed, I could have said there was no indication of a serial killer. The reporter is sensationalizing the murder and scaring people for no good reason. It's no wonder so many parents are driving their children to and from school after reading that news story. I'll talk to the Chief about news coverage. We need to get some accurate stories in the paper."

Brian looked up from the newspaper when a bag was plopped in front of him. A gum-chewing waitress was standing at the cash register. "What kind of salad dressing do you want, Mrs. Fowler?"

"Oh, I'll take low-calorie Italian, thanks." Karen smiled. "Aren't you Kat's niece?"

"Yep, that's me. Kat is a super aunt." The waitress looked at Brian with a smirk. "You're the hotshot detective who's in town, which means you're Natalie's divorced brother. It's your loss if you don't ask Mrs. Fowler out. She's very nice." The girl winked at Karen. "That'll be $14.92."

Karen looked at the waitress, totally aghast. "Hey, hold on there, I can get my own dates, okay?"

"You've not been dating anyone since you've moved here, so I thought I'd help you out." The waitress looked only slightly distressed. "Sorry, my Aunt Kat always says I have a big mouth."

Looking at Brian, she said, "You've got utensils and napkins, and I put in three packets of ketchup. Do you want more than three?" Brian shook his head. "Yeah, I could tell you're not a real southern Iowan boy. If you were, you'd want 6 or 7 packets of ketchup at least." Brian handed over $20 to the waitress and told her to keep the change. As he left, she was smiling at her five-dollar bill.

"Cripes, small towns. That was embarrassing." Karen's cheeks were flushed.

Brian laughed. "She seemed to take a real interest in your love life. Perhaps we should go out, once this investigation is complete. What do you say?"

"Sure. Obviously, there are many people interested in my dating life. Perhaps a nice outing or dinner will quiet them all down."

Once they got to Karen's office, Brian quickly laid out the food for both of them, and then took an enormous bite of his Maid-rite. "Delicious. What is it about Maid-rites? I would never choose to eat that kind of sandwich in Chicago, but come to Chaldea and all of a sudden Maid-rites, tenderloin sandwiches, and green bean casseroles all seem delicious."

Karen was sitting back in her chair, grinning at Brian. "I can see that you're in love with that Maid-rite."

"I haven't had a Maid-rite in fifteen years, at least, but this sandwich is the tastiest thing I've eaten in days."

Karen was scarfing down her salad. "So sorry, I have to eat fast. I still have to meet with a group of parents tonight."

"I'm sorry to lay more problems on you, but in the course of my investigation, it's come to my attention that your custodian, Jorge Costa, and your teacher's aide,

Brandon Leary, have been smoking marijuana in the upstairs custodial closet."

Karen stopped eating, her fork hung in midair. She rested her head on her hand, her elbow on the chair arm. "You're kidding? Those stupid fools! Smoking pot in a school! There goes one of the best teacher's aide's we've had in a long time. We'll have to fire Brandon. He's only been here a short time—didn't even make it through the probationary period. And Jorge, good heavens, he's been here forever. What do I do about him?" She looked at Brian helplessly.

Brian tapped his fingers against Kat's desk. "It's a misdemeanor, but it took place in a school. Jorge confessed, so I'd suggest that he throw himself on the mercy of the judge and hope for community service. Then perhaps the Board of Education could hire him back on probation, since he's been an employee in good standing."

"I can only hope it will go that way. Because, frankly, what would I do without Jorge? He's the only one that knows the building and all its idiosyncrasies. We'd be without heat, air conditioning, and hot water if it weren't for Jorge. Sometimes, I think he goes down to the basement and beats on the boiler to get it going. Smoking pot? I ought to laugh—Jorge and Brandon toking up in the custodian's closet. But today, all I can do is worry about keeping the school going."

Karen sat up straighter in her chair. "Would you submit a written report I can take to the Board? Anything else?"

Brian took another bite of his sandwich. "What can you tell me about Milly Landon, the reading specialist? She generally dashes out of the room when I appear at the door, and her answers during the police interview were two-word sentences."

Karen looked thoughtful. "I don't know much about her. Honestly, I'm not sure any of the teachers know anything about her either. Sherry hired her fairly recently, I think. She's awfully quiet. Quite a few students go to her for reading help. They don't complain about her, and they're making progress." She shrugged. "But that's not what you want to know, is it? You want to know how she related to Sherry or something about her private life. I have absolutely no idea. Do you want me to ask around about her? I probably have Milly's resume in Sherry's office." She paused and shook her head. "Nope, I don't. The police took away the files. You have it."

"I'll have Officer Speck take a look at her resume. But I would appreciate it if you would quietly ask around about her."

"Aye, aye, sir! Now I'm a principal and a sleuth," Karen smiled. "Oh, by the way, Jessamyn quit this afternoon. She flounced into the office, grabbed her phone, and said she never wanted to be a teacher. Then she blurted out that you'd suggested that she find something that made her happy."

"Uh, well, I kind of did that. I suggested that if she disliked being a teacher so much, perhaps she should think about a different profession."

"Well, she's run home to daddy in Plain View, if you need to speak to her again. You know, I feel as though you've gotten a bad impression of student teachers. Jessamyn was a bit of an anomaly. I've probably had seven or eight student teachers throughout my career, and most of them were dedicated, intelligent young individuals who went on to become an asset to the field of education."

Brian smiled. "Don't worry; I've been around plenty of really lousy cops. All professions have losers. I'm glad Jessamyn quit. She definitely was not cut out to be a teacher."

Just as he was about to leave, Brian inquired, "Do the classrooms lock?"

Karen shook her head no. "Locks have been proposed for as long as I've been here, but there never seems to be enough money in the budget. Why do you ask?"

"I'm wondering who got the lab jacket from Bobbi Nelson's room and how he or she managed it."

"So it was Bobbi's lab jacket. But it seems unlikely Bobbi would murder Sherry. I mean, she hated her. But somehow, if she murdered her, I think, well, she'd announce it to everyone, probably waving the knife, and saying something nasty. Oh, I really shouldn't have said that. I'm tired."

"Hmm, so you think she's not a likely suspect." Karen made a face and shook her head. "Thanks for all your help today. I'm going to give Officer Danzy a call and have him pick me up. I've got more work to do down at the police station. Crap, it is awful not having a car."

"I heard Joe recommended a Ford Explorer that Brad Melrose is selling."

"How in the heck do you know that?"

"I'm going to apply to be a detective; you need some competition. The name, Melrose, that's Lucy's maiden name, the woman you met at Pinky's last night. And Brad Melrose is her brother." Karen smiled sweetly at Brian. "News gets around."

A group of parents, led by her friend Lucy, filed into the office. They were meeting to plan the memorial service for Sherry Trandon, to be held Friday at the school. Karen waved good-bye to Brian and turned her attention to the meeting.

Chapter Ten
Wednesday Evening

When Brian arrived at the Chaldea police station, he started planning what he would say to the Chief. Nodding at one of the police officers standing in the lobby, he stopped and asked him to fetch Mrs. Fitch's car from Kennedy School and drive it to her house. The police officer frowned at the assignment but begrudgingly said he'd do it.

Brian thought that the police officers of Chaldea had probably had several interactions with the Fitches. He almost felt sorry for the officer as he knew the poor guy would be sworn at when the keys were returned. However, that was police work. You often couldn't choose the tasks you wanted to do.

Brian entered the squad room and walked to the Chief's office in the back. The Chief waved him into a seat and told him to shut the door. "Okay, where are we in this investigation? I've already heard from Phillip Nash, who's royally pissed at you. Of course, he is kind of a prick, but an excellent hunter. I enjoy deer hunting with him. Really knows how to handle a gun. Has a collection of hunting knives, too, from around the world."

The Chief stopped talking and looked at Brian. "I guess that was a rather unfortunate statement about Phillip, but he does have an entire gun and knife collection—handguns, rifles, and even some weird assault weapons. Uh, he keeps them locked in his basement, and the knives too." The Chief paused and then stopped talking. There was an uncomfortable silence, and then the Chief said, "The problem with homicide is that sometimes your friends and neighbors become suspects. I never like that part."

Brian nodded in acknowledgment. "Phillip Nash is up to something, but I'm not sure how or if he's connected to the murder." Brian then continued to sum up what he and his team had done that day. He listed pieces of the investigation that needed to be followed up, including a closer investigation of Sherry Trandon's past, identifying the child who was under the principal's window at 7:10 on the morning of the murder, and Trandon's missing cell phone. It was bothering him that it hadn't shown up.

Brian asked the Chief about the school district's finances, but Chief Daniels just shrugged. According to him, there were no problems with school finances. Sure, there'd been a teacher's strike several years ago and parents were constantly complaining about all the supplies they had to buy, but all school districts were short on money. What else was new! It was pretty much an unsatisfactory meeting. Brian had no clear suspect, and the Chief still had to deal with a town that was convinced there was a dangerous murderer on the loose. No police officers, especially Brian, seemed to think this was a random murder done by someone who had just happened to wander through town.

Brian checked in with Officer Speck, who was looking tired and annoyed. She had piles of files on her desk and was hunched over her computer. She barely acknowledged that he was there and kept pecking away. Danzy was busy, putting reports on Brian's desk. He glanced down and saw the lab jacket results, a list of items taken from Sherry's house, and a report by Speck on Kennedy School employees, based on their personnel files. Sitting in the middle of his desk was Sherry's address book.

"Danzy, I want you to pull Milly Landon's personnel file. Go through it for anything unusual, and then leave your notes and the file on my desk. Then I want you to start on Sherry Trandon's home computer. The tech unlocked it, so you can access all the files now."

"Yes, sir."

"I'm stopping by Natalie's for a short time, and I'll bring you some supper and lots of coffee. We've got lots of tedious work to do." Brian still hadn't solved his car problem, so he borrowed a police car. He really ought to stop by his apartment and get his other laptop to use later that evening, but he didn't want to run into the Fitches. He drove back around the square and turned onto Jackson Street. Pulling up in front of Natalie's house, he saw Josh playing basketball in the driveway with three neighbor kids.

Josh ran up to his car. "Hey, Uncle Brian, come play basketball with us."

"Sorry, kiddo. I can't. I need to get some food for my fellow police officers and then get back to work."

The other two boys were staring at Josh's uncle. "Are you a detective?" asked one boy. Brian nodded. "Do you carry a gun?" Brian nodded again.

"Can I see it?"

"Another time, maybe," responded Brian. "I'm in a bit of a hurry right now."

"Yeah, he has to catch old Trandon's murderer. My dad says there was probably a line of people who wanted to kill her, mostly teachers 'cause she was a she-devil. She was mean to work for. Anyway, that's what my dad heard," said the other boy knowingly.

"There are a lot of theories out there. We're still investigating." Brian took the stairs three at a time, opened the front door and headed toward the kitchen.

Natalie was just pulling a mac and cheese casserole out of the oven. It smelled delicious. Smiling, Natalie said, "Good timing. Let me get the Jello out of the fridge and we're all set." Reaching into the fridge, she pulled out orange Jello containing carrot pieces and topped with whip cream. "This is Josh's favorite." She turned the ring so that Brian could see where a section had been eaten. "As much as Josh wanted to eat with his uncle, he couldn't wait."

"I can understand that," replied Brian. "I was always hungry at his age. I hope you don't mind, but I already had a Maid-rite with Karen Fowler. But I promised Danzy and Speck I'd bring them some food. Mac and cheese and a big helping of Jello—it's probably their favorite Chaldea meal." He beamed at Natalie.

"*Oh là là.* Dinner with Mrs. Fowler. How nice. I heard you've been hanging out with her."

"No, not you too. Half this town seems to think we're dating. She's just assisting with the investigation. I can't date someone who's involved in it."

"Sure, sure. I was told she had inside knowledge from you."

Brian put his head in his hands. "Small towns, what am I going to do? I'm not sharing secrets with her. Karen's been in on a few interviews because the person involved requested her. That's all."

"Okay, don't get your dander up. I think it's cute." Brian made a face, grabbed a bowl, and took a big helping of Jello.

"Hey, I thought you'd eaten."

"Well, now I'm hungry."

"So poor Rebecca and Bradley are having a late night? That's got to be hard with Brad's new baby."

"Huh? Bradley has a baby?"

"Good grief, Brian. You don't even know the people you're working with."

"I guess. I've been thrown into this murder and I'm working with people I don't know. I haven't had a minute to stop and learn about them."

"I'll pack up some mac and cheese and Jello for them. Would you like a big thermos of coffee?" asked Natalie.

Natalie went off to make coffee and Brian helped himself to some mac and cheese. Yeah, he'd eaten dinner, but it was going to be a long night, and he loved Natalie's mac and cheese. He started shoving casserole down his throat.

He should learn to eat slower. But Brian felt like he had spent a lifetime bolting down food as fast as he could. His Mom had always been late with supper and he remembered eating as he ran out the door to band practice. Then it'd been college, where he'd worked a part-time night job, so eating on the run had become a way to save time. As a beat cop, it seemed like every time there was a plate of food in front of him, there'd be an emergency call. Now he ate fast out of sheer habit.

Brian left the house with Tupperware dishes of food and a huge thermos of coffee. He sat down at his desk in the police station and set the coffee on the shelf above the computer. Pulling out the goodies from his sister, he called over to Officers Danzy and Speck. "Hey, Natalie sent you some mac and cheese, Jello, and peanut butter cookies. Come on over and get it." He set the Tupperware containers on the counter. Both Officers slid their chairs over.

"Tell Natalie thanks. We're going to need sustenance tonight." Officer Speck scooped up her Tupperware containers and returned to her desk.

Swiveling around in his desk chair, Brian asked, "Hey, any luck tracking down Douglas Vanderhoot?"

"Oh yes, Douglas Vanderhoot is Congresswoman Elyse Vanderhoot's son. He's ten. What would you like me to do?"

"The kid is ten and he's been left $300,00. We'll plan a meeting with the mother. Ask the lawyer to arrange it for tomorrow morning, late, at his own office. It'll be more neutral territory than the police station."

"Your sister is the greatest cook. Her casseroles for the church potluck are always gone first." Officer Danzy carefully picked up his containers and smacked his lips. "Many thanks."

Brian poured himself a cup of coffee, put on his reading glasses, and prepared to pore through reports and files. Picking up the lab jacket report, he read that there was a large grease stain on the left sleeve, near the cuff. *It doesn't let Bobbi off the hook for the murder, but it does clear up whose lab jacket was used. Bobbi is manipulative. She wouldn't be likely to use her own lab jacket to murder the principal. She would probably take the lab jacket of someone she disliked.* With no locks on classroom doors, almost anyone could have taken the jacket from her closet.

Next was Milly Landon's resume. Skimming it, Brian read Officer Danzy's notes about it. She graduated from the University of Illinois twenty years ago. She had only three years of teaching experience, and that had been more than ten years ago. The teaching experience looked skimpy, and there were gaps in her employment. There was nothing listed for the past ten years. Why would Trandon, who seemed to want perfection in her teachers, hire this woman? *Surely, there are more qualified teachers, even around Chaldea. It's time to re-interview Ms. Landon.* He was not looking forward to it. She was one of the most uncooperative people in this case.

The address book was sitting in the middle of his desk. After gulping down some coffee, Brian slid it over to take a look. Thumbing through the pages, he didn't find much. If Sherry had a cell phone, why was she keeping a separate address book? The addresses and names didn't even make sense. There were initials for names and what looked like a code for phone numbers. He decided to send it over to the specialists in the Major Crime Team and see if they could decode it. Sherry Trandon was awfully complicated for a principal of an elementary school in a small town. How did she manage this secret life while living in a fishbowl like Chaldea?

Picking up the report on the results of the search of Trandon's house, Brian was disappointed that nothing new was found. No more partially hidden cabinets! And nothing unusual was found in drawers. *Bummer!* However, he'd been right about the furnishings being expensive. The living room couch was worth $15,000. He looked around for the box of photos from Trandon's closet that he'd told Danzy to get out of the evidence room. There it was. He pulled the box from under his desk, where it'd been pushed. Opening the box, he dumped dozens of photographs on his desk. Staring up at him were pictures of Sherry Trandon, younger and very naked.

Brian raked his hands through the pictures and started sorting them by making two piles, one of Sherry Trandon and one of the unknown naked women. Were these women she knew or simply random pictures of naked women? He continued to sort, staring hard at the unknown women. Perhaps he'd recognize someone from Chaldea.

Brian's hand hovered over a picture of a young woman with long, dark hair. She was sitting, completely naked, on a swing in a backyard. He reached into a drawer and pulled out a magnifying glass. Carefully, he examined the face. Damn, if he wasn't looking at a younger Milly Landon. Good grief, was that a tattoo? It looked just like the one that Sherry Trandon had on her crotch. He moved the magnifying glass closer. Yep, it was almost identical to Trandon's. Quickly, he sorted through the rest of the pictures. By the end, he had six pictures of Milly Landon.

This should make for a very interesting interview. Milly Landon, where did you come from, and what's your connection to Sherry Trandon? Brian slid the six pictures into a manila envelope. The rest of the pictures he dumped back in the box and labeled it for the evidence room. Brian felt hopeful that some pieces of the puzzle were starting to fit together.

Sipping his coffee slowly, Brian started running down his list of suspects. He'd have to explore the Milly Landon issue more. Something was happening with Dr. Nash. That prickly feeling was there. But how would Nash have murdered Trandon? It just didn't seem likely that Nash donned Bobbi's lab jacket and then snuck down to the teacher's lounge, grabbed the cake knife, and killed Sherry. The egotist idiot would have done the murder differently. But something was off with him.

As for Rhonda, she seemed like someone to pity—an abusive husband who didn't work and about to lose her job, which would have ended her career as a teacher. But a murderer? She seemed a bit scatterbrained. How could she have planned a murder? And the little kid—who was he and what had he seen or heard? Finding that little kid and asking a few questions could really help determine what happened Tuesday morning in Trandon's office.

Officer Speck pushed her chair back and sighed. "My God, I need a break. These numbers are driving me crazy."

Officer Danzy looked up from examining Trandon's computer. "My eyeballs are sticking to the back of my head." He stood up and stretched. "I'm gonna call Linda and see how she's doing with the baby. He's been a bit colicky the last few days." Danzy wandered to the back of the squad room and pulled out his phone.

Officer Speck also stood up and started to meander to the back of the squad room. "How old is the baby?" Brian asked.

Officer Speck turned around. "Oh, little Michael Danzy. He's about 4 weeks now. Cute, cute, cute! Ask Brad to show you a picture. He has dozens." She continued to the restroom and disappeared inside.

Brian glanced at the clock on the wall. *Lordy, it's almost midnight. Well, maybe we should call it quits for tonight.* He knew Brenda Sousa would be coming in some time tomorrow morning, but the group could meet at 9 a.m. for a briefing. And Danzy could get to work searching for Trandon's phone. It had to be somewhere.

When Speck and Danzy returned, Brian told them to call it quits for that evening. Everyone was tired, and they needed to be fresh for tomorrow. Promising to be ready for a meeting at 9 a.m., both officers shut down their computers and put everything in the evidence room. With a quick goodbye, they were both out the door.

Brian gathered up some loose papers, shoved them in his desk drawer, and locked it. He stumbled out to the car. Every bone in his body was tired. Driving back to his apartment on empty streets, he thought about how quiet Chaldea really was. It was just midnight and no one was out and about. How that contrasted with Chicago, where cars and people were everywhere, regardless of the time. Perhaps there were advantages to living in Chaldea. A good night's sleep was what he needed.

Turning down McKinley Street, he could see police lights ahead. *Oh no, what happened? So much for a quiet night!* He sped up and pulled to a halt in front of the house where he was renting the apartment. A police officer was on the porch, and he could see another through the open door.

Bounding out of the car, Brian stopped and peered in the police car. Logan and Sheldon Fitch, the two kids who lived on the first floor, were sitting in the back seat with a blanket draped over them. The police officer on the porch turned and spoke, "Sir, may I help you? Please don't come any further."

Brian stopped in his tracks and said, "I'm going to pull my badge out of my pocket. I'm Brian Kerns, a detective from Chicago, on loan to the Chaldea Police Department."

The police officer walked down the steps and shone his flashlight on Brian's badge. "Sorry, sir, I didn't recognize you. We've had an incident. Why are you here?"

Brian nodded toward the second door. "I am renting the apartment upstairs from the Fitches." Brian and the officer turned around quickly as a man came stumbling out of the house.

"That woman is a witch," he sputtered. "She tried to kill me."

From inside, the two officers could hear a woman shouting, "You're a lousy creep! Get out of my house."

Brian put his arm on the man. "I'll keep an eye on this gentleman. You go check on your partner." He propelled the man to a porch chair and pushed him into it. "You stay here until this is sorted out."

"Gladly, just keep me away from that crazy woman."

Brian gingerly sat down on the porch railing. "What happened?"

"Aw shucks, I was at Pinky's, having a drink when that there woman shows up. We had a few drinks, danced a bit, and she invited me home. After the sex, when she thinks I'm asleep, I find her going through my wallet and taking my money. I asked her what in tarnation she thought she was doing? She said she was just getting paid. I said no way. What we did was con—conten—contsensual sex. She wants to know what the heck that is. I told her it meant we both wanted it. That's when she started hitting me. I threw on most of my clothes and before you know it, she's got a knife and she's chasing me around the living room. I thought I was gonna die. The kid called the police. Probably saved my life."

Brian made a face and said, "The word's *consensual*. You might need it for your police report."

"Yeah, that's what I said, contsensual sex." The man pulled matches and a cigarette out of his pocket and lit up. "Guess I'll be here for a while."

"You are to stay on the porch chair and don't move. I'm going to go check on the kids. Got it?" The man nodded and puffed on his cigarette.

Brian walked down the steps and tapped on the police car window. Logan unrolled the window and frowned at Brian. "I just wanted to check and see if you're okay," Brian asked. Logan shrugged. He put his fingers to his lips and motioned to Sheldon, who was sound asleep on the car seat.

"I'm okay, I guess. Sheldon's asleep. Mom pulls this crap every once in a while. It's embarrassing. She's a lot better when my dad is around 'cause she's scared of him."

"When does your father get out of prison?" Brian asked.

Logan grunted, "If all goes well, he should be home by Christmas. I just don't want to end up in foster care. The cops will probably drive us to Plain View and put us in the group home for the night. Then they'll try to put Sheldon with a family and he'll hate it and run away again. We'll be separated, I'll miss school, and this is my last year." Logan pounded his fist against the front seat. "Things just never go right. I was applying to the University of Iowa for next year and I have a chance at a full scholarship. This will ruin everything."

"I'm sorry, Logan. Let's get through tonight, and then perhaps some plans can be made that will work for you and Sheldon." Brian and Logan looked up as the police officers emerged from the house with Mrs. Fitch in handcuffs. One police officer was holding a bag of frozen peas against his face. Brian strode over to converse with them.

"The woman hit me; we're taking her in. A night in jail may calm her down," said the officer holding the frozen peas against his face. "The gentleman, Mr. Poe, wants to press charges, so he's going to follow us down to the police station in his car. I guess one of us will have to drive the kids to Plain View for the night."

Brian glanced down the street and saw what he thought looked like Karen Fowler's sports car zooming down the street. It soon pulled up in front of the house and a teenaged girl jumped out and ran over to the police car.

"Logan, are you okay? How's Sheldon?" She stuck her head through the window and began a heartfelt conversation.

A slightly disheveled Karen emerged from the car. "Brian, I didn't expect to find you here." She was wearing a coat over her pajamas, and her hair was mussed. "I look a sight."

"No, not at all. You look like someone who's been dragged out of bed. I am surprised to see you here," Brian replied.

"Not my idea at all. Logan called Gabby," she pointed toward the teenager, "who woke me up and insisted on coming over here to make sure Logan and Sheldon were okay. Teenagers." Karen looked slightly irritated.

Brian looked at the police officers and then back at the kids in the car. "It's nearly 1 a.m. and everyone is dead tired. How 'bout I take responsibility for the kids for tonight? I'll get them to school in the morning, and then you can contact Human Services and they can deal with it." Both officers looked relieved and said they'd fill out the necessary paperwork at the station.

Brian walked back over to the police car and opened the back door. "Logan, you and Sheldon are staying with me tonight. I'll drop both of you at school tomorrow where Human Services will contact you."

Gabby, who was squished in beside Logan, squeezed his arm. "This is a great idea. It'll be better for Sheldon, too. And my Mom says the detective is really nice."

Startled, Logan said, "Really? Okay. Look, why don't Sheldon and I just sleep in our own rooms and you can wake us in the morning? It's not like we haven't been home alone before."

"Sounds good to me," Brian responded. "I'll leave my door unlocked and give you my phone number. You have a working smoke alarm and carbon monoxide detector?"

"Yep, my dad put them in right before he went to prison." Logan nudged Sheldon awake. "Come on kid, we're staying in our own beds tonight. Gabby, thanks for coming over, you didn't have to do that. I hope your Mom isn't too mad."

"She'll get over it." Gabby gave Logan a quick kiss. "I'll see you at school tomorrow."

Logan, with his arm around Sheldon, staggered up the porch stairs and disappeared into the house. Brian waved good-bye to Karen and followed Logan into the house. He thought he was prepared for a messy house but entering the Fitch's home was both startling and disgusting. The front room was a complete disaster. Couch cushions were on the floor, chairs were pulled out willy-nilly, papers covered the floor, and dirty dishes were strewn across every horizontal surface. As he headed down the hallway after the boys, he could hear his feet crunching on what felt like popcorn. Brian glanced into the kitchen and saw that the sink was piled with dirty dishes, as was the stove, the table, and all the counters. There was a distinct smell of rotting food. He braced himself for what he'd see in the boys' bedrooms.

Logan was pulling off Sheldon's shoes and pushing him into bed. Other than a few dirty clothes sitting on the chair, the room was spotless. There was a desk with spiral notebooks neatly piled on the desktop. A row of books was tidily arranged on the shelf above the desk. A dresser stood in the corner with all the drawers pushed in and the top of the dresser was completely clear. Logan glanced up at Brian. "Yeah, Sheldon is quite picky. He lives in his room; he can't stand the messiness in the rest of the house."

As if he had read Brian's thoughts, he continued, "Besides failing at many other things, my mother is a lousy housekeeper. Sheldon hides in his room, and I've been really busy this year with school, so the mess continues." Logan stood up, turned off the light, and closed the door of Sheldon's room. "He'll sleep like a log until I wake him."

Brian pulled out his cell phone. "You have a phone, right? Give me your number." Logan recited his phone number, and Brian typed it in. "I'm sending you a text so you'll have my number. So, what time should you be up tomorrow morning?"

"I'll get up around 7 a.m. and make sure Sheldon is up too. We both need to be at school by 8 a.m."

"Okay, come knock on my door by 7:20 and I'll have something for both of you for breakfast. Call me if you need anything during the night. See you tomorrow." Brian turned and walked back down the hall. *Am I beginning to go soft? I've seen many desperate people in difficult circumstances, but as a police officer, I've been trained to stay out of victims' personal lives. What is happening to me? I'd better get back to Chicago soon or I'll never be able to handle all the homicides that happen in a big city.*

By 7 a.m. the next morning, Brian was showered and dressed and digging through the refrigerator and cupboards, looking for food that two hungry boys could eat. Thank goodness he'd recently gone grocery shopping. Getting out a large skillet, he started scrambling eggs. Reaching into the refrigerator, he pulled out bacon from Jerry's Meat

Market. He couldn't believe Jerry's was still on the square after all these years. The meat from Jerry's was known throughout the county. Best grass-fed beef in the state, everyone said.

Brian opened up a new loaf of bread and started toasting slices. *What else can I make? Aha, canned peaches in the cupboard. Who cares if they're loaded with sugar?* Picking up his can opener, he deftly opened the can and dumped the peaches into the bowl. He was just sliding the scrambled eggs onto a dish when he heard a knock on the door. Glancing up at the kitchen clock, he saw that it was 7:19.

Hollering "Come on in," Brian poked the bacon with a fork. Dumping it on a plate, he set it on the table. The two boys were standing at the table with their mouths open.

"Are you expecting a visitor, sir?" asked Sheldon.

Logan poked him in the ribs. "I think breakfast is for us, Sheldon."

"Sit down and dig in," responded Brian. "Surely you're hungry."

Both boys sat down and piled eggs, bacon, toast, and peaches on their plates. There was complete silence as the boys practically inhaled their food. Brian sat down with his second cup of coffee and observed them quietly. They had made an effort to tidy up and wear clean clothes. Their backpacks were sitting in the corner of the kitchen. As the boys started to slow down, Brian felt like he could ask a few questions.

"Logan, when do you turn eighteen?"

Logan started to answer when Sheldon piped up, "Next week! Gabby is going to take him out for a surprise."

"Gabby... is she a girlfriend?" Logan nodded and kept eating.

"Logan's, like, in love," Sheldon announced. At this Logan stopped eating and punched his brother lightly on the arm.

"Cut it out, Sheldon. That's private business."

"You boys know that Human Services will be contacting you at school today. I don't think your mother will serve time for hitting a police officer, but I'm uncertain about the charges Mr. Poe will bring. With that uncertainty, they will want to place you temporarily in foster care.

"So here's my thinking. Logan, you'll be eighteen next week and that will make you a legal adult. You might be able to convince Human Services to let you stay in the house until your father or mother returns from jail. I would suggest that you make a strong case for staying in Chaldea High School. Tell the social worker and/or judge about your potential scholarship. Ask the judge to appoint a Human Services Guardian to oversee finances and a social worker to see to your welfare. You might want to thoroughly clean the house before Human Services visits."

Sheldon had stopped eating and was staring forlornly at Brian. "But what about me?"

"I'm not sure about you, Sheldon. The best scenario would be if you could temporarily stay with a family in Chaldea. Do you have any relatives in this area?"

"Just a dumb cousin, but she got murdered," said Sheldon.

Brian set his coffee cup down. "What? Do you mean that Sherry Trandon is your cousin?"

Both Logan and Sheldon nodded, but Logan spoke first. "Ms. Trandon is my dad's first cousin. They didn't exactly get along. She pretty much ignored my mom and dad, and she never even acknowledged publicly that Sheldon and I were related to her. She did pay me well for mowing the lawn and trimming bushes."

"How often were you over at her house?"

"At least once a week, either mowing, raking leaves, painting trim. I guess you'd say I was a handyman."

"Did you ever see or hear anything unusual?"

Logan scrunched up his face. "I guess, sometimes. Ms. Trandon made it pretty clear I wasn't to mention anything to anyone. Of course, she's been murdered, so..."

Sheldon looked at his brother. "What about that time Mrs. Burgess showed up crying and Ms. Trandon yelled at her to get in the house? I was sitting in Logan's car reading, and Ms. Trandon gave me the meanest look."

"Oh yeah, that was kinda weird. It happened a few weeks ago. Mrs. Burgess seemed pretty upset, and Ms. Trandon got nasty with her."

Brian rubbed his chin. "Anything else? Anyone else show up while you were there?"

"There was another woman, kinda small. I saw her from a distance, but she dashed into the house really fast, like she didn't want to be seen. She's from Sheldon's school too. I think she's new."

There was a pause, then Logan spoke again. "I guess the weirdest was Monday. Ms. Trandon had a passenger in her car, but she drove straight into the garage instead of leaving the car in the driveway, like she usually does. There's a short, connecting breezeway to the house, and she rushed this woman through the breezeway and in through the back door fast. All I saw of the woman was a headscarf. And there was already another woman in the house. I saw her through the kitchen window when I was trimming the hedges and as soon as she saw me, she whisked the curtains shut."

"Monday, that's the day before she was murdered. I wonder what was up."

"I dunno. There were kinda weird noises coming from the house, then Ms. Trandon came out, paid me, and said I was finished. I wasn't anywhere near done and she overpaid me. But she seemed disturbed, so I left and figured I'd give her the extra money back next week."

"Logan, that's helpful information. Probably nothing to do with the murder, but every bit of info helps an investigation." Brian took another sip of coffee. "I'm interviewing your dad's other cousin today, Brenda Sousa. Have you ever met her?"

Sheldon shook his head, but Logan looked up from spreading jam on his toast. "Yeah, I met her a long time ago when Sheldon was really little. She seemed a lot nicer than Ms. Trandon. I remember that she brought us presents."

"I can't promise anything, but I will let Mrs. Sousa know about your situation. You never know, sometimes cousins come through."

Glancing at the kitchen clock, Brian stood up. "We've got to get going. Dishes go in the sink and then we're off to school."

Both boys chorused, "Thank you for the breakfast." Logan scraped the few bits of food that were left into the garbage can and carefully stacked the dishes in the sink. Both boys picked up their backpacks and headed down the stairs.

Brian dropped Sheldon off at Kennedy Elementary. He waved at Karen, who was outside with her megaphone, working to keep the line of parents' cars moving. Next, he dropped off Logan at the high school. "Good luck with Human Services," he called through the window. "You have my phone number. Call me if you need anything."

Chapter Eleven
Thursday Morning

Karen entered the school at 6:45 a.m., ready for another day. Being a principal was godawful hard work, especially with all the upheaval over the death of Sherry Trandon. She had a long list of things to do today: figure out state testing issues, discuss the memorial service with the teachers, see how Rhonda was coping, meet with the Watsons. *There just isn't going to be enough hours in the day to accomplish everything.*

Walking into the office, Karen flipped on the lights and idly wondered when the principal's office would be ready for her. She'd like to get it re-painted and find some new furniture, but mostly she relished the thought of working in a quieter environment. The main office was so noisy. Karen set her bags down, shrugged off her jacket, and practically stumbled over Jessamyn, who was sitting in a chair at the side of her desk. "Land sake's alive. What are you doing here?"

Jessamyn was huddled in her jacket, with just her red splotchy face peeking out. "I've come back to finish my student teaching," she stuttered.

Karen sat down at her desk, gulped down some coffee, and studied her. "What's wrong Jessamyn? You're not here because you want to be."

"My dad says I have to finish what I started." Jessamyn started to cry. "He says he doesn't care if I flunk student teaching, but I need to finish out the two weeks I have left. It's supposed to make me stronger."

Karen looked at Jessamyn with dismay. "This is not going to work. The substitute teacher is furious that you cursed at her and Mrs. Hart emailed me from her conference that she's glad to be rid of you."

"I know," wailed Jessamyn. "But my dad says I can't take the trip to Europe this summer unless I finish student teaching, so I'm here to finish. I don't care if you flunk me, I'm going to finish." She slumped down in her chair and glared at Karen.

Oh sweet Mother, she just keeps turning up like a bad penny. We can't get rid of her.

As Karen started to speak, Jessamyn said, "Wait, wait, don't say anything yet. Wait! You know what I can do. I can re-design all the hall bulletin boards for you, plus the ones in this office. They're all disgusting. So boring." She rolled her eyes. "Doesn't anyone around here understand design? You know that I do great bulletin boards. Remember that one I did for the main hallway for parent-teacher conference night?

"Also, I can draw in the mural on the gym, like the art teacher has been planning forever. Then the kids can take turns painting. The art teacher can supervise, though. I'll do anything but be around kids. And—and I can put together a photo display of Ms. Trandon for the memorial service. What about that?" Jessamyn looked at Karen hopefully.

Karen sighed. *It might be easier to have Jessamyn work around the school than tangle with her father. And she is a talented artist with a flair for design.*

"Okay, Jessamyn, it's a deal. But I want you here at school from 8 a.m. to 3:30 each school day, with no excuses. I'll give you some directions, but you'll also have to take instructions from Kat with absolutely no giving lip. You're going to have to work independently at times. I just don't have time to supervise you. Cause me any trouble, any trouble at all, and you're done—out—kaput! I'm notifying your college supervisor that you've flunked student teaching. She can take it from there."

"Oh, thank you, Mrs. Fowler. This will get my dad off my back. And you won't be sorry, not sorry at all. I'm great at photo displays, bulletin boards—really anything to do with art. I'll start by gathering photos from people for the memorial. You'll want that first." Jessamyn got up and actually bounced out of the office.

Kat was standing by her desk gaping at Jessamyn as she practically danced out the door. "I have never ever seen that girl with a smile on her face. That's amazing. What'd she do, win the lottery?"

Kat laughed when Karen told her Jessamyn was working for them for two weeks because her father wouldn't let her quit. Just as they were finishing up talking about possibilities for bulletin boards, Michael, the fifth-grade teacher, dashed into the office. "Karen, you might want to go to the reading specialist's room. Milly's packing up in there. She told me she's quitting today."

"Oh, why would she do that?" Karen exclaimed. "We need a reading specialist." She hurried down the hall to the reading specialist's room. Indeed, when she arrived, Milly was tossing stuff into a cardboard box.

"Milly, what's happening?"

"I'm sorry, Karen, but I'm done. I like teaching kids and it was okay as long as Sherry was alive, but she's dead, so I'm off."

"I don't think I understand, Milly. You're quitting, with no notice, in the middle of the year?" Karen's voice rose higher with each word.

"Yep, that's right," responded Milly tartly. "That's it, exactly."

"I didn't realize that Sherry's death affected you so much. Were you friends?"

"You could say that." Milly picked up her box and started toward the door.

"Breaking a contract is very serious, Milly. You won't get hired in Iowa again."

Milly turned around and grimly smiled at Karen. "Honey, I don't need to teach. My father left me a trust fund. I'm off to gay Paris," she said with her fake French accent, and she flounced out the door.

Karen watched as Milly walked down the hall and out the front door. *Unbelievable! What am I going to do for a reading specialist? Milly and Sherry were friends? I never saw them together.* She walked out the door and straight into Bobbi Nelson, who was loitering in the hallway.

"So, our quiet little Milly Landon has quit, hasn't she? I figured we'd see the backside of her after Sherry's death."

"Why's that?" asked Karen.

"They were friends all right. Good friends, I think, if you know what I mean. Earlier this fall, pretty much right after Milly started, I saw Milly and Sherry embracing in the office. At first, I thought something had happened and Sherry was consoling her, but then they started laughing and kissing. I do think Sherry had a female lover. That would not have gone down very well with parents, which is why they kept it so quiet.

"I asked Sherry about it. She was livid and told me to shut up. She said they'd been friends for a long time, and I was wrong about what I'd seen. Very defensive, Sherry was. And coincidentally, after that, she missed my annual observation and never followed up. Yay for me, I hate observations."

"I don't know what to say, Bobbi. I'd just like to get through the memorial service and let the kids say good-bye to their principal."

"Don't worry so much, Karen. I'm not going to say anything to anybody. I've got my own life to think about.

I'll be retiring soon, probably at the end of this year. Keep it in mind." Bobbi smirked and wandered off around the corner and up the stairs.

Karen continued to the teacher's lounge. After pouring herself a cup of coffee, she sat down across from several of the teachers. "I think we're having some problems with children arriving at school before the playground supervisors are out. Have you been aware of any?"

The teachers mostly shook their heads, but Michael, predictably, had a few comments. "There's always Brooke. Once in a while, her Mom drops her off early because she has to teach an early class out at the community college. But I don't think that's happened since Sherry hollered at the mom to get her act together." Michael started laughing. "Remember? Brooke's mom got out of the car and started screaming at Sherry. It was a true 'girl fight.' The mom got so agitated she spilled coffee all down the front of her suit. Her mom hasn't dropped Brooke off early since."

"Thanks, Michael, for reminding us of that scene," Karen replied drolly. She checked with Jorge and Kat. Neither of them had any ideas about children being dropped off early. As Karen was coming back from talking to Jorge, she bumped into Fran Gumper, the substitute teacher for Mrs. Hart. "How's it going, Fran? Do you have any questions about the class?"

Mrs. Gumper shook her head. "Things will be much smoother now that student teacher has left."

"I completely agree, Fran. I've put Jessamyn to work on some hall bulletin boards. She won't be in the classroom again."

Karen started to leave when Mrs. Gumper spoke again. "I'm a bit worried about Freddy Moser, though. He's so quiet and timid. His father really should stop dropping him off so early. It's hard on him."

"What, Freddy is being dropped off early? I thought we'd put a stop to that a long time ago."

"He's been dropped off early the two days I've been here."

"Really? I'll speak to the father about that, Fran. Don't say anything to Freddy or the dad. I'll take care of it." Karen realized she probably had found the child who'd been hiding in the bushes. She'd ask Freddy about the early arrival and then contact Brian.

After helping with the carpool line, Karen sank down into her chair behind her desk. *Those stupid tests will start Monday unless Nash gets a delay. The meeting with the Watsons is coming up and there is no quiet place to meet. I need an office.*

Right on cue, the Watsons walked in the door. Karen rose to meet them and escorted both of them back to her corner. "You need an office," remarked Vince Watson. "This really won't do at all."

"I'm not sure when the police will be done with the principal's office. Soon, I hope. I agree it is hard to meet with parents out here in the open."

Karen looked at Mrs. Watson. She seemed particularly flustered today. She was absently rubbing her hands together and wasn't even making eye contact. Mr. Watson appeared distracted too. He was sitting and staring out the window behind her desk.

Karen started, "When we scheduled this meeting, Sherry and I both planned to meet with you. Tragically, that meeting will never happen now. I'm glad we could reschedule. Preston is having a difficult time focusing on work, turning in assignments, and maintaining good relations with his peers."

She paused and looked expectantly at the Watsons. Usually, they were full of questions. Today, both Watsons just looked back at her, politely. There was a long pause while Mr. Watson continued to stare out the window and Mrs. Watson looked down at her lap. Karen continued, "As you recall, last month we met with the social worker and the district psychologist who suggested that Preston's opportunities to be successful in the classroom are severely hampered by his lack of attention. At this time, I'd like to discuss the possibilities of medication." Both Watsons just sat in their chairs and looked at Karen. Silence prevailed.

Finally, Mr. Watson stood up abruptly. "Yes, we'll take Preston back to the doctor and try medication." He turned and walked quickly out of the office. Mrs. Watson continued to sit in her chair and rub her hands together.

"Mrs. Watson, are you okay?" asked Karen. *Are Stepford Wives ever okay?*

"Oh yes, I guess I am. Don't let Vince bother you. He's preoccupied with the dis… about something. It has him quite frantic. He and Phillip Nash have been talking on the phone, constantly. You'd think they had done something illegal." She gave an embarrassed laugh. "I'll make an appointment for Preston to see the doctor, Mrs. Fowler." Mrs. Watson stood, shook Karen's hand, and walked out of the office.

Could today get any weirder? First Jessamyn, then Milly Landon, and now the Watsons. What is up with this family? Usually, they ask lots of questions and Mr. Watson likes to act like a prosecutor, grilling whatever school employee is talking about Preston. Today they didn't ask for any information.

Karen picked up the tentative program for the memorial service. She smiled as she read that the kindergarteners were drawing pictures of Sherry, the first graders were making hearts with sayings about Sherry, and the second graders were writing a book titled *A Day in the Life of Principal Trandon*. The third graders were writing five-paragraph essays—*uh, really? Sherry was so test conscious she'd probably like that*— the fourth graders were singing a song, and the fifth graders were writing poetry. This would work.

There would be a short speech from Superintendent Nash, from herself, and a prayer by the Presbyterian pastor. Karen wondered if she should include something from the parents. No, the service would be long enough as it was. The kindergarteners couldn't sit for that long. She just wanted it to be over soon.

Karen looked up from her work to find a woman who bore an amazing resemblance to Sherry Trandon standing in front of her. She wasn't as tall, but the hair was that same straight cut, the eyes matched exactly, and the body build was a bit stout, just like Sherry. When the woman opened her mouth and said, "Hello," Karen practically fell off her chair. The voice was Sherry Trandon's.

"I see that I've startled you, dear. I'm Brenda Sousa, Sherry's sister."

Karen stood up and shook hands with Brenda. "I'm Karen Fowler, acting principal. I'm so terribly sorry about Sherry, Mrs. Sousa. It's been a tragedy. I'm sure it was an appalling shock for you. What can I do for you? Please, have a seat."

Brenda sat down in the chair next to Karen's desk. "Mostly I just wanted to see where Sherry worked. She was so proud of Kennedy Elementary School. She talked about it to me whenever we chatted on the phone."

"Why don't I give you a tour of the school?"

"That would be lovely, Mrs. Fowler. I'm just not ready to check in with the police and the thought of going into Sherry's house, well, it gives me the shivers."

Karen stood up and ushered Brenda out of the office. "Mrs. Sousa, you look remarkably like your sister, so you may get some strange looks as we walk around."

"Oh my, I hadn't thought of that. I don't want to upset any children."

"It'll be okay," Karen assured her. She showed off the classrooms, the art room, the gym, and the specialists' rooms. This was the first tour she'd ever given of the school, and she felt immense pride. When she showed Brenda the Learning Center, she gave most of the credit to Sherry, who'd overseen the complete remodel of the Center and found the money to equip it with technology. They had just rounded the corner to the kindergarten wing when a child skipping down the hall gave out a shriek and dashed into the classroom. Karen hastened into the kindergarten room. "Jeremy, come here, it's okay. That wasn't Mrs. Trandon you saw in the hallway. That's her sister, Mrs. Sousa."

Jeremy was hanging onto the teacher's skirt and crying. "I saw a ghost, I saw a ghost." All the children had stopped their activities and were staring at Jeremy.

"Jeremy," Karen said calmly, "you and I are going to walk out into the hallway and meet Mrs. Sousa."

As Karen took Jeremy's hand, she said to the other children, "Mrs. Sousa, who is Ms. Trandon's sister, is going to come in the classroom and say hello to all of you in a few minutes."

Clutching Karen's hand, Jeremy timidly peeked up at Mrs. Sousa. "This is Jeremy, Mrs. Sousa."

"Hi there, Jeremy. I'm Ms. Trandon's sister." Brenda smiled down at Jeremy.

Jeremy took another look at Brenda. "You look like her and your talking voice is like hers. But you're shorter and fatter and your voice isn't mean."

"Jeremy, I think that's enough description," said Karen firmly. "Let's just all step into the classroom and Mrs. Sousa can say hello." Taking Jeremy's hand once more, all three trooped into the kindergarten room.

"Children, this is Mrs. Sousa, Ms. Trandon's sister. Can everyone say hello?" Karen looked around the room encouragingly.

All the children chorused, "Hello, Mrs. Sousa."

One little boy with bright blue eyes called out, "You do look a lot like Ms. Trandon, 'cept she was taller."

Mrs. Sousa smiled. "You're right. But sometimes people did get us confused. We look a bit alike and our voices are very similar."

A young girl with long blond curls spoke up next. "We're very, very sorry that Ms. Trandon is full of dead. I'm drawing a picture of her for you and it's going to be in a book."

"Thank you. I'm looking forward to seeing your picture. I'll let you all get back to your activities now." Brenda started backing up toward the door.

Karen quickly followed her out. "Thank you for handling that so well. Young children do get confused and sometimes say inappropriate things. I'm sorry that Jeremy made unflattering comments about you and Sherry."

"Oh, I've been around children lots. I find their honesty refreshing. I am heavier than Sherry, and I can imagine that Sherry ruled the school with a firm hand. She was that kind of person." Brenda looked at Karen. "In fact, my guess is most of your teaching staff disliked her. She was always complaining about the teachers when we talked. Do you think one of the teachers killed her?"

Karen stopped and looked at Sherry's sister with consternation. "I sincerely hope not, but the police have not arrested anyone yet."

"Hmm, well, Sherry particularly complained about a Bobbi Nelson a little too much at times."

"Bobbi is cantankerous and very outspoken, but I can't think of a reason why she'd murder Sherry." *Bobbi can join the line of suspects. It seems like everyone had some kind of motive.*

"Well," Brenda pursed her lips. "I wondered about their friendship."

"Their friendship? They had a friendship? I thought you said Sherry complained about her?"

Brenda stopped in the middle of the hallway and gave Karen a searching look. "Yes, she did. I think there are things you don't know about my sister, and it's probably best to leave them unsaid." *No doubt, there are lots of things I don't want to know.*

Karen and Brenda continued walking toward the office, and Karen told her about the memorial service planned for the next day. "Would you like to say a few words to the students at the service?" Karen asked.

Brenda stopped and thought for a moment. "Yes, I think I would. It'll only take a few minutes, but I'd like to talk about how Sherry always wanted to be a principal of an elementary school and how proud she was of Kennedy. I'll keep it short—I know how antsy young students get. But thank you for asking, I appreciate it. Thank you again for the tour. I'll see you tomorrow. And don't worry about what I said about Bobbi Nelson. I've just always wondered about their relationship." Brenda shook hands again with Karen.

What relationship, other than they couldn't stand each other? Karen wondered. Bobbi was having an affair with Nash, not Sherry Trandon. She wished Brian Kerns would solve this case soon. It was driving her crazy.

Karen looked down at her desk and saw a message from Dr. Nash. The testing had been postponed for two weeks. *Hallelujah!* she thought. The teachers would be so relieved.

It was time to talk to Freddy Moser. If she went to the Learning Center and talked to him while the class was checking out books, it should look innocent enough. Entering the Learning Center, Karen saw that the librarian was just finishing up with his story. The third graders were starting to mill around the library stacks looking for books.

Finding Freddy squatting by a book stack, Karen asked him to bring his book over to a table in the corner. At first, she just chatted with Freddy about his book. Then she said, "Freddy, I need to ask you something. You're not in any kind of trouble, but I need to know the truth. Has your dad been dropping you off at school before the playground supervisors are out?"

Freddy hung his head. With a shaky voice, he said, "I don't want to get my dad in trouble again."

"You won't, Freddy. Your dad and I will talk and figure out something so you don't have to be dropped off early. But are you arriving early?"

"Yes, Mrs. Fowler."

"Before the playground supervisors are out?"

"Yeah."

"Where do you go, Freddy, until the playground supervisor comes out?"

"I hide in the bushes at the front of the school." Freddy hung his head again. "I'm in trouble, aren't I? Ms. Trandon is going to yell at me." Then he looked up at Mrs. Fowler with a horrified look. "Oh, she can't, she's dead." He started to cry.

"Now, Freddy, stop it. You're okay. Have you been doing this every day this week?"

"Yes'm."

"So you did it today?" Freddy nodded. "And yesterday?" Freddy nodded again. "And the day before that, Tuesday? And Monday?" Freddy kept nodding his head.

"Yes'm, every day for a long time."

"It's okay, Freddy. I don't want you to worry. As I said, I'll talk to your dad, and we'll find some before-school care. Now go check out your book." Freddy got up and hurried over to the check-out desk.

Karen walked slowly back to her office, past Rhonda's classroom. She was definitely worried about her friend. She had looked awful before school. There were huge black circles under her eyes, and she had looked even more bedraggled than usual. Karen had asked her if she wasn't sleeping well, but Rhonda muttered that she had to get to her classroom and pushed by her. Now she could see Rhonda in her reading chair, with a group of students around her and the rest of the students working at reading centers.

Reaching her office, Karen decided that it was time to call Brian and let him know the child under the bushes had been identified. It was time to call the father, too. A before-school daycare arrangement had to be made. It wasn't even lunchtime yet, and Karen was beat. *Time to get another cup of coffee.*

Brian picked up his phone on the third ring. "Hi, Karen. I'm about to sit down with Brenda Sousa."

"I've identified the child who was under the bushes Tuesday morning," said Karen. "It's Freddy Moser, a third-grade student. If you're going to interview him, I'd suggest that I should be present. He's very shy and liable to freeze up on you. Freddy's quite small for his age and a bit immature. You'll have to go easy on him. Also, his father will want to be involved in the interview."

Before they hung up, she added, "Oh, one more thing. Milly Landon quit this morning. She was close friends with Sherry, possibly lovers, as Bobbi Nelson saw Milly and Sherry kissing in the office. That's a shock. If you want to talk to her, she's leaving town for Paris quite soon, I think."

"I will. It's essential that I talk to her. Do you have an address for her?"

"Sure, let me pull it up on my computer. That's odd. It's the address for the Liberty Hotel, room 315. Why would she be living in a hotel? God, that's got to be expensive."

"Karen, thank you. You've been most helpful. I'll try to arrange the Freddy Moser interview for this afternoon, and I'll track Milly down as soon as I can."

Kat was standing at her desk when Karen hung up the phone. "Hey, did you know the Fitch boys stayed with your detective last night? I guess Mrs. Fitch landed in jail and Detective Kerns took care of them so they wouldn't have to go to a group home in the middle of the night. Human Services is here now talking to Sheldon."

"Brian isn't exactly my detective, Kat. I did know that about the Fitch boys, and I'm really glad Detective Kerns could take them in last night. It must have been awful seeing their mother dragged off to jail. Those boys have been through so much."

I hope Human Services can work something out for them. Karen looked at the piles of files on her desk. *I've got to plan an upbeat faculty meeting. Morale is plummeting due to all the stress. We'll all feel better when the murderer has been arrested. Oh, please, someone has got to be arrested for this crime.*

Chapter Twelve
Thursday Morning

Brian met with Speck and Danzy at exactly 9:00 a.m. Things were starting to fall into place.

"Okay, here is what I have to date." Brian told the two officers about the lab jacket results. The sleeve did have a grease stain on it, confirming it was Bobbi Nelson's. He quickly described his interview with her and his re-interviews with Ms. Jessamyn Babcock and Dr. Nash. He explained that he'd reported the marijuana use by Jorge Costa and Brandon Leary to the school principal and the school district would follow up on this.

Both officers were intrigued by the photos found in Trandon's closet cabinet. Brian also described his interview with Pastor John about Sherry and Sean and Rhonda Burgess. Officer Danzy looked at Officer Speck and then back at Brian. "You know, sir, that church has a bit of a reputation for being rather unusual, even for Chaldea."

"How's that, Officer?"

Officer Danzy looked at the floor and then back at Brian. "I haven't seen it, but it's rumored that church members walk over hot coals to prove their faith. It's a very closed-off community. Nobody in the church talks about what goes on in the church so, of course, people speculate. My gut instinct tells me that something just isn't right." Speck nodded in agreement.

Brian looked thoughtful and said, "We'll explore it further if we have to. Officer Speck, what did you find in the files from Trandon's home and office desk?"

Officer Speck reached for a list on her desk and handed it to Brian. "Here is a list of the home files and a generalized description of the contents. As you can see, the files are mostly bills paid, warranties, and directions for using appliances. I spoke to the lawyer, and he thinks the will is pretty straightforward. Everything goes to the sister, except for the $300,000 left to Douglas Vanderhoot. There's a box that's been left for his mother, Elyse. He has no idea what's in the box, only that it is located on the top shelf of the bedroom closet, labeled 'Toots.' Our meeting with the lawyer and Mrs. Vanderhoot is scheduled for 11:30 this morning. She only has a few minutes available before she has to go to a speaking engagement at 12:30.

"The school files have been organized and I've made general comments about each file. There were some weird things in the school file about equipment and supply purchase orders. I can't quite figure it out. I thought about calling the business manager for the school district, Mr. Watson. But then I found some very strange withdrawals that make no sense at all." Speck paused to take a breath. "Sir, I need to consult the city accountant, Milford Ashton, again. He walked me through some of the finances yesterday, but I found more questions than answers last night while studying the files. Things just aren't adding up. I think we may need a warrant for school district records."

Brian grimaced. "I have no idea how district finances connect to Trandon's murder, but we'd better follow it up. Work with the accountant, and if things are not right with the district finances, we'll ask for a warrant."

Turning to Danzy, Brian said, "The phone, have you located it?"

"Yes, sir. With help from AT&T, we found it out at Trotter Creek. That's the creek that got all the waste from the meatpacking plant. The plant hasn't been open for years, but there's still an old gravel road that leads to it and the creek. The phone was partially covered by a log that was next to the water." Officer Danzy made a face. "We had to return for wader boots. That creek is toxic. But we have the phone, and the Major Crimes Team is working to take the information off it. I've been working on Ms. Trandon's home computer. I have a list of her files and a general description." Danzy's face turned red. "There are a lot of porno sites."

"Male or female?" asked Brian briskly.

"Um, female/female. There were also online forums and blogs that Trandon participated in. The language in the blogs is, well, really raunchy."

"Okay, I'm going to get you some help. I want those sites and blogs thoroughly checked out. Maybe Trandon developed some relationship that went sour. Call Neal over at the Major Crimes Team and ask him to help you go through all of it. And while you've got him on the phone, see if he had any luck with Trandon's address book. It's in some kind of code."

"Yes, sir."

Officer Danzy looked at Officer Speck and almost chuckled. "Neal, in Tech, is not going to mind this assignment."

"Let's keep it professional," Brian reminded both Speck and Danzy. They nodded. "This was good work, both of you. Keep me informed."

"I'm off to interview Milly Landon. It should be very interesting." Brian picked up his brown bag, flung his jacket over his arm, and dashed out the door.

Brian paused for a minute outside the police station. Glancing at his watch, he was appalled to see that it was already 10 a.m. He wondered how Logan and Sheldon were doing with Human Services. *I really shouldn't get involved. Of course, the question is—could I do more?* He was somewhat ambivalent about calling Logan to see what was happening after interviewing Milly Landon.

He parked cockeyed in front of the hotel, in clear violation of the parking rules, and dashed inside and over to the elevator. Both the door attendant and the receptionist had followed him. He punched the button. "Sir, you can't park out front like that." Brian whipped around and pulled out his badge.

"Police business," he growled. Turning to the receptionist, he asked, "Has Milly Landon checked out of the hotel?"

"Oh, she's checking out this morning, but I don't think she wants company. She's very particular about who goes to her room," said the receptionist in a slightly panicked voice. "Maybe I should call up first."

"Absolutely not," Brian bellowed at her. The elevator opened and Brian dashed in and punched the third-floor button. The elevator seemed to take forever. Racing down the hallway, he knocked on door 315.

"I'm not quite ready yet, bellhop," came a voice from inside. "You're early." Brian continued knocking.

Milly jerked the door open. "Look, I said I wasn't quite ready—" Two suitcases were by the door, a garment bag lay open on the bed, and a small tote was partially filled with what looked like cosmetics. "Oh, you," she said. "I'm not talking to the police."

"Either you talk to me here or down at the station, Ms. Landon. Right now, it's a friendly chat, but I can certainly read you your rights and take you down to the station."

"All right, come in." Milly turned around and threw herself down in the desk chair. Brian pulled out another chair from a small dining table and took out his notebook.

Looking around, Brian said, "You're packing up? What about your job?"

Milly looked at Brian and snorted. "I'm done teaching kids. I'm good at it, but I'm tired of doing it. Sherry's dead and there's no reason to stay in this dumb little town."

"And what was your relationship with Ms. Trandon?"

Milly laughed derisively. "Oh, you policemen! You're so careful with your questions. Sherry Trandon was my lover, but, to be clear, not a partner. It would never have been a long- term relationship. Yes, we knew each other a very long time ago. We reconnected, rather passionately, I'd say."

"And just how did you reconnect?"

"It was through a dating site, womenscupid.com"

"So, how long ago did you know Sherry?"

"I knew Sherry when she was traveling around the country with Lauri, at least twenty-five years ago. She and Lauri landed in San Francisco and stayed with a friend of mine. We became lovers then, but it got a bit volatile for my tastes, with Lauri also hanging around. So I bugged out. Who would have thought we'd find each other again?

"Then we reconnect through this dating site, and all of a sudden, I'm traveling to Iowa City, Des Moines, Chicago, Davenport, you name it—just to meet her. It got expensive, mostly for Sherry. So she suggested I come stay in Chaldea and teach at her school. What a lark. There we were, sneaking kisses in the faculty bathroom, having little rendezvous out in the countryside, and pretending to be just your run-of-the-mill teacher and principal. On weekends, we'd head for some city and really let loose. Sherry loved the secrecy. It turned her on."

Brian crossed his arms and looked steadily at Milly. "But then she got murdered. What light can you shed on that?"

For the first time, Milly looked downcast. "I don't know. I've gone over and over it in my head. As far as I know, everything was fine at the school. The superintendent liked her, the board liked her, most of the parents were okay with her, and the teachers tolerated her. What more could you want?" Milly looked at Brian and said, "I'm in total shock that Sherry's dead. I keep expecting her to walk through the door."

"Did Sherry talk about any problems at school or church or anywhere?"

"Well, she was convinced that puffed up superintendent was stealing from the district. I told her to leave well enough alone. You never win when you get tangled up with stuff like that. I think she stopped investigating. She certainly stopped talking about it.

"I guess her previous lover was sort of a problem. It was someone here in Chaldea who just couldn't let go of her. Sherry thought it was funny, and she refused to tell me who it was. She said if I knew, I'd have less respect for her and it would show how low she'd had to go. The woman was a total frump-cake, according to Sherry. Supposedly the woman knew nothing about passion and sex, but once she got going, it was terrific."

"Do you have any suspicions about who it might have been?"

"Not really. I know she called one night and Sherry got mad at her. I know she's married because Sherry told her to go do it with her husband and show him what's what. Sherry can be a bit crude and cruel. That's what made her so interesting. Plus, she was great in bed.

" Sherry did not let a lover down easily. Maybe you should look for jilted lovers as suspects in her murder, although her past lovers live all over the Midwest. That's why I never got deeply involved with her. Sherry is not to be trusted with feelings."

"Do you know an Elyse Vanderhoot?"

"No, never heard of her. Is she one of Sherry's jilted lovers?"

"How about Toots?"

Milly blanched. "Toots, why do you ask?"

"Have you heard of someone by that name?"

"Cripes, I don't want to get involved with you people. Sherry had someone, a woman she was in love with— actually, she was crazy about her, named Toots. That's all I know."

"Have you ever met her?"

Milly shook her head. "No, I don't think so. Listen, detective, I liked Sherry. We had a great fling. She was a great partier and a terrific dancer. But neither one of us was serious about settling down or anything like that. As you have probably found out, Sherry was not easy to get along with. I'm very sorry and sad Sherry's gone. But I have no ideas about her murder."

"Why are you so anxious to pack up and leave?"

Milly shrugged. "There's nothing left here for me. I only came to this God-forsaken town for Sherry. I hate funerals and I don't want to meet, or even see, her sister. I'm leaving and that's all there is to it."

Brian looked down at his notebook and then up at Milly Landon. "Ms. Landon, you are a person of interest and I'm going to ask you to stay in Chaldea for a few more days. Should you need to leave for any reason, you will need to notify me."

Milly clenched her fists and glared at Brian. "You're kidding! I am out of here."

"I'm sorry, but no. Read a book, see a movie, or honor your teaching contract, but you will need to stay in Chaldea. I can't tell you how important it is that you not violate this request. I do not want to put out a search bulletin for you. Do you understand?"

"I suppose so." Milly sat back in her chair and picked up the newspaper. "It seems as if I have a bit of free time in this dirty, little town. Perhaps I'll go to Pinky's and get drunk."

When Brian returned to the police station, he could already see a woman sitting in the Chief's office. Probably Brenda Sousa. He tossed his jacket and brown bag on his chair and went to the Chief's office. "Good morning. You must be Mrs. Sousa. I am so sorry for your loss."

A woman, considerably shorter than Sherry Trandon, stood up and shook his hand. There was a family resemblance, especially the eyes, but this woman looked a bit kinder and gentler. Although she appeared tired and sad, there were laugh lines around her mouth and eyes. Her hair certainly resembled Sherry Trandon's, but overall Brenda Sousa looked more like a grandmother figure, dressed in a moderately dumpy but practical dress, wearing wire-rim glasses, and carrying a large pocketbook.

"Detective, I'd like to hear about my sister's death and then whatever you can share about the investigation."

"Certainly. Can I get you some coffee or water?"

Brenda Sousa shook her head no. Brian proceeded to gently but vaguely describe the murder scene. When asked how she had been murdered, Brian acknowledged that she'd been killed with a knife. He asked when Brenda was planning to go to Sherry Trandon's house. He warned her that the police had been careful, but the house had been searched and the home files and computer had been removed to the police station. These items would be returned when the investigation was concluded. There were some interesting leads, but no suspects yet. He was actively pursuing the case with the help of several police officers.

Brenda nodded. "I see. This has certainly been a shock. I never thought Sherry would be murdered, and at the job she loved?" Brenda reached into her purse, took out an old-fashioned cloth handkerchief, and dabbed her eyes. "I'll have to let John and Louise know."

"John was informed and I've already interviewed him. We haven't been able to locate Louise. Do you have an address for her?"

"No, I don't. I can try one of her old addresses, but she moves around so much, I'll probably have to wait for her to contact me." Mrs. Sousa smiled sadly at Brian. "We're not a close family."

"Mrs. Sousa, I do have some questions for you. I must get to know your sister as that often leads to the murderer. Did Ms. Trandon have any enemies, or do you know of anyone that had been giving her trouble for the past few months? Do you know an Elyse Vanderhoot?"

Brenda Sousa looked baffled. "No, I've never heard that name. I don't know much about Sherry's life here in Chaldea. We were different people, detective, and didn't have much in common. But she never talked to me about anyone giving her trouble. Well, except for one teacher at her school. She complained a great deal about a Bobbi Nelson."

Brian looked up from his notes. "Tell me more about that."

Brenda paused and then said, "She complained a lot about this woman's sarcastic remarks. It made me wonder why."

"What kind of complaints?"

"Oh, she said the woman was a lazy teacher who didn't know how to teach, that kind of thing. And she was always furious about this woman's comments about her. I guess this Bobbi said some unflattering things. There was one time we were having dinner together and she went on and on about this Bobbi Nelson. I said she and the teacher had a love-hate relationship and Sherry blushed, and I've never seen Sherry blush in my life."

"I see. Do you think they were involved?

"I don't know. The subject never came up again."

"Okay, if you remember anything else about Bobbi Nelson and your sister, I'd appreciate you letting me know. I wanted to ask you about your sister's house. I found some unusual items in her closet and some photos that were in a partially hidden cabinet."

Brenda pursed her lips. "Oh, those! Well, I suppose you would ask about that. Sherry would be mortified if she knew people were poking around in her closet and her private affairs. She did lead rather a double life, one that she liked to keep very quiet."

"So, Ms. Trandon had photos that show her and others in rather compromising positions, and the women appear to be in their twenties. Is there a chance you'd recognize any of the women if I showed you the photos?"

Brenda looked at the detective. "No, I wasn't a part of her life then, but I can tell you that if she were alive, she would be devastated if those pictures got out, or were seen by anyone else."

"They're evidence in her murder investigation, but unless the pictures directly pertain to her murder, I don't see any reason why they would need to be seen by anyone else."

Brenda looked relieved. "Those pictures are from what I call her 'wild period.' Sherry ran off with this girl Lauri during her junior year of college. They were lovers and traveled around the country. That's when she got her tattoos, which I'm sure you saw in the autopsy." Brian nodded.

"She didn't communicate with the family much. Sherry showed up at home after a couple of years. I'd have to think back to get you the exact dates. My father was furious with her, said she'd ruined her life, etc. My father kicked her out of the house and told her never to come back. She went straight to our aunt and negotiated a loan to finish college. As far as I know, when she graduated, she moved to

Chaldea with her teaching certificate and got a job. Sherry and I weren't talking much in those days, so I'm not sure."

"Have you talked to her much since?"

"Some, Sherry called me occasionally and I called her. We usually get together for the holidays. I'm divorced and she's single, so it's nice to have some family around. We talked about our careers and shared our love for gardening. Once in a while, we'd get together with John."

"Did Ms. Trandon recently have a partner, or do you know if she went out to bars and parties?

Brenda tightened her lips. "Why do you ask, Detective? Did she have someone special here in Chaldea? Surely, not this teacher, Bobbi. She was very protective about her school and made sure no information ever got back to the community about her, uh, other activities."

"We haven't found evidence of a partner here in Chaldea, but I did wonder about her closet. One side of it is full of business clothes and the other side is full of party clothes, things like sheer shirts and sparkly dresses, things you just wouldn't wear around Chaldea, or frankly, anywhere where you might see parents."

"I've never seen her closet, detective. There were times when she said she was busy, but that could have been anything. And one time some woman answered her phone. When I asked for Sherry, she said that she had accidentally picked up Sherry's phone. It was a very awkward conversation, but I didn't think anything of it at the time. You think having a girlfriend or attending parties pertains to the murder?"

"I don't know if parties and possible unknown partners pertain to the murder. I ask questions, Mrs. Sousa, and I try to follow up on all puzzling things. And Sherry's closet and photos from the past puzzle me."

Brenda gave Brian an almost disdainful look as she replied, "Of course, I knew my sister was a lesbian and partied a lot. It was something we both acknowledged, but never discussed in any detail. Sherry's private life was off-limits. She got very prickly about it if I said anything."

"Just one more question," said Brian. "We've been in contact with your brother, who says he wasn't on speaking terms with Sherry. What do you know about that?"

"John and Sherry never got along, even as kids. John's got a lot of strange ideas regarding Christianity, which he likes to foist on both Sherry and me. Sherry had no patience for it, and she and John would end up screaming at each other. I tended to ignore his preaching. I'll make the obligatory visit out to see him while I'm here. My guess is he won't even come to the memorial service. He sees Sherry as a fallen woman."

"Does he know Sherry was a lesbian?"

"Yes, she threw it in his face three years ago at Thanksgiving. He almost threw up at the table. John stormed out of the house, and we haven't gotten together since."

"There is one other matter I wanted to discuss with you that has nothing to do with Ms. Trandon's murder."

Brenda looked at her watch and said, "Okay, I've got a few minutes before I meet with the Presbyterian minister to go over funeral details."

"I'm renting an apartment above the Fitches." Brenda rolled her eyes and crossed her arms. "Last night there was an incident and Mrs. Fitch got arrested. With your cousin in prison, the two boys are about to be pushed back into foster care." Brenda was shaking her head heatedly.

"Just a minute, let me finish. Logan is almost 18 and is doing very well at school. In fact, he's applying for a scholarship to the University of Iowa. I suggested to him that he ask Human Services to let him stay in the house until one of the Fitches gets out of jail, since he turns eighteen next week. Sheldon, the younger boy, needs a family to stay with in Chaldea. I know you don't know the boys well, but if an adult could sponsor him, just for a couple of weeks, then he could be near his brother. By then, the situation with Mrs. Fitch might be resolved."

"I don't know why you got involved with those ornery Fitches, young man. Roy Fitch may be my cousin, but my mother and father wanted nothing to do with the Fitch family. From what I understand, they were always asking my parents for money. And believe me, they did not approve of their irresponsible behavior. I can see you're trying to do right by the boys. I will be in town for a while to finish up my sister's affairs. But really, take care of two boys?" Brenda crossed her arms.

"Logan is responsible. I don't think you'd have to do much as both of them are really self-sufficient. You just need to contact Human Services." Brian leaned forward in his chair. "Those boys need a decent break."

"You are asking a lot. I'll think about it, and I'll talk briefly to Human Services and the boys and we'll see. But please don't count on it. I can't imagine myself taking care of two young boys."

"Mrs. Sousa, thank you. And thank you for sharing about your sister. I'm going to have a police officer help you connect with Human Services."

Brenda stood up. "Thank you for your time. Please keep me informed. I'm staying at the Liberty Hotel on the square for now. When I was little, we used to run past the Liberty as fast as we could because there was always a line of old men sitting on some straight-backed chairs outside the hotel, and they would yell vulgar comments at us. It was terrifying. What a welcome change the remodeled hotel is."

After Brenda left, Brian sat down and put in a call to Mr. Moser at his work. He explained that Freddy was a witness to events involving the murder of Sherry Trandon. Mr. Moser was horrified. Finally, after much discussion, Mr.

Moser agreed to have Freddy questioned at Kennedy School, with both Mrs. Fowler and him in the room. The boy was extremely sensitive as it was, and he didn't need Detective Kerns to scare him.

Brian then called Karen to confirm the appointment. "I talked to Mr. Moser and he's available right after school."

"Okay, I won't have Freddy take the bus, so you should be able to interview him sometime around 3:30."

"Thank you, Karen. I appreciate this. Your friend, Lucy, told me that the memorial service is tomorrow at 10:30. I'll be there."

"Yes, thank you; we're ready for it, I guess," said Karen. "I've never had a memorial service at an elementary school, and I hope I never have to again… Oh well, it has to be done and it'll be over tomorrow. Right now I've got to get out to recess with the first graders. The supervisors are complaining that the kids are fighting over soccer rules. First graders! It's like the U.N. out there, with each first grader arguing that his or her rules are right and everyone else's is wrong. I guess that makes me either Dictator of the World, or Secretary-General of the U.N. Lucky me!"

Brian laughed. "Oh, be Dictator of the World. You can make all the rules and do whatever you want. It sounds like so much fun."

When Brian hung up, he called over to Officer Speck. "We've got to get to Babcock's office. Damn, take a patrol car and put on the siren. The office is over in Plain View."

Officer Speck and Detective Kerns found Elyse Vanderhoot sitting impatiently in William Babcock's office. She set down her cup of coffee and looked at them haughtily. "Detective, I only have a few minutes. What is this about?" The woman was snobby without even trying. Her blond hair was pulled back in a bun, she had an expensive suit on and the strand of pearls around her neck must have cost a fortune.

Detective Kerns sat down and took out his notebook. Officer Speck already had her notebook out, but it gave him a minute to assess the situation. "I'm sure that Mr. Babcock has informed you that your son inherited $300,000 from Sherry Trandon. Can you tell me how you and your son know the late principal of Kennedy Elementary School?

"My son doesn't know Ms. Trandon at all. I've been friends with her for several years. I don't remember exactly how we met. I think it was at my husband's campaign office. Sherry was a tireless worker."

"So, were you surprised when Ms. Trandon left your son, who you say doesn't know our victim, a large sum of money?"

"Why, yes, I was."

"So were you close friends? Did you socialize much?"

Mrs. Vanderhoot made a show of looking at her watch. "Listen, detective. I'm in total shock about the money. I have no idea why Sherry Trandon would leave my son this large sum. Now, I must get to my luncheon." She stood up.

Detective Kerns and Officer Speck also stood up. Brian tried one last question. "Do you know what was left for you in the box labeled Toots?"

"No idea whatsoever." Elyse Vanderhoot walked sedately out of the office and climbed into a limousine outside the door.

Brian was visibly irritated. "Let's stop by Sherry Trandon's house and look for this mysterious box. It wasn't listed with the items taken from the house by the Major Crimes Team."

It didn't take long for Brian to retrieve the box from the bedroom closet. Heads were going to roll at the Major Crimes Team. How could they have overlooked this box in their search? Sitting in the patrol car, he slipped on gloves and opened the box. He was staring at an array of sex toys. He heard Officer Speck's mild gasp. He picked up some black velvet handcuffs with one finger. "I think Mrs. Vanderhoot has a bit more explaining to do. I'll talk to the Chief and we'll arrange another interview with the aloof Elyse, or should we call her 'Toots'?"

After talking to the Chief about Vanderhoot, they decided another interview was in order and the detective would contact her. Brian left the office, feeling irritated about the congresswoman, and called over to Danzy. "Let's go take a look at where this cell phone was found." They climbed into a police car and Brian started driving in the direction of Trotter Creek.

Following Danzy's directions, they arrived at the gravel road that led to the meatpacking plant near Trotter Creek. Turning down the road, Brian remarked, "This is so isolated. I wonder how Trandon's cell phone ended up way out here." Reaching the end of the road, Brian got out of the car. "Okay, show me exactly where the phone was found."

Danzy marched off through the weeds and trash toward the creek. Arriving at the creek bed, he pointed to a log and told Brian how the phone had been wedged there. Brian looked around at the weeds, the trash, and the creek and said, "Who would want to meet here? Do you think the murderer came here to get rid of the phone or was this a meeting place? It would certainly be isolated enough for a rendezvous, perhaps between Sherry and the mysterious lover."

"I just don't know, sir. Possibly."

As Brian and Officer Danzy stood staring at the creek, they could hear rustling from further up the hill. A man was making his way down the path. He had a floppy old hat on his head, a rifle of some sort over his shoulder, and appeared to have a string of rabbits on a line. "Well a-what in tarnation do we have here?" he hollered out. "This place is getting downright crowded. I'm gonna have to move further out."

Brian stood up and called to him, "Sir, we'd like to speak to you. We're from the police."

"Shucks, I don't want to get messed up in some sorta police business. Y'all leave me alone."

Officer Danzy called out, "Bill Foxmore, is that you? I haven't seen you in ages. How have you been?"

"Been better." Bill spit a wad of tobacco out on the ground. "What's with your people, Brad? Y'all all over the place yesterday. It's just not private anymore, not private at all since those two wimin been coming out here."

Brian looked at the old guy curiously. "Two women? What do you mean?"

Bill set his line down, rested his gun against a tree, and pulled out his pipe. After tamping it down and lighting up, he said: "Well, those two wimin come out here all the time, messin' up the place, and carryin' on."

"Please, sir, I need you to describe exactly what you saw." Brian took out his notebook.

Bill leaned against a tree and took a long puff on his pipe. "One of the wimin drived a fancy, blue car, and she had 'nother wimin with her. They'd drive to the end of the gravel road and park, just like them teenage kids sometimes did. Only the teenagers ain't comin' out here anymore." He chuckled. "Not since I scared them on Halloween. They's think the place is haunted. But those wimin! They don't scare so easy. They then did disgustin' things in that car. Me and Frank couldn't watch. Disgustig." He again spat on the ground.

Brian looked puzzled. "Frank?"

Officer Danzy responded, "His dog."

"That's the end of it. They was bad wimin. One of them used ta cry and carries on. They hasn't been out here for a bit. I's hope they gone away, 'specially after the fight."

"What fight and when did this happen?" Brian asked.

"Well, I don't have a fancy calendar. It was a while back. Well, they did them nasty stuff and then one wimin gets out of the car and she was a cryin' and carryin' on. The other wimin got out of the car and she shouted and hollered at the first wimin and told her she wuz stupid. She was a mean'un."

"Can you describe these women?"

Bill scratched his head with a stick he was holding. "I don't know I can do that. They wuz just wimin, you know. One pretty much looks like 'nother."

"It's important," Brian stated firmly. "Please try."

Bill sat down on a boulder, and Officer Danzy and Brian attempted to look comfortable sitting on logs. "I guess I can tell you what they all looked like. One wimin was big, really big and she had a big voice. She, uh, had short hair. The other wimin had brown hair, pulled back in a whatcha call it? you know, a bun. Her voice wuz not loud. She wuz shorter. There, that's all I remember. I need to be gettin' home. I've got to skin these here rabbits." Bill stood up and picked up his rifle.

Brian stood up too. "Wait a minute, sir. I need you to describe these two women to a police sketch artist. It's very important. I also want you to look at some photos of people."

Danzy looked at Brian quizzically. As an aside, Brian murmured, "Show him staff pictures from Kennedy School. He may be able to identify one or both women."

Bill Foxmore continued to complain. "No, I'm not goin' into town. No way." He shook his head vehemently.

Officer Danzy stood up. "How about I go along with you and help you skin your rabbits and then you can take me back to town in your pickup truck? That still runs, right?" Bill nodded. "And when you drop me off at the police station, you can come inside, we'll buy you a nice dinner, and you can describe the women to a police artist and look at some photos. How 'bout that?"

"Huh, you still remember howta skin rabbits?"

Officer Danzy nodded. "You know my grandpappy taught me well." As they walked off through the woods toward Bill's house, Brian could hear them discussing fried chicken, mashed potatoes, and green beans for Bill's supper. Brian pulled out his cell phone and put a quick call in to Officer Speck to see where she was with the District's finances.

"I've got the city accountant here, and we both agree there's something wrong with the district books. It looks as if sums of money have been taken out regularly over several years. With Chief Daniel's permission, we have a call into the auditor. Also, the Chief is going to subpoena the district financial records. An expert accountant for the state police has been contacted to examine the school district finances. This has gone beyond what I can do. Sir, it looks as if Vince Watson and Dr. Nash have been siphoning off funds. We just need to confirm it."

"Good work, Speck. Keep on it and keep me informed." Sherry Trandon was right about corruption in the school district. That made Dr. Nash a person of interest in the murder. It was possible she was trying to expose him.

Brian pulled a piece of paper from his pocket with the name of the social worker that Officer Danzy had given him. A Ms. White was handling the Fitch case. He hadn't heard from Logan, but it was time to see what was happening. *Darn, if I haven't started feeling responsible for those kids.*

Ms. White answered on the second ring. Brian identified himself and asked for an update on the proceedings. She suggested he should get in touch with Brenda Sousa as she was taking over temporary custody of both Logan and Spencer. He thanked Ms. White and put in a call to Brenda.

When Brenda answered the phone, Brian could hear a vacuum cleaner in the distance. "Oh, yes, I'm taking over temporary custody of the boys. I talked to Logan for a long time. He's a very mature young man. Right now, the boys and I are cleaning the house from top to bottom. I cannot abide a dirty house. It looks as if my cousin's wife will be in jail for several weeks, so I'm planning to move some things from Sherry's house over to this one if the police are through with the house—you know, sheets, blankets, dishes—things like that."

"The police are almost done with the house. I'll have a police officer accompany you to retrieve the items you want."

"I spoke to a lawyer this afternoon, over in Plain View, a Mr. Babcock. I am the beneficiary for everything in the house and all cash reserves, except for that box and $300,000 that goes to a Douglas Vanderhoot. I have no idea how my sister got ahold of so much money. And this Douglas must be a very special person for her to leave him so much money. There are loads of things to work out, so it won't be a problem caring for the boys for several weeks. If it goes beyond that, well, then we'll have to see."

"I'm so glad this worked out for the boys. They finally got a well-deserved break. Logan must be particularly happy. I'm currently renting the upstairs apartment, so let me know if there's anything I can do to help." Brian slid his cell phone back in his pocket with a real sense of satisfaction. At least something had worked out okay.

He really needed somewhere to think. Everything was rattling around in his head.

Sitting once again in the back of the diner sipping coffee, Brian reached into his brown bag and pulled out a tablet of paper and all his notes. Sifting through his notes, he doodled on the paper. It had always helped him to think if he could draw lines and squares and curlicues all over a piece of paper. He remembered, with some satisfaction, that he'd written an essay on doodles that helped get him admitted to Northwestern University.

It seems as if there are several possible suspects. Dr. Nash and Vincent Watson, although I can't place Watson at the scene yet. Rhonda Burgess was in the building and upset with Sherry over the possibility of losing her job. Milly Landon, who seems to have appeared out of the past, and the mysterious lover, whoever that could be, are all highly suspect. Then there's Bobbi Nelson. She lied to protect Nash, but maybe she was lying to protect herself. Was she involved with Sherry Trandon too? What about this Elyse Vanderhoot? Toots? There's more to this friendship with Sherry than she's letting on. And who leaves $300,000 to some kid she supposedly doesn't know?

He really needed old Bill Foxmore to work with a police artist to render a decent sketch of the women who were seen out at Trotter Creek. Perhaps his hunch would pay off and Foxmore would identify a staff person from Kennedy by looking at photos. After all, if Trandon's phone was found out at Trotter's Creek, maybe Sherry had been a regular visitor. And then there is Freddy Moser, the worrier. What had he seen and heard? Brian could feel the case starting to close in on him. It was like pushing his way through a fog. He reviewed his notes and fretted. *Where is the missing key to this murder? If the lover in Sherry's car could be identified, perhaps some questions would be answered.*

Brian left some money for the bill, stepped out into the back alley and put in a call to Officer Danzy. He got Neal, the technician. "Have you found anything of interest on the computer?"

"Yes, I've pulled some stuff from various online forums. Sherry definitely had a lover or partner in Chaldea or nearby. She references her with great derision. You should stop by. We've got some text messages isolated too. No luck with the code in the address book. I am starting to wonder if it's even a code."

Several people waved at Brian as he opened his car door. Chaldea was a friendly place, he admitted to himself, but overall, all this friendliness made him a bit uncomfortable. There was something about the anonymity of Chicago that he liked. In Chicago, Trandon probably wouldn't have needed to create such a secret life.

Brian strode into the Chaldea police station and straight over to Officer Danzy's desk, where Neal had temporarily set up his computers and equipment. Tossing his jacket and brown bag on his chair, he said, "Show me what you've got."

Neal pushed several sheets of paper at Brian. "Take a look for yourself. These conversations are from a forum called forevergaygirl." Brian looked down and read a conversation between "amontillado" and "lovinit." He blinked. Trandon was describing someone she was involved with.

Neal chuckled. "Don't you love the handle name— amontillado? My uncle drinks that kind of sherry. He says it goes great with cigars. And yeah, the description of the sex is way out there. Totally X-rated reading."

Brian nodded and read on. *This is like reading a porn novel, or at least what I think a porn novel would read like.* Looking at another sheet, he could see that Trandon had been actively involved in setting up parties and gatherings in places like Iowa City, Davenport, and Cedar Rapids.

After reading a description of what she was planning to wear, he could begin to see a use for the clothes in the closet. *It must have cost a lot for Trandon to travel to all these cities and party.* Then there was a description of a gay cruise in the Caribbean. It looked like she had gone to that since Neal marked that it coincided with spring break. Brian read through all the paperwork that Danzy and Neal had provided. It certainly confirmed that Ms. Trandon liked to party.

The description of her lover in Chaldea depicted an unhealthy relationship. Trandon appeared to have the upper hand in this relationship as she described ordering this other woman around. It was truly repulsive what she had supposedly made her do, sexual antics that Brian hadn't even heard of, or maybe she was just bragging. Either way, it was emotional abuse of this other woman. He was beginning to feel sorry for Sherry Trandon's lover.

According to Trandon, this other woman was naïve and thought she was in love with her, something that Trandon ridiculed over and over in her conversations with various people in the online forum. Brian re-read a paragraph. She seemed to refer to seeing this lover at work. *Was it someone on the school staff? Who could it be?* He cast his thoughts back to the school staff. Bobbi Nelson didn't fit the description of a meek lover. Mary Nash did and so did Rhonda Burgess. Jessamyn Babcock didn't fit, but maybe that other student teacher, the shy one in the second grade he'd interviewed. *Stop it, I am stretching way beyond any evidence I have.*

Brian pulled out the paperwork from his brown bag that had been collected on the staff at Kennedy. Passing over the men, he concentrated on the women. No one else seemed to fit the description, but he didn't know many members of the staff. He really needed to ask Karen to share her perspective on her staff's personalities. Perhaps she'd have some insights.

"Any text messages of interest?" he asked.

Neal sat at the desk passing the phone back and forth from one hand to the other. "There's nothing of interest on this phone. I think this is her business phone, and if she has another one, that's what she uses for personal stuff. However, I can't find any evidence of a second phone. AT&T is the only company that services this area, and they don't have a phone registered to a Sherry Trandon. I think she used a burner phone, that's what I think. And I think she purchased them when she traveled. Buying burner phones in Chaldea would be noticeable."

Brian sat and rubbed his forehead. "We didn't find any trace of a burner phone at her house, the school, or her car. We can't trace it if we don't know the number. I think we've reached a dead end there. Sorry, Neal. Keep working on the address book. Has Officer Danzy arrived with Bill Foxmore?"

Neal grinned. "Yes, they're washing up. I guess skinning rabbits is a messy business." At that moment, Danzy and Bill Foxmore walked out of the men's room.

Brian slammed his fist on the desk. "You know what, Officer Danzy? First, show Bill pictures of the staff at Kennedy. They're all in the personnel files. Maybe he'll recognize someone. I'm not even sure we need the police sketch artist now. Yeah, maybe we're just getting a bit closer to the truth. We can hope. I've got an appointment at Kennedy School to interview a witness, and then I'll be back."

Chapter Thirteen

Thursday Afternoon and Evening

Karen collected Freddy from his classroom and brought him down to the office. "Just sit here for a few minutes until your dad comes and then we'll go back to your classroom." Freddy sat on the bench, gloomily swinging his legs back and forth, and even when Kat offered him chips, Freddy didn't perk up.

"There's my dad, Mrs. Fowler. " A smile lit up his face and he bounced out the door to greet him. Karen quickly followed, shook hands with Mr. Moser, and told him they'd be meeting in Freddy's classroom.

Brian arrived at the third grade classroom at that moment. "Good afternoon, Mr. Moser. I appreciate you allowing me to talk to Freddy." He glanced at Freddy, who appeared to be reading a book. Since the book was upside down, Karen was pretty sure he was pretending. Brian casually walked over and sat on a beanbag chair across from Freddy. The detective would have to approach the issue carefully. Freddy looked scared to death. His freckles stood out on his face, his hands were shaking, and he kept turning to look fearfully at his dad.

"Hi, Freddy. I bet you know who I am."

Freddy nodded.

"Hey, I see you're wearing a Blackhawks T-shirt. Are you a fan?"

Freddy nodded solemnly. "My dad and I listen to their games and sometimes we watch them on TV."

"I'm from Chicago and I'm a big Blackhawks fan."

Freddy looked at Brian wide-eyed. "Have you ever been to one of their games?"

"I saw them win the Stanley Cup in 2015. That was a great game, the greatest game. Patrick Kane was terrific. You know, I met him once."

"You did? Wow, you are so lucky. Dad, this detective met Patrick Kane and he's seen a Blackhawks game for real."

Mr. Moser, who had been watching the exchange carefully, smiled. "The detective is a very lucky man. Someday, Freddy, we'll get to a game."

Karen had been listening to the conversation, surprised at how good Brian was with kids. *He finds out Freddy's interests and gains his confidence using sports, of course. Don't males always do that?*

"Freddy, Mrs. Fowler, and your dad have probably talked to you about how important it is for you to tell me what you saw Tuesday morning when you were sitting under the bushes by the principal's office." Freddy looked up at Brian with a worried frown.

Karen spoke up. "You're not in any kind of trouble, Freddy, although you and your dad do need to figure out some before-school care. I'll help with that."

Brian looked back and forth between Mr. Moser and Freddy. "Mr. Moser, what time did you drop Freddy off? The time is very important."

"I knew you'd ask that, and I'm trying to remember exactly when. It was very close to 7 a.m. I told Freddy to hang low so he wouldn't get in trouble for getting to school so early. That's why he was hiding in the bushes." Mr. Moser looked embarrassed.

Turning back to Freddy, Brian asked, "Freddy, during the time you were in the bushes, did you see anyone go into the school?"

"No, I was trying to stay invisible, like Harry Potter in his invisibility cloak. I wish I had one. Do you like Harry Potter? My dad read me all seven books."

"I do like Harry Potter, and you're right, an invisibility cloak would come in really handy as a detective. So you didn't see anyone go into the school?"

"I didn't see anything, but I did hear some shoes go by, and once I heard talking as some people went into the school. But I didn't look."

"I want you to think hard about this next question. Did you hear or see anyone in Ms. Trandon's office? Did you perhaps hear voices or take a peek in the window?"

Freddy was now rubbing a spot on his hand and his worried frown was even more pronounced. With a quavering voice, he asked, "Is the murderer going to get me?"

"That's a fair question, Freddy. Have you told anyone about what you saw or heard?"

Freddy vigorously shook his head and whispered, "No."

"I think you're safe then. The murderer won't know that you talked to me. Your dad and Mrs. Fowler won't say a word. However, I think you should stick close to your dad for a few days until we clear this whole thing up."

Freddy looked relieved. "Okay, I think I can tell you then. You're Patrick Kane's friend, so it's all right. I was in the bushes looking at my comic book when I heard loud voices in the principal's office. I thought it was someone getting in trouble because Ms. Trandon has a big voice and she was very angry." Brian looked at Freddy encouragingly. "There was a man's voice hollering pretty loud and Ms. Trandon and this man were yelling at each other a lot."

"Could you hear anything they were saying?"

Freddy sighed. "Mostly it didn't make sense. It was about money though. Ms. Trandon kept shouting, 'You took the money' and then something else. The man just shouted that she was wrong." Freddy continued, worried, "I don't think you can tell Ms. Trandon she's wrong 'cause she was always right. She always said so anyway. After a while it got quiet. I don't know if he left or not.

"Later, I was getting some crackers out of my backpack to eat when there was more noise. This noise wasn't quite so loud at first. Mostly, the person was crying. Well, I guess it was kind of noisy 'cause she cried really loud. Ms. Trandon was talking to her, but I couldn't hear what was said. After some more time, the crying lady started yelling at her. She screamed stuff like 'You're mean,' and 'I hate you.' My dad says you shouldn't ever say you hate someone."

Brian asked, "So they were arguing?"

Freddy shrugged. "I guess. Ms. Trandon didn't say much except 'You're stupid' and 'You're ugly.' She sounded irritated, kind of like when I don't clean my room and my dad has to remind me over and over again. Then it was quiet for a while, and I thought the person had left or maybe both of them had left, but then there was this loud kinda angry cry and then silence. I can't describe the cry 'cause it was creepy. Really creepy. Really, really creepy."

"Is that all?" asked Brian.

Freddy looked at the floor. Then he looked up at the detective. "Are you sure I won't get in trouble?"

Brian shook his head no. "You will not get in trouble. What did you see? Did you," he looked at Freddy quizzically, "did you peek in the window?"

"I did 'cause I thought I recognized the voice, and I was right. It was Mrs. Burgess. I know her because I have her for math."

Brian leaned forward. "Think hard, Freddy, and describe to me exactly what you saw."

Freddy looked over at his dad and Mrs. Fowler, and then back at Brian. "I peeked in the window and I could see Ms. Trandon sitting at her desk. She looked annoyed, like when the kids in my class misbehave because the teacher is out of the room and then she comes back and gets mad at the misbehaving kids. Ms. Trandon looked like that. Mrs. Burgess was sitting in the chair on the other side of the desk. She was rubbing her hands together and crying. That's what I saw."

"Okay, you're doing really well. Were you looking when the loud cry happened?"

"Nope, I was reading my comic. There was a loud cry and I got scared and I squished down in the bushes. It was quiet for a tiny bit and then I thought I heard some grunting and a voice again and then there was sort of a moaning sound, but I'm not sure. It was all so scary. Then after a while, all the teachers started coming out of the school. That's when I snuck around to the playground and stayed there. Then the police cars came and then the busses and I looked for some third graders to hang around with."

Brian patted Freddy on the shoulder. "You did well telling me what happened. Let me just go over this with you again. First, you heard a man's voice and you don't know whether he left, then you heard Mrs. Burgess's voice, then you heard a cry, and then just a little bit later you heard grunting and then maybe moaning. Do you think the moaning was coming from a man or a woman?"

Freddy started biting his lip. "I don't know, I just don't know. It could have been a man or a woman. It was a creepy moan."

"You're doing okay, Freddy. Just one more question. Was the moan high—sort of like this?" Brian made a moaning noise. "Or was it low—kind of like this?" Brian made a lower moaning sound.

Freddy shrugged helplessly and started to tear up. "I don't know. It was all very confusing and scary, very scary." Freddy continued to look at Brian apprehensively. "I don't understand how Ms. Trandon ended up dead. She was alive when I saw her. How did it happen?"

"I'm not sure how the murder happened, but I'm getting a lot closer to figuring it out. It's very important that you do not talk to anyone about this—not to a friend at school, not to anyone. Do you understand?"

Freddy nodded. "Yup, I get it." He slowly walked over to his dad, who put his arm around him and squeezed him.

"You did an awesome job, son."

Brian looked at Freddy, who seemed woebegone, with his face all scrunched up in a frown. "Freddy, you know, I think I can get Patrick Kane's autograph for you. Would you like that?"

Freddy's face lit up. "Oh yes, that would be great, really great."

"Okay, give me some time. I won't be back in Chicago for several weeks, but I have a friend who knows Patrick Kane super well. I'll see what I can do."

"Wow, that would be so awesome, wouldn't it, Dad?"

"It certainly would. Now let's go home and get you some dinner." Mr. Moser put his arm around Freddy, and they walked out the door.

Brian turned to Karen. "What you heard is highly confidential. You can't tell a soul."

Karen was sitting in shocked silence. "I know, I won't say a word. But Rhonda—why was Rhonda in Sherry's office crying? I don't get it. And who was the man?" *My God, so much goes on in this school that I don't know.*

Brian sat down. "I need your help, Karen. I don't know the staff at Kennedy very well. It has become evident that Sherry was having an affair with a staff member at the school. This person may be able to help us with the investigation. Do you have ideas who it could be?"

Karen put her head in her hands. "Oh my God, this just gets worse and worse. A staff member who was having an affair with Sherry? I already told you about Milly Landon. You think there's another person?"

Brian said, "Yeah, Milly confirmed the affair. But I think Ms. Trandon was also involved with another staff member."

Karen continued to shake her head. "I never saw even a hint of it. I have no idea, no idea at all."

"I think the affair happened before Milly arrived. What about Rhonda?"

Karen looked at Brian, completely appalled. "Are you kidding? She's married, she has a child, and she goes to a very strict fundamentalist church. Rhonda, having an affair? That's —I don't even know what to say." *Oh, no, not Rhonda. God would smite her dead for doing something so sinful.*

Karen stopped talking and looked reflective for a moment. "It is kinda weird, but Rhonda was acting strange last spring, not at all how she usually acts. She was, I don't know—perkier. She was taking better care of herself— fixing her hair, wearing cuter clothes. But she's taken a real tumble lately, acting almost depressed. But I'm sure that's all due to her husband. He's very difficult to live with.

"I'd say Bobbi was a possibility, but she's already having an affair with Phillip Nash. She didn't get along at all with Sherry, and I don't think it was an act. Besides, she's been in love with Phillip Nash for almost 30 years. Brenda Sousa was here earlier and hinted about some relationship between the two of them. But I just don't see it. There was genuine dislike, almost hatred." *I guess they could hurl insults at each other and then have makeup sex.* "Being a teacher in Chaldea is like living in a fishbowl. I just don't see how anyone could get away with an affair, especially between two women. Chaldea is quite conservative, you know that. Sherry, with a lover? In Chaldea? This is truly a disaster. I can't think of any other staff who might be involved, but then I'm still shocked about Sherry's private life, so I guess I don't notice things as much as I thought I did."

Brian sat and looked at Karen. "It's been pretty evident that someone here in Chaldea murdered your principal. It's a difficult idea to adjust to. You know all these people and now perhaps someone you worked or socialized with is a murderer. I guess time helps and people move on, but nothing will be quite the same again." Brian stood up. "I've got to get back to the police station. Keep a very close eye on Freddy when he's at school. I'm going to continue keeping a police officer stationed here. And please, give me a call if you think of something that might pertain to the case, even if it seems trivial."

Karen walked back to the office, bone-tired. *I knew a murder investigation would be bad, but this just gets worse and worse.* How could Brian suspect Rhonda? That was crazy. Now, every time she saw a staff member, she'd wonder if that person killed Sherry.

Sitting down at her desk, Karen opened up her computer. For the first time, she realized she was probably alone in the building. Kat had gone home, and the night custodians had not yet arrived. *I just want to go home. This is so creepy.* She shook her head. *Stop it,* she told herself, *I've got work to do.*

Just then the phone rang. Karen took a deep breath and prepared for yet another upset parent. "Hello, this is Karen Fowler."

An airy, breathless voice sounded in Karen's ear. "I'm so glad I caught you. This is Elyse Vanderhoot. I am desperate to talk to you. It's very important."

"Elyse, you are definitely a voice from the past. How are you?" Karen had gone to school with Elyse. In junior high they'd been best friends, pledging life-long loyalty to each other. That hadn't lasted long. Elyse had dropped her in high school for supposedly not being cool enough. Thanks to Elyse, her freshman year had been wretched.

"Karen, I need advice from an old friend."

"Advice, Elyse? You've got a whole congressional office full of people to advise you."

"I need your level-headed personal advice, Karen. You've been a true friend all these years. Could we talk now, in person? How about if we meet at the park bench by the band shelter, like old times? I'll bring you a latte."

"Well, the latte is new. Are we discussing boys? That's what we used to do."

"Kinda. Thank you, Karen. I'll see you in ten minutes."

The dial tone rang in Karen's ear. *God, that is so like self-centered Elyse. Calling me up after all these years and acting like we're best friends. I can't imagine what is so important that she needs my advice. Frick, I've got work to do. Elyse calls and I run out to help her solve some problem. Mom was right back in high school when she said I was better off without her. What a self-righteous prig.*

Karen grabbed her car keys, jacket, and purse. She turned off her computer and slammed the office door. When she parked on the square, she could see Elyse sitting on the park bench where they'd spent hours one summer, sharing boy crushes, hairstyles, and what have you. *God, she looks like a prima donna, sitting there.* Grumpily, Karen got out of her car and waved.

Elyse jumped up and hugged Karen. "You look great," she gushed. "And I heard you have a boyfriend." She handed the latte to Karen, who almost dropped it.

"Your sources are incorrect, Elyse. No boyfriend."

"Oh, I'm sorry. Someone told me they'd seen you going around town with that detective who's investigating Sherry Trandon's murder."

Karen looked at Elyse over the top of her reading glasses, which she'd forgotten to take off. "I was asked by Dr. Nash to provide the detective with any assistance that's needed. That's all. Beats me how people get a boyfriend out of that." She slipped off her reading glasses, dropped them in her purse, and sat down on the bench.

"I've got limited time, Elyse, as I'm sure you do. What gives?"

Elyse was twisting the napkin from her latte around her finger. "I'm worried, Karen. I hold a public office now and everyone notices what I do. There's always seems to be a reporter hiding behind a bush, just ready to catch me doing something wrong."

"Elyse, more power to you for getting into politics, but I'm not the person to confide in about whatever mess you've gotten yourself into."

"But you do know the detective on the murder investigation, and you're involved with it, right?"

"What in God's name are you asking me? You've got to be clearer than that."

"Okay, okay. It's hard to start. That detective interviewed me this morning about Sherry Trandon."

Karen stopped drinking her latte and stared at Elyse. "You knew Sherry?"

"Kinda. She left Douglas money."

"Douglas, your son? Why would Sherry leave him money? Did she even know him?" A group of people walked by and glanced curiously at Elyse and Karen. They waited for them to move out of earshot.

"No, she's never met Douglas."

"I'm lost, Elyse. 'Fess up. What's going on? You're talking like you did that time you stole Connor Andrews from me to take to the Homecoming dance freshman year. You're full of innuendos I'm not following." Karen was still thoroughly pissed about Connor. He was cute, and she liked him. *You were the bitch who could have cared less about him.*

Elyse grabbed Karen's arm. Tears were forming at her eyes. "Sherry and I had an affair years ago."

Karen's mouth dropped open. "You're gay." *I knew it, I always knew it! So did my Mom. She tried to tell me, but I didn't believe her.*

"Quiet, shh. Please, Karen, shut up. I'm not gay. I was experimenting."

"With Sherry Trandon?"

"Yes, but the relationship got messy. She was serious and I was, uh, experimenting. She was furious when I broke it off to get married. Like, oh my God, you won't believe what she did."

Karen continued to stare at Elyse, open-mouthed. "Try me."

Elyse's face reddened, and she slid her foot back and forth across the grass. Finally, she whispered, "She mailed a package of poop to me."

Karen was disgusted. "That's so gross." But then, Elyse had always been outstanding at ticking off people.

"Yeah, it was, and when I had Douglas, she mailed me another package of poop."

"Oh, Elyse. I don't know what to say. You were married twelve years, right?" Elyse nodded. "So you haven't had any contact with Sherry for a long time?" Elyse looked at the ground and almost, not quite, hung her head. "You're kidding me? You've seen her since you got married. Recently?"

"Over the years we've met several times in Chicago for a weekend. Don't judge me, Karen. Sherry is like a poison you can't get rid of. The experience, I don't know how to describe it."

"Oh, please don't. I don't want to hear about your passionate weekends. I still don't see why you've called me, Elyse. So, you had this affair, which you kept alive for fifteen years. I guess you need to confess it to Detective Kerns. I don't think it will become public knowledge unless it directly pertains to the murder. I still don't get why she left Douglas money? How much did she leave him?"

Elyse's face colored. "$300,000."

Karen's mouth dropped open. "Wow! Why?"

"It's a way to get back at me. I always told her I couldn't divorce my husband because Douglas was too important. She knows I'm always hard up for money. I would have spent the money; I have this tendency to spend beyond my means. Leaving it to him in a trust means I can't touch it. She's forced me to put Douglas first. God, she's such a bitch."

"Sherry's revenge, I guess. But where did Sherry get money like that?"

"Lower your voice, Karen, please. There are reporters everywhere. I think, well, I think Sherry was blackmailing people."

"For what?"

"God, you are such an innocent, Karen. You always have been. She had affairs with women and then threatened to tell their husbands."

"Oh, so as innocent Karen, I'll ask: She was blackmailing you, wasn't she?"

Elyse took a tissue from her pocket and wiped her eyes. "I wanted to meet in public so I wouldn't break down." She sighed. "Sometimes I wish we were back in junior high, talking about what to wear and how to fix our hair. I'm in such trouble, Karen. That detective is going to come after me."

"Right, because you're still not telling me the whole story. I know you, Elyse. Remember, we were best friends. You're holding something back."

"Oh, what am I going to do? I was at Sherry's house last Monday night. Little did I know she'd be murdered the next morning. She picked me up in Plain View, out at my lake house, took me back to her place, and then things got out of control. Another woman was there, Milly, and Sherry was on a complete power trip. It was so awful. She videotaped the whole thing because she said I was getting too big for my britches. Where do you think that tape is now?"

Karen sat speechless on the park bench. Finally, she said, "I don't know. Possibly the police have it. Or maybe Sherry put it somewhere and it hasn't been found yet."

"I have to find that video. Do you think we could get into Sherry's house?"

Karen scooted over toward the edge of the bench and gave Elyse an exasperated look. "Absolutely not. Are you crazy? The house is sealed due to the police investigation and the neighbor, Miss Brown, has laser eyes and would be sure to see you. Break in and you'd make front-page news, Elyse." *It would be kind of fun to see Elyse arrested for breaking and entering.*

"I know, it was a stupid idea. But it's bound to be in her house. She wouldn't have time to put it in a safe deposit box or hide it because she was murdered the very next day."

"Elyse, wake up. You and Milly were two of the last people to see Sherry alive. You need to take that information to the police."

"We're attracting attention. Let's walk." Elyse stood up and linked arms with Karen. "You know this detective. Could you arrange it, please? Perhaps we could meet at your house, so I'm not seen going into a police station."

Karen reached over and removed Elyse's hand from her arm. The woman had clenched it so tight it felt like she'd been bruised. "Let me give Detective Kerns a call."

Walking a few feet away from Elyse, she dug her phone out of her purse, called Brian, and told him about Elyse.

Back to Elyse, she said, "He'll be at my house in ten minutes. I'm living in my mom's house, so meet me there."

When Karen let Brian into the house, he said, "I've only got a few minutes." He looked around the living room. "Where is she?"

"Excellent question. She should have been here five minutes ago. Come on in the kitchen and I'll get you something to drink. Coffee? Tea? Vitamin water?" *Bet he wants coffee and donuts.*

Brian smiled. "Cops always drink coffee." As they sat drinking their coffee and chatting, Karen again reminded herself how easy Brian was to talk to. *Such a good listener and attentive.*

She was thoroughly enjoying herself when the doorbell rang. She went to open the door and found Elyse at her doorstep. "Good heavens, Elyse, did you get lost? Detective Kerns only has so much time."

"I'm sorry, Karen. I had to make a phone call."

"Come on back to the kitchen. We're drinking coffee."

As Elyse started answering the detective's questions, Karen watched with amusement as her old friend attempted to flirt, play the victim, and finally burst into tears. *Elyse is quite the drama queen. I don't think any of her playacting is going to work on Brian.* She handed Elyse a box of tissues.

When they got to the events of Tuesday morning, Karen tuned back in with interest. Elyse was talking about Sherry's threats and explaining to Brian how Sherry was in love with her. Elyse looked up and batted her eyes at Brian. "You can imagine how angry I was at Sherry for blackmailing me all these years, and then videoing me so she could jack up how much I pay her each month. I'm afraid we said some very nasty things to each other. In fact, Sherry was so angry with me, she refused to drive me back to Plain View and I had to ask that weird Milly to drive me."

"What time was that?"

"Oh, very early, around 6 a.m. I didn't want to stay one minute longer at Sherry's house." Elyse rolled to a stop and put her hand on Brian's arm. "You're such a good listener, Detective Kerns. You must be really good at your job."

"What time did Milly drop you at your lake house?"

"It was right around 6:30 a.m."

"What did you do next, and was there anyone else in the house?"

"I went upstairs to take a shower and my housekeeper brought me coffee. Then I answered some emails. You're welcome to interview the housekeeper and look at my computer."

"I'll be doing that." Brian continued to write in his notebook, then shut it and looked at Elyse. "Mrs. Vanderhoot, I am glad you finally came forward. To summarize, you've had an on-again/off-again affair with Sherry Trandon for approximately 15 years. It has been difficult at times, with Ms. Trandon hurting you physically." Elyse nodded. "You wanted to break it off after three years, but she didn't. She videoed you and has been blackmailing you ever since. And that's when you should have contacted the police to help you."

Elyse hiccupped. "I know that now."

"The most recent video, the one from Monday night, has disappeared. Now, no videos have been found at the house, but we'll take another look. If the one in question is found among the house contents, it would be the property of her sister, who inherited all of Ms. Trandon's possessions. If that happens, a good lawyer can probably help you retrieve it. After all, you didn't give permission to be taped."

"Oh, thank you, detective. You've been just wonderful. I am so hoping that we can keep all this confidential."

"We'll try. When and if this murder comes to trial, the District Attorney will decide what is important. As for Milly Landon, I have no idea if she'll keep Monday evening confidential." Brian paused before continuing, "One more thing. There's a box labeled 'Toots,' which I picked up today from the house," said Brian. "I believe it's yours. I'll notify you when you can pick it up, although it may be several months."

"I—I don't want it," replied Elyse faintly.

"Do you even know what's in it?" asked Brian.

"I think so. It's a green box, decorated with tinsel, right?" Brian nodded. "I definitely don't want it. I don't." Elyse, who had been looking hopeful, once again started to cry. "This affair is going to follow me forever, I know it. And it could ruin my career, just ruin it." She stood up and gave Karen a hug. "We'll have to get together in better circumstances, honey. I'll see myself out."

After Elyse left, Karen collapsed back in her chair. "What a piece of work—and to think she used to be my best friend in junior high. I wish I could offer you a glass of wine, but I bet you're still working, aren't you?"

"I wish I could, but I have so much to do. I'll take a rain check on the wine. Wine and dinner, for sure, when this is over. Thank you for getting Elyse to share this information. Every little piece of the puzzle gets us closer to the murderer. Do you think she's capable of killing someone?" Brian looked questioningly at Karen.

"I wish I could say a loud, sincere 'No,' but yes, I think she's capable of it. Elyse always looks after herself." Her old, narcissistic friend could off someone if it put her ahead. *And to think we all elected her to Congress. But then, Congress has a number of corrupt people.*

After Brian left, Karen got some supper and a large glass of wine. She was way too tired to return to school. She would watch some TV, relax, and not think about murder.

Chapter Fourteen
Thursday Evening

As Brian left, he pulled his cellphone from his pocket. It was lit up with several texts telling him to get back to the police station as soon as possible. He drove fast, pulling around the square above the speed limit, and raced into the police station. Things were beginning to fall into place. It looked like the murder suspects were down to Phillip Nash and Rhonda Burgess, but he needed to keep an open mind and be ready for the unexpected. *Who knows—there is always Milly Landon or Elyse Vanderhoot to consider. Or possibly Vince Watson, the business manager. Even Bobbi Nelson isn't off the hook yet.*

When Brian dashed into the police station, Officer Danzy, Officer Speck, Chief Daniels, and an unknown man in a suit were gathered around a computer. Neal was busily putting graphs and figures up on a large screen. Brian strode back to the Chief's Office. "What's up?"

Chief Daniels turned from examining the graphs and said, "Brian, Phillip Nash has been siphoning off funds from the school district for the past three years, with the help of Vince Watson. Oh, and this is the accounts expert from the state, Tom Turner." He gestured toward the man in the suit. "And Tom, this is our lead detective on the murder investigation, Brian Kerns."

The men nodded hello to each other. Brian turned back to the projection screen. "Can someone walk me through what you have?"

Tom came forward and started pointing out budgets for departments and bills paid. "You can see here and here where figures don't add up. Then, if you superimpose these particular bills that were paid with outgoing checks, you can see where we've circled places in which figures don't add up. It gets rather complicated and I've got more work to do, but I can say with certainty that both Dr. Nash and the business manager were taking money from the school district."

Brian turned back to the Chief. "Will you be bringing him in for questioning?"

Tom stood up from where he was bent over the computer. "Not so fast. I don't have all the evidence put together yet, but certainly both Nash and Watson are persons of interest. I should have enough evidence to take it to the District Attorney tomorrow. Your tech, Neal, and I will be working most of the night."

Brian turned back to the Chief. "Phillip Nash has become a suspect in the murder of Sherry Trandon. I am fairly certain I can place him in the office at least once the morning of the murder, and possibly twice. There is certainly a motive now. Sherry Trandon was working to expose him for taking money from the district. She may have confronted him about his embezzlement, perhaps the morning she was murdered. My witness is a child, which is always dicey to deal with. But I also think I can break the story Bobbi Nelson told me about Nash being with her in the school. I'll need to interview Nelson again."

Brian continued, "Chief, I can also place Rhonda Burgess in Trandon's office that morning. I will have to interview her again. We're still working on the identity of Trandon's lover. I'm hoping Bill Foxmore either recognized a staff picture or we got a decent sketch from the police artist."

Officer Danzy waved from across the room. "Sir, we've got an identity for the women out at Trotter Creek. Come check this out."

Bill Foxmore was sitting at Brian's desk, looking pleased with himself. A plate of fried chicken, mashed potatoes, green beans, and dinner rolls was in front of him, and he was noisily eating. Waving a chicken leg at Brian, Bill grinned. "Yup, I found all three of them there wimin. Absolutely, sure as the devil, these are the three wimin out at the crick."

"Three women? There were three women out there?"

Bill took a bite of fried chicken and chewed it for a bit. Brian looked as if he might reach over and throttle the man. Officers Danzy and Speck were standing there speechless. "Yup, three wimin! Of course, not at the same time. What are y' all thinking?" Bill chuckled.

Keeping his face expressionless and his voice controlled, Brian said, "Mr. Foxmore, we're in the middle of an investigation and time is of the essence. Please stop eating and explain how three women were out at Trotter Creek."

At Brian's tone, Bill stopped eating. "Hold your horses, young man. I be tellin' you. Like I said, this wimin and this wimin were out there quite a bit." He pointed at a staff picture of a rather serious looking Rhonda Burgess and a stern and forbidding looking Sherry Trandon.

"But then, this wimin," he jabbed Sherry Trandon's picture "and this here wimin," Bill had pulled a Kennedy staff picture of Milly Landon out of the stack, "were out at Trotter Creek several times in the last week or so. And they wuz arguin' and arguin', really loud. This one," Bill held up the picture of Milly Landon, "wanted money that the big woman wuz goin get for her and she want it right away. The other one, the big one, said they has to be patient. They argued something fierce and then they started kissing and stuff. You know what I mean." He winked at Brian.

Brian was flabbergasted. *So Burgess was the one having an affair with Trandon, but then, so was Milly Landon.*

Danzy spoke first. "I guess you aren't surprised about Rhonda Burgess. I was. Good God, she's married and has a child. This is going to be so hard on her family when it gets out."

Brian glanced at Bill, who seemed to be thoroughly enjoying all that was happening and said, "Officers, let's move over to the other side of the room for some privacy."

Officer Speck sat down abruptly when she got there and examined her nails. She finally looked up. "Somehow it doesn't feel so good to be closing in. People's lives are going to change and not for the better. I think Rhonda Burgess and Milly Landon are both prime suspects and Phillip Nash is another possibility."

"Right you are. We now have three persons of interest for this murder investigation and three outliers. Don't forget Vince Watson and Bobbi Nelson are both longshot possibilities, and I just interviewed a third possibility, Elyse Vanderhoot. She was at Trandon's house Monday night and she hated Sherry Trandon's guts. They'd been having an on-off affair for fifteen years, and Trandon had been blackmailing her with compromising videos."

Danzy and Speck both stared at Brian, shocked. "Sir, that's, that's—I don't know what to say. She's our congresswoman," said Officer Speck.

"Nuts, I even voted for her." Danzy looked disgusted.

"Also, I interviewed Freddy Moser and he heard a male voice in Trandon's office. I'm suspecting it was Nash, who has admitted to being at the school that morning. And Freddy Moser has identified Rhonda Burgess as being in the office. He peeked in the principal's window and saw her.

"But what about Milly Landon?" Brian questioned. "Did we overlook her? She seems to go back and forth between Kennedy and Lincoln. Where was she Tuesday morning? Officer Speck, get out your chart on who exited the building Tuesday morning. Is Milly Landon on it?" Officer Speck was already at her desk rummaging through files. Grabbing her chart, she rushed back over to Brian. Officer Speck and Brian bent over the chart.

Looking up, Speck said, "Sir, Milly Landon is listed with the group of teachers who exited Kennedy School after the announcement at 7:35 a.m. However, you didn't interview her until Wednesday."

"Yeah, and Milly Landon drove Elyse Vanderhoot to Plain View that morning around 6 a.m., so she had plenty of time to get to Kennedy." Brian looked thoughtful. "Let's not forget Vince Watson either. He didn't show up for his scheduled conference at Kennedy Tuesday morning. We may need to do some more investigation there. Stealing money from the District makes him a suspect." Brian was looking pleased and frustrated at the same time. Pleased they were making progress and frustrated because they still hadn't determined who'd murdered Trandon.

"Okay, now maybe we're getting somewhere. Officer Speck, send two officers to the Liberty Hotel to retrieve Milly Landon for questioning. If she's not there, try Pinky's. Be sure the officers tell her we just need to ask a few more questions.

"And then Speck, take an officer with you and bring Bobbi Nelson down to the station for questioning. I need to pull apart her story on when Nash arrived at school and exactly where he was. He certainly wasn't in her classroom the whole time, as she said. Perhaps we'll ask her about Vince Watson. Maybe she saw him at school Tuesday morning."

Brian turned to Officer Danzy. "Danzy, I want you to take an officer and go pick up Rhonda Burgess. She's to come down to the station to answer questions. Also, put a car on Nash's house—not a patrol car, for Pete's sake. Use an unmarked vehicle and verify he's home."

"How, sir?"

"Place a phone call and ask for him. If he's not home, ask the wife how you can reach him. Make it an urgent—school business. The point is, I want a cop on him while I interview Bobbi Nelson."

"Okay, but what if any of these people say no, they won't come down to the police station?" Danzy asked.

"Then arrest them," growled Brian.

As Office Speck was leaving, she called back over her shoulder, "There's fried chicken for you in the refrigerator."

Brian took off his jacket as he walked toward his desk. He was about to fling his brown bag on his chair when he remembered that Bill was sitting there, still eating his dinner and thoroughly enjoying himself. "Mr. Foxmore, I'm going to have you go sit at the table at the back." Brian pointed to the back of the room. "When you're finished eating, let me know, and I will have an officer drive you home. I appreciate your help today in identifying the three women. Thank you."

"Sure, the free grub tonight was worth it. I git a little tired of eating rabbit all the time." Bill picked up his plate, cup, and napkin, and ambled toward the back of the room. Brian looked at his desk, sighed audibly, and walked to the men's room to get a paper towel to wipe up the grease and crumbs. Then, remembering what Speck said, he took a short detour, stopped by the refrigerator, and pulled out a plate with his name on it.

After helping himself to coffee, Brian sat down at his desk and started munching on fried chicken. He was hungrier than he thought. Brian pulled out his notebook and started reviewing his interviews on Bobbi Nelson. She'd gone from saying she arrived at 7 a.m. and was alone in her room to admitting that Nash had shown up at 7:15 for coffee. Then she'd backtracked and said he'd followed her up to her room at 7 a.m. And then finally Nash had said he arrived before Nelson at around 7 a.m. and had left when the announcement was made to evacuate the school. What was the real story?

He could hear Bobbi Nelson before he saw her. She was jerking the door open and stomping into the police station. "Keep your hands off me," she snarled at Officer Speck. "I have rights."

Stopping at Brian's desk, Officer Speck asked, "Should I put Miss Nelson in the interview room?"

"Yes, I'll be with her momentarily."

Bobbi marched down the hall with Officer Speck herding her from behind. "This is just stupid, stupid, stupid. I have better things to do. Quit poking me," she spat at Officer Speck. "I told you, I have rights."

Officer Speck returned from the interview room, red in the face. "That is a difficult woman. I told her she was just here to answer a few questions, that she wasn't being arrested. But the woman just lit into me."

Brian stood up. "I guess I'd better go talk to her before she ignites and blows up the place." He grabbed his notebook. "Come on, I need you to take notes." Officer Speck followed him to the interview room.

Bobbi was sitting in a chair, fuming. The minute Brian entered the room, she started in. "Why am I here? This is ridiculous. I told you I didn't kill Sherry Trandon. Why would I? The next principal could be even worse." Bobbi crossed her arms and glared at Brian.

Brian sat down across from Bobbi. "You're here to answer some questions, Ms. Nelson. I warned you before

248 Fatal Lesson

about lying to the police and I'm warning you again. This is a very serious matter, and this time I want the truth."

"The truth about what?" Bobbi asked belligerently.

"I want you to stop and think about Tuesday morning. I want to know exactly when you arrived at school, when you saw Nash, where you saw him, and when he left."

"I see," drawled Bobbi. "Should I get a lawyer?"

"You are not a suspect presently, and this is just an interview. At most, we're looking for a witness statement. You can, of course, have a lawyer at any time. It is up to you."

"Oh, all right," said Bobbi with a defeated air. "Tuesday morning. Let's see. I arrived at school around 7 a.m. There were a few cars in the parking lot, but I didn't pay attention to them. I'm sure I did not see Phillip Nash's car because I would have noticed that. I went in the front door and up the stairs to my room, and I didn't see anyone. I made a cup of coffee and started reading the paper."

"Was anyone in your room when you arrived?"

Bobby paused, "No, I was alone."

"When did Superintendent Nash arrive?"

"I'm not sure exactly. He was a bit late. He was supposed to meet me at 7 a.m. He—he stepped into the classroom around 7:15 and said hello. He said something had come up and he had to tend to it before seeing me."

"When did he leave?"

"When the announcement came over the intercom to evacuate the school," responded Bobbi tiredly.

"Did you see anyone else Tuesday morning between 7 a.m. and 7:35? Think carefully before you answer."

Bobbi glowered at Brian. "No, I saw Phillip Nash and that was it until the announcement was made to evacuate the school."

"Okay. Officer Speck is going to read your statement back to you and then you'll need to sign it. Why did you lie about this?"

Bobbi shrugged. "Because Phillip asked me to, I guess. I didn't think it was all that important at the time, and I guess I'm still wondering why it's so important. I don't think Phillip Nash killed Sherry Trandon. He wouldn't be that stupid. We're both retiring at the end of the year and have plans to move to Florida. Why would he jeopardize that?"

Brian looked at Bobbi sternly. "All aspects of murder investigations are important. All aspects! Quit thinking about yourself all the time."

Bobbi managed to look chagrined. "Look, I really have no motive for killing Sherry Trandon. I don't think Phillip does either. I was just doing him a favor."

"A favor? Maybe you should stop and think about why he needed a favor regarding his whereabouts on Tuesday morning right about the time Sherry Trandon was killed."

Bobbi looked at Brian, aghast. "Well, I never... Well, I never... thought there was a problem. Are you saying Phillip Nash is a suspect in the murder of Sherry?"

"No, I'm not saying that necessarily, although there appears to be gaps in Dr. Nash's story." Standing up, Brian said, "Once we have finished the paperwork, you'll be free to leave. We're very busy at the moment, so typing up your statement will take a while." With that, Brian slammed the door; Officer Speck had followed him out into the hallway. "I've got to get Nash down here for questioning before we let Bobbi Nelson go. Take your time with the paperwork and with giving her a ride home. We need Nash on the way to the station before Bobbi gets access to a phone." Speck nodded and went to her desk to start the process.

Brian looked toward the front door and saw Officer Danzy coming into the police station looking downright flustered. Walking over to Brian, he said, "Sir, Mrs.

Burgess was not at her house, and her husband refused to say if he knew where she was."

Brian kicked the wall with his foot. "I should have foreseen this. Tell me exactly what happened at the house."

"Officer Thompson and I knocked on the front door and rang the doorbell. We were beginning to think no one was home when the door was flung open by Mr. Burgess. He looked quite disheveled. His shirt was hanging out, his hair was mussed, and he was rubbing one hand as if it hurt. He rudely asked us what we wanted. When we asked for Mrs. Burgess, he said he didn't know where 'the bitch' was and slammed the door.

"Officer Thompson and I looked around the property a bit. Two sets of grease spots were in the garage, indicating two cars, but only one car was there. We really couldn't look around much without Burgess's permission."

"Okay, I'll have another officer pull up all the information about the Burgess's cars. We're going to put out an all points bulletin to other law enforcement agencies. Maybe someone will spot the car. I want you to take an officer with you and start looking for Rhonda Burgess in likely places. Go out to Trotter Creek and look around. Then try the Spirit of the Word Church. Roust out the pastor. I'm pretty sure he lives on the premises. Ask him for any help he can give us about finding her. Tell him she might be a danger to herself and others if he balks at sharing information. Now go—we've got limited time to pull this all together."

Brian turned to Officer Speck who was looking at him with trepidation. "Get on the phone with Karen Fowler and see if Rhonda is at her house. Ask her where Rhonda might go if she were upset. Also, try that Noreen Denton who teaches with Rhonda. Check Burgess's file for relatives. Maybe she is headed to a relative's house."

Brian hurried into the Chief's office. "I think we need to bring Phillip Nash down for questioning. And we need to do it right away. His alibi has fallen apart and I think he was in Trandon's office during the time that the murder might have taken place."

Chief Daniels frowned and tightened his lips. "Okay, I'll go get him. He'll create less of a fuss if it's me. What an idiot to get caught up in a mess like this. He was such an easy guy to go hunting with, and he always brought the best beer. You're going to want to stay away from school finances as much as possible, Brian. The D.A. will be bringing charges tomorrow morning. Nash is bound to lawyer up and it's at that point we'll read him his Miranda rights. Right now, he's just a person of interest in a murder investigation."

Brian nodded and began pacing around the office. Every once in a while he'd stop and ask Speck to update him on her phone calls about Rhonda's whereabouts. Then he'd call Danzy and the officer would tell him about the lack of progress in his search around town. It was all so frustrating. Danzy had talked to Pastor John, who was horrified to hear that the police were looking for Rhonda. The pastor emphatically told them that she had not been out to the church nor had she sought his counsel. The woman seemed to have vanished.

As Brian was about to make the 15th circuit of the police station, the Police Chief and Dr. Nash walked in the door. Nash looked disgruntled and a bit worried.

"Detective Kerns, you can talk with the superintendent in my office."

Brian gestured to Officer Speck to come with him and followed the Chief and Nash into the office. The Chief picked up his briefcase and walked back out of the office. Brian sat down at the table; Nash sat across from him.

Officer Speck got out her notebook and prepared to take notes.

"Dr. Nash, I need to ask you once again about your movements on Tuesday morning. I have a witness who saw you going into Bobbi Nash's room at approximately 7:15. Bobbi Nelson has corroborated this."

Nash squirmed in his chair. "Well, yes, that is about the time I went into Bobbi's room."

"Start at the beginning with what time you got up, where you went, and who you saw. Keep in mind that I do have witnesses and I'm really, really tired of listening to your lies."

Nash's face reddened. "There's no need to get surly with me, Detective. I did get up around 6 a.m. and I did head into the office. I was supposed to meet Bobbi around 7 a.m., but I went to my office to get some paperwork that Sherry Trandon had requested. I thought since I was going to be at Kennedy, I'd stop by her office and clear up a misunderstanding."

"And what was that misunderstanding?"

"Oh, she had a real bee in her bonnet about the supply budget. She was just reading the finances incorrectly. It can get quite complicated. Not everyone can understand school finance, you know."

"When did you arrive at Kennedy?"

"Hmm, it was a bit before 7 a.m. and I parked around back and went in the front door, the only door that was open. I didn't see anyone, and I went straight up to Bobbi's room."

Brian pulled his chair up straight. "Wait, you said you went into Bobbi's room at 7:15."

"Patience, Detective Kerns. I got there before 7 a.m., Bobbi wasn't there, so I thought I'd go down and talk to Sherry. I went down to her office. Sherry and I discussed the finances, and then around 7:15, I went back up to Bobbi's classroom."

"You were in the victim's office, shortly before she was murdered, and you didn't tell me this on Tuesday." Brian looked at the superintendent in disbelief. "What the devil?"

Dr. Nash looked at Brian rather sheepishly. "I didn't want to get involved. People would ask why I was at school that early and what I was doing there. The fact that I was meeting Bobbi might have come out. You know how these things are."

"No, I don't know how these things are," said Brian. "I really don't. Tell me about the meeting."

"As I told you, Detective, we talked about the supply budget. There's nothing to tell. When I left, Sherry was very much alive."

"Do you want to elaborate on that meeting? I have a witness."

"Oh..." Nash looked a bit deflated. "A witness? You're bluffing."

"I do have a witness and I am not here to play games. You are in much bigger trouble than you think. Out with what happened." Brian was almost shouting.

"Keep your shirt on, Detective. I've lived in this town for many years and you're here temporarily from Chicago. Lower your voice and be respectful."

Brian tapped his pencil on the table, counted to ten, and said, "Superintendent Nash, if I don't get some cooperation from you, I'm going to put you in lockup overnight as a material witness to a murder." Brian glanced at his watch. "And it's way too late to have anything done about it. All court officers are fast asleep in their beds." Brian frowned menacingly at the superintendent. *Even though I can't do this, I can threaten. Nash won't know his rights.*

Dr. Nash said, "You wouldn't dare."

"Don't tempt me. After all, you just told me I'm here temporarily, so what do I care if I lock up the superintendent of schools?"

"Okay, okay, just simmer down! Yes, I was in Sherry's office from around 7 a.m. to 7:10 and yes, we argued about school finances. Sherry was yet again on one of her moral high horses and she doesn't listen when she's decided she's right. We, Watson and I, had borrowed from the supply budget to keep the busses running. And theoretically, you're not supposed to do that. But," Superintendent Nash shrugged dramatically, "what can you do—the busses have to run and the gas station's not going to give away the gas."

"And when you returned to her office?"

Superintendent Nash sat up and stuttered, "What?"

"What happened when you returned to Trandon's office a little while after 7:15?"

"And just what makes you think I returned, detective?"

"Remember, I have a witness."

"Oh, for God's sake. For the last time: I did not murder Sherry Trandon." Dr. Nash's face was red, and he was almost shouting. "And that's all I'm going to say. I came here voluntarily and I'm leaving voluntarily. If you want to talk to me again, contact my lawyer." Nash took out his wallet, sorted through some cards, and threw a business card across the table at Brian. Then he stood up and marched out the door. Pointing to an officer sitting at a desk, he said, "You, I need a ride home." The officer looked at Brian, who nodded. Nash walked toward the door, head held high, with the officer trailing behind.

Brian looked down at the card in his hand. Mr. William Babcock, attorney-at-law. Jessamyn's father, again. Weren't there any other lawyers in the area? Officer Speck stood next to Brian. "Do you think he murdered Sherry Trandon, sir?"

"I don't know. He certainly has motive and opportunity. Any word on Rhonda Burgess?"

"No, it's like she's disappeared off the face of the earth. Danzy hasn't had any luck either. Milly Landon has arrived and she's in the interview room. Sir, I think she's had a lot to drink. The officers found her at Pinky's. She announced to the entire bar that the officer was there to arrest her for murder. When the officers finally bundled her into the car, she fell asleep. I've been pouring coffee down her, but I don't know how much good it will do."

"Great, I'm going to interview a drunk. Come on, Speck, let's get it over with."

Brian and Officer Speck entered the room to find Milly sprawled in her chair, with her arms and head flung down on the table. Brian could smell the alcohol on her from across the table. "Miss Landon, I need you to sit up. I have some questions for you."

Milly opened one eye and moaned. "It's the super cute detective," she said with slurred speech. "Aren't I lucky to have such a little cutey asking me questions? Too bad I don't like men. I'd just eat you up." Milly made smacking noises with her mouth.

"Miss Landon, sit up and drink some coffee. The sooner I get some answers from you, the sooner you can go home."

Milly raised her head and moaned. Gulping down some coffee, she said, "Aw righteo, ask away."

Taking a deep breath, Brian asked, "When did you get to Kennedy School Tuesday morning, the day of the murder?"

"What makes you think I was at Kennedy? Tuesday's my day to be at Lincoln."

"You evacuated the building with the rest of the Kennedy staff, that's how I know you were at Kennedy," said Brian dryly.

Milly picked up her cup and had another gulp of coffee. Turning to Speck, she said, "Honey, this would go down easier with a slug of whiskey in it. Do you have some whiskey?" Officer Speck shook her head no.

"Come on, Ms. Landon, you're wasting time." Brian tapped his pencil against the table. "When did you arrive at Kennedy School Tuesday morning?"

"Aw right. Keep your voice down. I went to Kennedy around, I don't know, I don't keep a clock in my head. I suppose it was around 7 a.m. or 7:05 or maybe 7:10, something like that. I wanted to see if I could talk to Sherry before school because she was really angry at me and I wanted to clear it up."

"Why was she angry?"

"Oh, we'd had a little disagreement earlier that morning, that's all."

"I see. Was it about you driving Elyse Vanderhoot to Plain View?"

"Oh my, honey, you are well informed. Yes, Sherry was way pissed at little Miss Elyse; the dramatics were awful. Do you want to hear the lurid details?"

"No, I don't think so, not now."

"Good idea, because it's positively atrocious." Milly rested her head on the table. "I'm so sleepy."

"Ms. Landon, sit up right now. What did you do when you got to Kennedy?

"My plan to see Sherry didn't work so well. There was someone in the office when I got there; I had to go around the corner so they wouldn't see me. Clever, right?" Milly looked drunkenly at Brian.

Brian shrugged. "I guess, if you didn't want to be seen. Did you hear anything?"

"Well, obviously, I heard a voice, which was why I didn't go into Sherry's office. That would have pissed her off if I'd gone in while she was conducting business. Oh my," she treated the detective to a string of expletives. "Would I have heard about that." Milly giggled. "But I only heard voices for a second before I wh-whi-whisked around the corner. I heard the person leave and I was about to come back around when another person showed up. Sherry was so popular that morning." Milly giggled again. Brian stared straight ahead, and Officer Speck bent over her notebook.

"You people are such downers. No sense of humor at all. Frankly, I'm finding everything funny." Milly took another gulp of coffee."

"Ms. Landon, please continue on."

"All right, all right. Um, I could hear nothing from where I was, and I was getting mighty tired of being squashed into the corner by the file cabinet, so guess what? I left by the other door. No Sherry for me that morning. Of course, I didn't know I'd never see her again."

"So you're saying you didn't go into Trandon's office?"

"Right on target there, Opey. That's such a good name for you. You're just so clean-cut and morally correct. Yep, I hereby rename you Opey." Milly flourished her cup at Brian, spilling some on the table.

Officer Speck was looking at Brian with a puzzled look. Brian rolled his eyes. "Opey's a reference to the Andy Griffith show that was on in the '60s. He was a clean-cut kid with a conscience." Brian shrugged. "I have no idea why I'm being referred to as that TV character."

Brian turned and frowned at Milly. "Please concentrate, Ms. Landon. Did you recognize the first set of voices you heard?"

"Well, of co-ourse I recognized Sherry's. But I didn't hear the other voice. It was garbled."

"Did you see any of these people, a form, a shadow, anything?"

"You're clutching at straws. It was dark; I was around the corner, squashed next to the file cabinet. What do you think I would see?"

Brian frowned at Milly. "Let's move on to your conversations or fights you had with Sherry Trandon, out at Trotter Creek."

"Oh, that stupid Sherry, I told her somebody had been watching us. But would she listen? Noooo."

"What were you fighting about?"

"Oh, this and that, lover's quarrels, you know," said Milly vaguely. "I'm really tired. Can I go home now, Opey?"

"My name is Detective Kerns, as you well know, and no, you may not go home yet. Please describe the argument."

Milly blinked at Brian. "Really, Opey? You don't want me telling you we argued about sex. You'd get embarrassed."

"I'm beginning to lose my patience, Ms. Landon. What was the argument about, money? The information I have is, you wanted the money and Ms. Trandon wanted you to be patient. Tell me about that part."

"Oh well, really, I already told you. Sherry had a stick up her butt about Nash stealing money from the school district. She said she had proof and she was going to bleed Nash for it. I was and still am very sick of Chaldea and I wanted both of us to get out of this flea speck town. So I wanted her to move on Nash right away and she wanted to wait.

"So," Milly waved her coffee cup at Brian, "maybe Nash killed Sherry. He's a truly vicious prick who is quite capable of it." Milly laid her head back down on the table. "Maybe Sherry would still be alive if I hadn't pushed her so hard about the money. And now I need to go to sleep."

"No," Brian said sharply. "There's no going to sleep. Why didn't you tell me this when I interviewed you?"

Milly lifted her head slightly. "Do you think I'm that much of an idiot? I wanted to be out of this town, not stuck in it, answering questions from the likes of you. I have no motive for killing Sherry, so what could I offer your stupid investigation, Opey?"

"Ms. Landon, you've admitted that you were in the office. You could have killed Sherry and probably blackmailed Nash yourself. There's your motive."

Milly, who had slumped back down in her chair and had her head resting on the table, sat up. "You'd never prove it, you lame detective. I'm much smarter than you." Milly laid her head back down on the table and passed out.

Brian looked over at Officer Speck and said, "I'd love to throw her in jail for the night, but get an officer to drive her back to her room at the hotel. Tell him or her to make sure she gets safely there. Have the officer tell the receptionist I want to be notified if she tries to check out."

"Yes, sir. I suppose Ms. Landon could have killed Trandon. What do you think?"

"I think I need to sleep on it. We've got three good suspects with motive: Milly Landon, Rhonda Burgess, and Phillip Nash, but there is no physical evidence. And we've got the other three possibilities, but there's very little evidence to tie Vince Watson, Elyse Vanderhoot, or Bobbi Nelson to the murder." Brian yawned. "It's past midnight. Call Danzy and tell him to go home and get some sleep. I'm heading home too. Good night."

Chapter Fifteen

Friday Morning

Karen bustled around the office, preparing for the day. The memorial was at 10:30 and there was so much to prepare. Jessamyn had put together a beautiful photo display of Sherry. The girl did have talent. Kat was in the gym putting up the rolling bulletin boards to display the heart messages that the younger children had made. She walked into the gym and glanced at a few.

Thank you Ms. Trandon for keeping our school clean, read one.

Sorry, you are deaded, read another.

You made us follow the soccer rules, said another.

Well, at least they're honest, thought Karen. *You can always count on first graders to write how they feel.* She would be so glad when this was all over. It just needed to go smoothly and then everyone at Kennedy could move on.

As Karen turned to leave, Judith, the first-grade teacher, ran into the gym. "Karen, we need you, come quick."

"What is it?" Karen asked as she rushed to follow Judith out of the gym.

"It's Rhonda. She's in her classroom, crying, and she looks awful, just awful."

Rounding the corner, Karen dashed into Rhonda's room. She was sitting on a child's chair. Her head was down, her hair was a total mess, and she was dressed in yesterday's clothes. "Rhonda, take it easy. Tell me what the matter is," Karen said in a gentle voice. She pulled up another chair.

Rhonda continued to cry. Karen got up, looked around for the tissue box, and brought it over to her. When Rhonda looked up, she gasped. One of Rhonda's cheeks had a red welt on it and her lip was split. Rhonda slowly rolled up her sleeve; three ugly blue-purple bruises were displayed on her forearm.

"I'm so sorry, Rhonda. You must be in pain. Let's get you to a doctor."

"No, no way. I'm okay. Motrin and ice work just fine."

"Did Sean do this?" Karen asked quietly. "Did he?"

Rhonda nodded. "I'm just so tired, so tired of dealing with him. I don't think I can go on. I just want to curl up and die."

"No, Rhonda, no. Please don't think like that. You have friends and we'll help you. And, most importantly, you've got Sophie to think of."

Rhonda sniffled. "You're right, I do."

"You need to leave that absolutely vile husband of yours. We'll make a plan; you'll get Sophie and leave that man. He's a menace."

Rhonda nodded. "It sounds so simple, Karen, but it isn't. I don't think you understand."

"I don't think I do. I don't understand why the police were so determined to find you last night. Officer Speck said they just had a few questions for you about Sherry's murder, but why couldn't it wait until morning? Where were you, anyway? The police looked everywhere."

Rhonda shrugged. "After Sean beat me up, I just drove around thinking about how awful my life was."

"All night?"

"Yeah, time got away from me, I guess. I know the police have questions. Karen, I was in Sherry's office Tuesday morning," she looked at Karen beseechingly, "but I didn't murder her. How could I have done that? I'm a righteous person, a good Christian woman."

"You've already explained that to the police. You were just checking in with Sherry, right?"

Rhonda looked away and shrugged. "Yes, that's all."

"There's no way you can teach today. Why don't I call Detective Kerns and he can come over to the school and get you? Then you can talk to him and make some plans for what you're going to do next."

Karen reached out and patted her friend's arm. "Look, I've got an extra room at my house. You can stay there now, and later, you and I can go over to your house and pack a few things for you and Sophie. I don't want you running into Sean by yourself. Then you can stay with me until you sort things out." She reached into her purse and handed Rhonda a key.

Rhonda gave Karen a look of pure gratitude. "You're a real friend, Karen. Okay, let's do that. I'll just go use the restroom and freshen up and I'll meet you down in the office."

Karen hurried down to her office, picked up her cellphone and called Detective Kerns. He answered on the first ring. "Karen, what's up?"

"I've got Rhonda here at school. Sean beat her up last night. She's going to wait here so she can talk to you. Then please take her over to my house and get her settled. I don't want her staying at her house where Sean can find her."

"I've got some things happening here at the police station right now. I'm interviewing some witnesses and possible suspects. But I'll send Officer Speck over to collect Rhonda and bring her down to the station. Thanks for calling me." Karen sat down at her desk, busied herself with some paperwork, and waited for Rhonda to get out of the restroom.

Karen looked at the clock and rose from her desk. Where was Rhonda? She walked back to the staff bathroom in the teacher's lounge and knocked on the door. "Rhonda?"

"No, it's me, Bobbi. Can't I even go to the bathroom in private? What do you want?"

"Sorry, I was looking for Rhonda."

"Haven't seen her, thank goodness. She's so mealy-mouthed, maybe she's hiding under the sink. No, not here."

Karen looked at the teachers in the lounge and asked, "Has anyone seen Rhonda Burgess?"

The teachers looked up from grading and reading the newspaper. Most shook their heads; Michael called out, "Rhonda never comes in the lounge."

Karen rushed back to the main office. "Kat, make an announcement over the intercom for Rhonda Burgess."

Kat said, "An all-call to everywhere in the school?"

"Yes, an all-call. I can't imagine where she went."

Just as the announcement was being made, Officer Speck entered the office. She glanced at Karen and said, "You can't find Rhonda?" Karen shook her head no. "What kind of car does she drive?"

"Oh, it's an older gray Honda. I saw it when I came in," said Kat. "It should be right out there." She pointed out the window. "Uh, it's not there."

Officer Speck got on her phone to Brian. "Sir, Rhonda Burgess has left Kennedy School. I'll check with the staff, but I don't think anyone knows where she's gone. Yes, sir, I'll start looking around town." She hung up her cell. "Mrs. Fowler, do you have any idea where Rhonda would have gone?"

"She's scared of Sean, so I don't think she'd go home. I offered her my house for a few days; perhaps Rhonda went there. She might be over at Lincoln checking on her daughter."

"All right, I'll go over to Lincoln and see if I can find her. Then I'll check out your house. Could you loan me a key in case she doesn't answer the door? Detective Kerns is worried about her." Karen opened her desk drawer, rummaged around a bit, and handed Officer Speck a key.

Karen sat back down at her desk but couldn't concentrate. "Kat, I'm going to drive over to Rhonda's house, just to make sure she didn't go there." *Surely Rhonda wouldn't go home. What if Sean is there?*

Karen rushed out to her car and drove as fast as she dared through the streets of Chaldea. She caught up to Rhonda just as she pulled into the driveway of her house. She rolled down the window. "Rhonda, I don't think it's a good idea to be here. What if Sean shows up? And, for Pete's sake, why did you leave Kennedy without telling me? We looked all over the school for you and Officer Speck was going to take you to the police station."

"I'm sorry, Karen. I just can't face the police right now. I have to get a few things from the house so Sophie will be comfortable at your home. Sean left early this morning to drive to Des Moines for some financial consultation. He was very secretive. Look, the garage is empty, so he's long gone."

She unlocked the back door and made a beeline for the bedroom. Reluctantly, Karen followed. Taking down a large suitcase, Rhonda started tossing in clothes. Next, she moved to Sophie's room. Not working quite so quickly, she explained to Karen that she was trying to remember Sophie's favorite clothes and stuffed animals. "It's important that she feels safe and comfortable."

"Is that a car?" Peering out the window, Karen saw the neighbor unloading groceries. "Thank goodness, it's just your neighbor, but let's hurry up."

Finishing up, Rhonda dragged the suitcase into the hallway. Grabbing the luggage from Rhonda's bedroom, Karen moved toward the back door. Rhonda stopped in the kitchen to get the emergency cash out of the flour canister.

That's when they both heard the lock in the backdoor.

"You bitch, what do you think you're doing?" Sean rushed across the kitchen floor and smacked Rhonda on the face. She rubbed her face and glared back at Sean.

Karen pulled out her phone to call 911, but Sean knocked it out of her hand; it slid across the floor. He gave Karen a vicious shove and pushed her into the corner. "Stay out of my business, you stupid bitch."

"Leave my friend alone, Sean. I'm leaving you and I'm taking Sophie with me. I've had enough. I fell in love with you when I was young and naïve. You were so handsome, so full of energy and ideas. I didn't know at that time just how evil you are. I'm not in love with you anymore."

"You're not leaving me. You'd never survive out there in the real world. You're too stupid."

Karen started to ease out of the corner and around to the door. Sean turned on her and brandished a steak knife he lifted off the table. "Stay back, Karen, this is between the whore and me."

Rhonda stopped leaning against the cabinet and stood tall. "I'm not stupid, Sean. I'm the one who earns the paycheck. And you have no idea what I'm capable of—no idea." Rhonda pushed her shoulders back, lifted her head, and glared at Sean.

"I know you've been having an affair, a sinful affair with that woman principal. She called me and gloated about the affair. Said not to blame you as you were a real idiot. You'd better get down on your knees and start praying. You're an evil woman, Rhonda Burgess." He reached for her, but she scurried backward. "Everybody in town probably knows you're fornicating with that woman too. What will happen when Sophie finds out? Heh?" He smirked at Rhonda.

"I was in Sherry's office when she called you, Sean. I know that you know about the affair," replied Rhonda tiredly. "I truly don't know what got into me. But I do know I am through with you."

"Don't you move away from me, you sinful woman."
Sean reached out to grab Rhonda by the arm.

Rhonda put her hand back against the counter, braced
herself, and prepared to be pulled across the floor by Sean.
Out of the corner of her eye, she could see a meat knife
sitting on the counter. Reaching out with her hand, she
grabbed it.

Sean stopped and backed up a step. "You wouldn't dare,
you little scaredy-cat." He swung the steak knife at her, but
it slipped out of his hand and clattered to the floor. "You're
so weak, you little bitch." Sean lunged toward Rhonda.

With all her strength, Rhonda sank the knife into Sean's
chest. She looked with horror as blood started to spurt out
and began to pool on the floor.

Rhonda stood and looked helplessly at Sean as Karen
jumped forward. Karen felt for the artery in his neck.
*Maybe I'm not in the right place. I don't feel anything. He
can't be dead.* Totally panicked now, Karen looked at his
chest. It was rising and falling. "Rhonda, call 911 now."

But Rhonda was leaning over the sink and throwing up.
When she turned around, she gave Karen a tight, little
smile. "I hate him. He's a worthless bag of crap." She
looked at Sean, who was moving around weakly on the
floor. "I'd push the knife in further, but he is Sophie's
father. I can't do that to her. My, I feel dizzy."

Karen shoved Rhonda in a chair and pushed her head
down between her legs. Grabbing her phone off the floor,
she dialed 911 and asked for an ambulance. She knelt down
beside Sean and felt for a pulse. "I think I feel a faint beat."
Blood was pooling all over the floor.

She leaned closer to Sean. *Was he saying something?*
"Rhonda, he's trying to say something."

Rhonda just sat in the chair, staring into space.

He looked up at Karen. "I didn't think she'd do it," he
whispered.

"I didn't think so either. Rest. The ambulance is coming." *You pushed Rhonda beyond what she could endure. Everyone has a breaking point.*

As soon as she heard the siren, Karen ran to the front door. Two paramedics glanced at her; wordlessly, she pointed toward the kitchen. One paramedic started taking Sean's blood pressure, and the other one examined the wound. Karen could hear one paramedic saying the patient was going into shock. Taking out a syringe, he gave Sean a shot. The two paramedics picked up the stretcher and hurried out to the ambulance. Karen followed them to the curb and watched as Sean was put inside.

Running back into the house, she grabbed Rhonda. "Come on, we've got to get to the hospital."

"Okay," said Rhonda, weakly. "I've got to lock the front door. Sean will be angry at me if I leave the front door unlocked."

Karen roared down the street in her car with Rhonda beside her. "Rhonda, are you okay? You're looking so pale."

Rhonda took ahold of Karen's arm and shook it. "I can't do this. Drive to Kennedy and leave me your car. I'm just going to drive and drive. I won't have to deal with Sean, and I won't have to answer questions from the police. Sherry should never have threatened to tell my family about the affair. That was such an unchristian thing to do. It is what set off this whole miserable set of events."

Karen looked at Rhonda strangely. "I think you're in shock. Just concentrate on breathing and we'll be at the hospital in a few minutes."

At the hospital, Rhonda stood against the wall, tears welling up. "Why hasn't the Doctor been out to tell me how Sean is? Surely he will be okay. Maybe I shouldn't have told the nurse that I was the one who stabbed him. She looked at me really weird, Karen, and said she'd have to notify the police."

"I had to call the police too, Rhonda. They have to be informed. Sean's been seriously hurt. You'll have to answer some questions."

Karen looked up at the clock on the wall. 9:00 a.m. It was getting late and she had so much to do before the memorial service. But she could hardly leave Rhonda at the hospital by herself. *She isn't even making sense.* "Come on, sit down, Rhonda. Talk to me."

Rhonda looked at Karen wearily. "This is not how my life was supposed to be. It just isn't. I went home to pack; you know that. I didn't expect Sean to show up. You saw how he came toward me, ready to beat me up once again. I don't know what made it different this time. He called me weak and stupid and I just couldn't take it anymore. I—I—I went crazy. I can't believe that I picked up the knife and stabbed him. I hate what he's made me and—and I hate what I've become." She rubbed her hand across her forehead.

"It was self-defense," Karen said. "I was there. He had a steak knife in his hand and dropped it while he was lunging toward you."

"I don't know what happened, it's a blur. He said I couldn't do it. He looked at me with that superior, smug look and called me a scaredy-cat. But, you know, I wasn't scared anymore. I knew I could do it. I stabbed him in the chest. I'd done it before." Rhonda started shaking.

Karen felt a stab of fear go through her. "What do you mean, Rhonda, you'd done it before?" Karen started to pull away. She looked up to see Brian standing in front of Rhonda.

"Mrs. Burgess, you need to come with me now. We're going to the police station."

"Oh no, I can't do that right now. I have to wait here for Sean. He'll want to see me as soon as he wakes up. He's very particular."

"Mrs. Burgess, I'm sorry, but Sean won't be waking up. He died in the emergency room from his chest wound." Brian paused. "I'm arresting you for the murder of your husband, Sean Burgess." He read Rhonda her Miranda rights. Rhonda just looked at Brian in disbelief. She didn't seem to understand what was happening.

Karen looked shocked. "Brian, it was self-defense. I was there."

"I'll need to get a statement from you, Karen."

Karen looked at Rhonda with both compassion and shock. "This is tragic, Rhonda. You need to get yourself a lawyer right away." Karen scribbled a number on a piece of paper. "Here's the number for William Babcock. He's a good lawyer, even though he's related to Jessamyn."

"A lawyer, I guess so. I don't know what to do." Suddenly she looked up at Karen in horror. "But what about Sophie? Who's going to pick up Sophie from school? Oh, what have I done?" She hung her head and started to cry again.

Karen sat back down, put her hand over Rhonda's, and said, "I'll have Gabby pick up Sophie from school." She looked at Brian and said, "I'm not sure about the legalities. Can Sophie stay with me until plans can be made for her?"

Brian nodded. "Yes, I'll contact Human Services and Rhonda can sign over temporary custody to you until things are sorted out on a more permanent basis."

"Thank you, Karen, oh thank you. You're a good friend." Rhonda clutched at her friend's hand. Karen gently disentangled herself.

"I've got to get back to school for the memorial service!" Karen stood up. "Rhonda, I'll check on you later. I'm so sorry, but I have to go." To Brian, she said, "I'll come down right after the service and give you a statement." She grabbed her jacket and hurried out the door.

Rushing into the gym, Karen saw that all the classes had arrived and were sitting quietly on the floor. Kat was gesturing to her from the fourth row, where Rhonda's class was seated. "Where have you been? I'm less than thrilled about being in charge of Rhonda's class."

"At the hospital. I'll tell you about it later."

"Where's Mrs. Burgess?" chorused several children.

"She's not feeling well and won't be attending," said Karen, firmly. "Now sit quietly and get ready for the memorial service."

"But Mrs. Burgess will want to be here," said Connor in a loud voice. "I'm sure she's sad that Mrs. Trandon died. When I had detention I had to wait for my Mom in the office. I saw them hugging once and I think there was kissing, too. Then they closed the door. I think they forgot I was there."

"Yuck, ick, kissing, that's disgusting," said Mary Lou, who sat beside him. "And I don't think you're supposed to kiss another girl, are you?"

A murmur of voices arose as several children started to debate kissing. Karen looked at the children with that special don't-give-me-any-trouble teacher look. "Now, no more talking. Mrs. Davis," she pointed at Kat, "will report any child who misbehaves to me and there will be consequences."

"Oh my," whispered Connor to Mary Lou. "Mrs. Fowler is in a very bad mood." *You bet I am. So, you all had better behave. Oh my God, I sound like Sherry.*

On her way to the front of the gym, Bobbi Nelson walked over and stood in front of Karen. "I see that Mrs. Burgess is not here. How come she doesn't have to attend this dreary function?"

"I'm in no mood to put up with your snarky comments today, Bobbi. It's none of your business."

Bobbi gave Karen an appraising look. "Kat said you had to run an emergency errand. And you were looking for Rhonda earlier. You'd never leave the school before the big memorial service unless there was some real trouble happening."

She gave a little laugh. "Oh my, I can tell by the expression on your face, Karen. Your friend Rhonda's been arrested for murdering Sherry. And you just put the pieces of the puzzle together. You're a bit slower than your detective buddy. I think he was downright suspicious of Rhonda several days ago." She grabbed Karen's arm. "We should have all the kids bring food for a bake sale."

Karen gave her a puzzled look. "What?"

"You know, to raise money for Rhonda's bail."

Karen shook Bobbi's arm off. "It's a very good thing you have tenure, Bobbi. Otherwise, I'd let you go. So watch your step, I'm in no mood for your nastiness today or any day. Now, get out of my way."

Bobbi backed up. "Sorry, Karen, I guess I went too far."

You bet your floppy boobs, you did. I can't even process that Rhonda may have killed Sherry. Could it have been an accident? Her thoughts were running wild. *With a knife in her back? Get real.*

Karen straightened her shoulders and walked up to the front of the gym to greet the Presbyterian minister, who started the ceremony with a moment of silent reflection. Karen gave a short speech about how they'd never forget Ms. Trandon, how much she had done for the school, and the plans to plant a tree in her honor.

Starting with the kindergarten, each class filed up to the front to say something about Ms. Trandon and show their projects. Half the first graders forgot their heart messages, the two third grade girls chosen to read their essays started giggling partway through and the fourth graders sang off-tune. For a school function, things were moving along fairly smoothly. But where was Dr. Nash? He was supposed to say a few words. Looking around, Karen couldn't see Vince Watson either. *Damn those men, skipping the memorial. How rude.*

Reverend Wilmot, the Presbyterian minister, tapped Karen on the shoulder. "John Trandon is here and he's headed straight toward you. I'd say, he looks very anxious and very determined."

John walked up to Karen and said, "I'd like to say a prayer at my sister's memorial."

"I'm sorry, John, that's not something we do in a public school these days due to the Supreme Court ruling."

"That's ridiculous. God is everywhere." John's face had turned red and he started muttering.

"Let's walk over to the side of the gym, John. You're starting to draw attention." Karen gently took his arm and started to guide him. "Brenda is about to speak to the students."

John jerked away from Karen, marched up to the microphone, just as the last fifth grader read his poem, and bellowed, "Let us pray." He grabbed the microphone from the kid, who ran back to his row, scared. His sister, walking to the front of the gym, gave him a horrified look. She reached for the microphone, but he smacked her hand.

Karen started forward, but Reverend Wilmot stepped up. "Let me help." As John exhorted his audience for a minute or so about evil ways, death, and sinful people, Reverend Wilmot stood by his side.

Brenda walked back over to Karen. "I can't believe he's doing this. Sherry would be aghast at this display from John."

When John paused to breathe, Reverend Wilmot leaned into the microphone and said, "Ms. Trandon loved 'My

Country 'Tis of Thee.' Let's all sing." As the teachers and staff started singing at the top of their lungs, the children joined in. It was the loudest rendition of the song ever sung at Kennedy Elementary.

When the last note was sung, Karen dismissed the students, and they quickly filed out. John was left standing at the front of the gym, looking angry and confused. "I was rudely interrupted."

"Rudely interrupted? You jerk, I never got to give my memorial speech for my sister." Brenda made a fist and hit him in the stomach. John doubled over and started gasping for air.

Karen looked at John and said, "I think you richly deserved that. I'd appreciate it if you never came back to Kennedy Elementary."

She thanked Reverend Wilmot for leading the school in song. "It was a good ending to the memorial. I'll let you see yourself out." Karen walked out of the gym and into the office. *I've got to get back to Rhonda.*

Chapter Sixteen

Friday Morning and Afternoon

After Karen left for school, Brian settled Rhonda in the patrol car, hopped back into his car, and followed the patrol car to the police station. Both Officers Danzy and Speck looked up from their desks as Rhonda was escorted to an interview room. She dropped into a chair and told Brian her lawyer was William Babcock. Brian told her that Mr. Babcock happened to be in the police station and he'd go get him.

William Babcock had spent the early morning as Superintendent Nash's lawyer, while Brian had spent his time interviewing Nash about his argument with Sherry Trandon. Brian caught up with Mr. Babcock just as he was climbing into his car. The man was unusually short, wore ultra-thick lenses, and had olive-toned skin. After spending part of the morning with him, Brian respected him as a lawyer. Briefly, he wondered how he could possibly be related to Jessamyn. *She's so much taller than he is, and— well, dumber.*

"I've brought Rhonda Burgess in for questioning regarding the death of her husband. She's requested you as her lawyer."

Mr. Babcock slammed the car door and looked at Brian, with a puzzled frown. "Rhonda Burgess is being questioned about the death of her husband, is that what you said? She's been formally charged?"

"Right now we're questioning her."

Mr. Babcock paused and just gazed at Brian. "Business is almost too good these days." Sighing, he said, "Okay, let me meet with her."

Mr. Babcock returned to the police station and walked back to the interview room. Brian unlocked the door, and Mr. Babcock entered the small room.

The Chief, Officer Speck, and Officer Danzy all descended on Brian. "What happened?" asked Danzy.

Brian told them Sean Burgess had been stabbed and Rhonda Burgess confessed to a nurse that she'd stabbed him. The patrol officer driving her to the station reported to Brian that Rhonda told him twice that she'd killed him. As soon as the lawyer talked to Rhonda, he and Speck would interview her.

Mr. Babcock stepped out of the interview room and beckoned to Brian. Officer Speck and Brian entered the interview room. Rhonda was sitting at the table, completely dejected. Her bruised arms were showing, her split lip looked painful, and there was puffiness around both eyes.

After informing Rhonda that the video camera was running, Brian gently asked, "Mrs. Burgess, I need you to tell me exactly what happened between you and Sean this morning when he returned to the house unexpectedly."

Rhonda looked up at Brian with a blank look on her face. "I plunged a knife into his chest."

"Yes, Rhonda, that's true, but let's back up just a bit. You were packing up your things and Karen was helping. You were about to leave when Sean came in through the back door, correct?"

"Yes, that's right. He started calling me names, horrible names, and saying I was sinful. I got angry, which was surprising. I never get angry. Instead of curling up in a ball on the floor—what I'd usually do—I backed up against the kitchen counter. I honestly don't remember all the things he said. Such a detestable man! I don't know why I ever married him." She shook her head back and forth. "I just remember being angry, so angry, I could hardly stand it; the anger filled me up. I felt hot like I was on fire. When he called me a scaredy-cat, I thought, 'I'll show him.' He came at me with a steak knife and I sunk the meat knife in his chest. I don't remember what happened after that. I know Karen was there, and eventually, we ended up at the hospital."

"Were you afraid for your life?"

Rhonda blinked at Brian. "Afraid, I've been afraid ever since I married the man. Scared to death all the time wondering when he was going to kill me." She started to laugh, a high-pitched screechy sound. Tears were rolling down her face and her shoulders started to shake. "Scared?" She slapped her hand down on the table. "You know what, I'm not scared anymore. I guess you can throw me in jail forever and every day I'll wake up and say, 'I'm glad Sean Burgess is dead.'" Suddenly, Rhonda's face paled. "Poor Sophie, what horrible parents she has. What will happen to her?"

"Human Services will work with you to arrange something."

"So you've got your confession, detective. I killed Sean Burgess. I did, little old scaredy-cat Rhonda. And I'm not even sorry." Officer Speck slid a glass of water across the table toward Rhonda. She picked it up and drank thirstily.

"I have just one more question, Mrs. Burgess. Did you think Sean was going to kill you with that steak knife?"

Rhonda set down her glass. "Oh, he would have killed me, all right. I'd had an affair with a woman, a sin that can never be forgiven. He wanted me dead." With that, she put her arm on the table, rested her head on her arm, and slumped forward in the chair. "I'm just so tired, so very tired."

Brian, Officer Speck, and the lawyer exited the room. All three looked completely worn out. Babcock said, "I'll talk to the district attorney, but it sounds like self-defense to me. I doubt he'll want to take it to trial. This domestic abuse has been going on for years. Once we start digging around for incidents, we'll have so much evidence the prosecution won't want anything to do with it. Who would have thought such troubles existed for the Burgesses? I didn't know them well, but," he shook his head, "who would have thought?"

Brian leaned against the wall and said, "Sir, you need to ask Mrs. Burgess if she wants you to represent her on the next charge."

"What charge?" Babcock looked perplexed.

"I'm about to charge her with the murder of Sherry Trandon."

The lawyer looked dumbfounded. "Oh," was all he could say. "Oh. I see."

Mr. Babcock sighed. "I'll be back after lunch. I'm going to the office to get my partner. Honestly, I have too many cases at this point. I've been told that Phillip Nash and Vince Watson are also being charged this afternoon with embezzlement." He walked out the door, climbed into his BMW, and drove off.

"Danzy, why don't you order in some pizza?" Brian took out his notes and began the painful task of going through all the interviews he'd done and jotting down questions. Lunch was ordered for Mrs. Burgess, but Officer Speck reported that she didn't eat anything. Mrs. Burgess was just sitting in the interview room with her hands folded neatly on the table, staring into space.

Detective Kerns, Officer Speck, and William Babcock all entered the interview room at 1 p.m. After formally charging Rhonda Burgess with the murder of Sherry

Trandon, Brian and Speck left her to talk to her lawyer. Then the formal videotaped interview began.

Brian sat across from Rhonda and thought about what a sad person she was. Since confessing to killing her husband, she'd obviously sunk into a depressed state. Brian looked at her with kind eyes and said, "Tell me about how you became lovers with Sherry Trandon."

At first, Rhonda didn't stir. She just twisted a strand of hair around her finger and looked toward the window. Then she turned back and looked Brian full in the face and started talking.

"It's a bit hard to say. Sherry started being noticeably nicer to me last spring. She'd compliment me on my teaching, say my hair looked nice, and ask me about Sophie. I was just grateful she wasn't yelling at me as she did the other teachers. Then she started asking me to stay late after school, and one afternoon she put her arms around me and kissed me. It was shocking, absolutely shocking. But I was drawn to it. Sherry told me I was pretty. No one had ever told me that before. I was like a big old fat fish on a hook, and she was reeling me in. Sherry continued to flatter me, making me feel confident and alive. Do you have any idea what that was like, after living with Sean, who did nothing but cut me down?" Brian shook his head no.

"Anyway, Sherry kept up the compliments and started bringing me little presents. Sometimes it was flowers, sometimes perfume. I kept all of the presents at school, of course. She'd write me notes, lovely notes, which I kept locked in a box in my desk. It was wonderful. I didn't even think I was being wooed or whatever. I thought we were friends, just good friends." A tear rolled down Rhonda's face and Officer Speck reached over and handed her a box of tissues. "The kiss was weird, but Sherry just said she'd gotten carried away. But I kept thinking about that kiss. I thought about it lots." Rhonda returned to staring out the window.

"Mrs. Burgess, why don't we move forward to the morning you killed Ms. Trandon."

Rhonda turned the saddest eyes on Brian. She glanced at her lawyer and the color rose in her face. "No, you have to hear how evil she was, how unbelievably evil she was." Her voice cracked and she started to choke up. She grabbed the glass of water and took a huge gulp.

"Sherry started giving me back rubs and touching me. She would make some excuse to put her arm around my shoulder or smooth back my hair. It was so stealthy. It seemed like one day it was back rubs and hugs, and then, and then, without even realizing it, we were lovers. That tormented me and went against everything I believed in as a Christian. And the more it tormented me, the nastier Sherry got. She threatened to tell Sean and send pictures of me to Sophie. How could she do that to an innocent child? If I tried to back off, she'd threaten me more. I hated her but I loved her."

Rhonda looked down at her hands which she was twisting round and round. "We met out at Trotter Creek, her house, and sometimes at the school. I was scared to death because she kept taking more and more chances. It was if she wanted us to be found out. I'd sneak over to Sherry's after I put Sophie to bed, but if I was late, she'd call Sean and then hang up. She loved making out in the staff bathroom. Once, Bobbi almost caught us."

Rhonda stopped talking and stared mournfully at Brian, Officer Speck, and William Babcock. "Why do I get involved with people who punish me? First Sean, then Sherry." Her statement was meant with silence from all three. Rhonda squirmed in her chair.

"The affair became more difficult to contain, but I couldn't let go. Sherry had a hold on me. I thought I loved her, despite all the things she did to me. But then, Milly Landon showed up in town this fall. Sherry dumped me overnight. I tried to talk to her about it, but she refused. I begged her to take me back, but she just laughed in my face and called me stupid and ugly. Milly was working at the school and it was pure agony for me. I became depressed, very depressed. It seemed that Sherry deliberately set things up so I'd see her with Milly and know what it meant."

Rhonda sat back and started to cry, uncontrollably. Officer Speck leaned forward and patted her on the shoulder. Brian turned off the video recorder. "Let's take a short break, Mrs. Burgess. How about I get you a soft drink? Sprite? Coke?"

Rhonda looked up. "A coke, please. You and Karen would make an excellent couple. It's like you're made for each other. I know Karen likes you. I'm just sorry I won't be around to see it."

Brian looked slightly embarrassed as he left the room. Officer Speck actually smiled. "Well, that brightened up a dreary confession, sir."

"I guess so." Brian walked off to the back of the police station. Babcock wandered over to the snack table to get a cup of coffee and a donut and then sat down and started reading the paper. Officer Speck got Rhonda her coke and went back into the interview room to keep an eye on her.

Minutes later, they reconvened in the interview room and Brian reminded Rhonda she'd been talking about Milly. "I went over to Sherry's once because I was desperate to see her. Unfortunately, the yard boy was there, so Sherry was furious I'd shown up. I talked her into going out to Trotter Creek a few weeks ago. It didn't go well, I cried, and she yelled at me. She just wasn't interested in me anymore now that Milly was around. And I couldn't get her out of my system. She was an addiction."

Rhonda sighed and took a sip of her coke. "I think it was when Sherry called me down to the office about my fake resume that I started to hate her. That's the day she called Sean, with me standing right next to her and crying. She told him we'd been having an affair. I left that part out when I told you the story before, Detective Kerns. I was just too ashamed. Sean beat me black and blue when I showed up at home. I thought he was going to kill me that time. And poor Sophie, she just cried and cried in her room. It was terrible. I realized that Sherry was truly evil. She'd ruined me and my family. And that's when I decided to kill her. It was my Christian duty. She was truly Satan."

Rhonda looked down at the table, cleared her throat, drank another swallow of coke, and said, "Now for the part you've been waiting for. I took Bobbi Nelson's lab jacket Monday afternoon. I knew she wouldn't miss it. And the woman is always so grumpy and nasty. Secretly, I guess I wished she'd be blamed for it.

"By Tuesday I was starting to feel uncertain about it all. I decided to just talk to Sherry, but I put the lab jacket on anyway, and I hid the knife inside my pile of papers. I went down to the office to do some photocopying and talk to Sherry. But Dr. Nash was already there and he and Sherry were having a screaming match in Sherry's office. I squatted down beside the photocopy machine and waited. Soon Nash stormed out and that's when I entered the office." Rhonda stopped and blew her nose. "This is hard to retell."

"You're doing fine, Mrs. Burgess, continue."

"Sherry was sitting at her desk, red in the face. She was so angry, and I knew I should have left. But instead, I sat down in the chair, wept, and begged Sherry to take me back. And Sherry laughed at me. She called me stupid and ugly again. I told her I loved her and she laughed, almost delightedly, and said, 'Tough luck, bitch.' And all of a sudden I didn't love her anymore at all. I could see her for what she was, an evil, evil woman.

"I got up to leave but then I sat back down and calmly put on the blue latex gloves I brought with me. Sherry asked me what I was doing and I smiled at her. Can you believe Sherry said, 'What do you plan to do, strangle me?'

"Then I walked behind Sherry's desk and she laughed and said, 'Oh, Rhonda, you're so stupid and dramatic.' Sherry didn't even take me seriously when I stood there with a lab jacket and gloves on, ready to kill her. I was so angry I was shaking. But then it was like all my pent-up rage went into my hands and I took out the knife from between my papers and with all my strength, I drove the knife into her back. Sherry let out a cry and then there was all this blood—*all this blood.*"

Rhonda started to cry again. Officer Speck offered her more tissues. "I looked at Sherry with a knife in her back and blood pooling on the floor, and I knew there was one less evil woman in the world. I called 911 and then it was a bit of a blur. There were a bunch of teachers around and then someone said we had to go outside. I know I talked to Karen and Noreen. Mostly, I just felt ill." Rhonda's voice wound down and she slumped forward. Everyone was silent for a moment as the information sunk in.

Rhonda looked up and said, "It didn't stop there, though. No, when I got home Tuesday, after killing Sherry, Sean was furiously angry and beat me again. Sophie cried and tried to stop it, and for the first time, Sean pushed his daughter. I screamed at Sophie to run to her room and lock the door. I crawled out to my car after the beating and drove out to Trotter Creek. I threw the phone I'd taken off Sherry's desk into the bushes. But I was pretty sure it was the wrong phone. It looked different.

"The rest of the days have been a complete blur. I was worried about keeping Sophie safe, but I didn't think Sean would really hurt her. I worried that I'd left evidence behind at the scene. I was never sure what Sherry was writing in this address book she was so fussy about, so I was scared the police would find it. And Sherry told me she kept a diary that detailed all the things we'd done. I was desperate to find that diary but too frightened to break into her house to look for it. What, oh what, is going to happen to me?"

Babcock, who had been sitting silently through the confession, said, "Mrs. Burgess, you are exhausted. I will wait to see what the district attorney charges you with, but you should be prepared for a murder charge in the case of Sherry Trandon. Your husband's death may be, I stress, may be ruled self-defense."

Rhonda looked down at the table. "They were both evil, very, very evil."

When Brian left the interview, he saw Karen across the room, sitting at his desk. She was looking extremely worried. "Your Officer Danzy took my statement. How is Rhonda?"

Just as Brian started to tell her, Officer Speck came out of the interview room with Rhonda. "Detective Kerns, I'm taking Mrs. Burgess to the ladies' room."

Rhonda saw Karen and stopped in the hallway. She looked forlornly at her friend. In a small, sad voice, she said, "I killed Sherry, Karen, little, old passive me." Rhonda's voice got stronger and she looked at Karen, almost defiantly. "She was an evil woman and she betrayed me in so many ways. You know that, Karen. I had to do it. It was all in God's plan."

Karen looked at Rhonda with both pity and compassion. Taking Rhonda's hand, she said slowly and softly, "No, Rhonda, it wasn't God's plan. It was just plain old murder."

Karen pursed her lips so she wouldn't start crying. She waved a quick good-bye to Brian and picked up her purse and coat. She walked out of the police station and climbed into her car. Briefly, she rested her head on the steering wheel while tears slid down her face. *Poor Rhonda, poor messed up Rhonda.* Then with a determined set to her face, she started the car and drove toward Kennedy School.

Epilogue

Superintendent Nash and Vince Watson were convicted of embezzlement of District school funds and are both serving a 15-year sentence in the state penitentiary.

Milly Landon left Chaldea and has not been heard of or seen since. Rumor is she is living abroad in Paris.

Brenda Sousa has decided to stay in Chaldea and is currently living in Sherry Trandon's house. She provides before and after school care for Freddy Moser.

Bobbi Nelson is still teaching at Kennedy Elementary School. Her caustic comments have gotten worse; she seldom smiles and insists that she'll be retiring as soon as she possibly can. She also says she's sworn off men. They're all untrustworthy and irresponsible.

Jessamyn Babcock moved to the big city of Des Moines and is currently working for a real estate company, offering advice to sellers on how to declutter their homes. Her father is hoping she'll go back to college and get a degree in Art and Design. He has the college already selected for her.

Elyse Vanderhoot was defeated in the next congressional election. Her affair with Sherry Trandon never became public knowledge and the video was never found. Brian Kerns wonders if it ever existed.

Rebecca Speck passed her detective's exam and is now serving as a detective for the Chaldea Police Department.

Sheldon is now living with his father, Mr. Fitch, who has been released from prison. Mrs. Fitch closed out the checking account at the local bank and took off with the family car. It is rumored that she is living in Chicago. Logan is attending the University of Iowa and is majoring in Drama. He still sees Gabby Fowler regularly.

Gabby Fowler joined the Drama Club, is president of the honor society, and is vice president of Future Business Leaders of Tomorrow. She goes to visit Logan at the University of Iowa as often as her mother allows.

Rhonda Burgess did not go to trial for either the murders of Sean Burgess or Sherry Trandon. She pled guilty for both. Sean's death was ruled self-defense and Sherry Trandon's death was ruled murder in the first degree. She is serving a life sentence in a Midwest penitentiary, but her lawyer is working for a lower sentence. Neither of the Burgesses had any close relatives, so Rhonda signed over formal custody of her child, Sophie, to Karen Fowler, her good friend.

Sophie Burgess is a lovely child, quiet and artistic. She is attending Lincoln School as a fourth grader and is receiving weekly therapy for the traumas she's endured. She misses her mom terribly and Karen has promised that after some time has passed, she will take Sophie to visit her mom in prison. In the meantime, Sophie writes her a letter twice a week.

Brian and Karen did go out for dinner at the country club in Plain View, once the murder investigation was over. They had a wonderful time together and never talked about murder, once.

Brian Kerns has returned to active duty as a homicide detective for the Chicago Police Department. He calls, texts, and emails Karen regularly. They're planning to spend spring break together. His cat, Sibelius, hissed at him upon his return, but Brian is working to get back in the cat's good graces by feeding him gourmet cat food. Brian sent the signed hockey puck to Freddy Moser, who tells everyone it is his most prized possession.

Karen Fowler became the permanent principal of Kennedy School. She threw out most of Sherry Trandon's rules and created a democratically elected teacher council which serves as an advisory board for all school decisions. The staff and students at Kennedy are much happier.

THE END

ABOUT THE AUTHOR

Kathy Johnston grew up in southern Iowa and read all the time as an escape from the doldrums of small-town living. After spending forty-one years in education she grew tired of correcting students' writing and decided to write for herself. *Fatal Lesson* is the first book in her Karen Fowler series and combines her love of education and the murder mystery genre.

When not writing, Kathy loves to travel with her husband (30 countries and 48 states), read, hang out with her two adult daughters, and chase her cat, Sibelius, around the house. Giving piano lessons keeps her teaching skills from getting rusty.